DON'T BLINK

JAMES PATTERSON is one of the best-known and biggest-selling writers of all time. He is the author of some of the most popular series of the past decade – the Alex Cross, Women's Murder Club and Detective Michael Bennett novels – and he has written many other number one bestsellers including romance novels and stand-alone thrillers. He lives in Florida with his wife and son.

James is passionate about encouraging children to read. Inspired by his own son who was a reluctant reader, he also writes a range of books specifically for young readers. James has formed a partnership with the National Literacy Trust, an independent, UK-based charity that changes lives through literacy. In 2010, he was voted Author of the Year at the Children's Choice Book Awards in New York.

Also by James Patterson

For more information about James Patterson's novels, visit
www.jamespatterson.co.uk

Or become a fan on Facebook

JAMES PATTERSON

DON'T BLINK

& HOWARD ROUGHAN

arrow books

Published by Arrow Books in 2011

5 7 9 10 8 6 4

Copyright © James Patterson, 2010

First published in Great Britain in 2010 by Century

Arrow Books
Random House, 20 Vauxhall Bridge Road,
London SW1V 2SA

www.randomhouse.co.uk

Addresses for companies within The Random House Group Limited can be
found at: www.randomhouse.co.uk/offices.htm

The Random House Group Limited Reg. No. 954009

A CIP catalogue record for this book
is available from the British Library

ISBN 9780099553724
ISBN 9780099525349 (export edition)

The Random House Group Limited supports The Forest Stewardship Council
(FSC®), the leading international forest certification organisation. Our books
carrying the FSC label are printed on FSC® certified paper. FSC is the only
forest certification scheme endorsed by the leading environmental organisations,
including Greenpeace. Our paper procurement policy can be found at:
www.randomhouse.co.uk/environment

Typeset by SX Composing DTP, Rayleigh, Essex
Printed and bound by CPI Group (UK) Ltd, Croydon, CR0 4YY

For Isabel Morris Patterson. —*J.P.*

To Elaine Glass, one of the bravest I know. —*H.R.*

Prologue

IN THE WINK OF A BLINK OF AN EYE

One

LOMBARDO'S STEAKHOUSE ON Manhattan's tony Upper East Side was justly famous for two things, two specialties of the house. The first was its double-thick, artery-clogging forty-six-ounce porterhouse, the mere sight of which could give a vegan an apoplectic seizure.

The second claim to fame was its clientele.

Simply put, Lombardo's Steakhouse was paparazzi heaven. From A-list actors to all-star pro athletes, CEOs to supermodels, rap stars to poet laureates—anyone who was anyone could be spotted at Lombardo's, whether they were brokering deals or just looking and acting fabulous.

Zagat, the ubiquitous red bible of dining

guides, said it best: "Get ready to rub elbows and egos with the jet set, because Lombardo's is definitely the place to see and be seen."

Unless you were Bruno Torenzi, that is.

He was the man who was about to make Lombardo's Steakhouse renowned for something else. Something terrible, just unbelievably awful.

And no one seemed to notice him...until it was too late...until the deed was almost done.

Of course, that was the idea, wasn't it? In his black three-button Ermenegildo Zegna suit and dark-tinted sunglasses, Bruno Torenzi could have been anybody. He could have been *everybody*.

Besides, it was lunch. Broad daylight, for Christ's sake.

For something this sick and depraved to go down, you would have at least thought nighttime. Hell, make that a full moon with a chorus of howling wolves.

"Can I help you, sir?" inquired the hostess, Tiffany, the one person who did manage to notice Torenzi if only because it was her job. She was a young and stunning blonde from the Midwest, with perfect porcelain skin, who could turn more heads than a chiropractor.

But it was as if she didn't even exist.

Torenzi didn't stop, didn't even glance her way when she spoke to him. He just waltzed right by her, cool as a cabana.

Screw it, thought the busy hostess, letting him go. The restaurant was packed as always, and he certainly looked like he belonged. There were other customers arriving, getting in her face as only New Yorkers can. Surely this guy was meeting up with someone who was already seated.

She was right about that much.

Table chatter, clanking silverware, the iconic jazz of John Coltrane filtering down from the recessed ceiling speakers—they all combined to fill the mahogany-paneled dining room of Lombardo's with a continuous loop of the most pleasant sort of white noise.

Torenzi heard none of it.

He'd been hired because of his discipline, his unyielding focus. In his mind there was only one other person in the busy restaurant. Just one.

Thirty feet...

Torenzi had spotted the table in the far right corner. A special table, no doubt about that. For a very special customer.

Twenty feet...

He cut sharply over to another aisle, the heels of his black wingtips clicking against the polished wood floor like a metronome in three-quarter time.

Ten feet...

Torenzi leveled his stare on the bald and unabashedly overweight man seated alone with his back to the wall. The picture he'd been handed could stay tucked in his pocket. There was no need to double-check the image.

This was him, for sure. Vincent Marcozza.

The man who had less than a minute to live.

Two

VINCENT MARCOZZA—WEIGHING in at three hundred pounds plus—glanced up from what remained of his blood-rare porterhouse steak, stuffed baked potato, and gaudy portion of onion strings. Even sitting still the guy looked woefully out of breath and very close to a coronary.

"Can I help you?" asked Marcozza, seemingly polite. His raised-on-the-streets-of-Brooklyn tone, however, suggested otherwise. It was more like, *Hey, pal, what the hell are you staring at? I'm eating here.*

Torenzi stood motionless, measuring the important man. He took his sweet time answering. Finally, in a thick Italian accent he announced, "I have a message from Eddie."

This amused Marcozza for some reason. His pasty complexion spiked red as he laughed, his neck fat jiggling like a Jell-O mold. "A message from Eddie, huh? Hell, I should've known. You look like one of Eddie's guys."

He lifted the napkin from his lap, wiping the oily cow juice from the corners of his mouth. "So what is it, boy? Spit it out."

Torenzi glanced to his left and right as if to point out how close the nearby tables were. They were too close. *Capisce?*

Marcozza nodded. Then he motioned his uninvited lunch visitor forward. "For my ears only, huh?" he said before breaking into another neck-jiggling laugh. "This oughta be good. It's a joke, right? Let's hear it."

Over by the far wall a waiter stood on tiptoe on a chair, erasing the Chilean sea bass special from a large chalkboard. Hustling by him, a busboy and his gray bucket carried the remains of a table for four. And at the bar, a waitress loaded up her tray with a glass of pinot noir, a vodka tonic, and two dry martinis with almond-stuffed olives.

Torenzi stepped slowly to Marcozza's side. Placing his left hand firmly on the table, he unclenched his right fist, which was tucked neatly behind his back. The cold steel handle of a scalpel fell promptly and rather gracefully from his sleeve.

Then, leaning in, Torenzi whispered three words, and only three. "Justice is blind."

Marcozza squinted. Then he frowned. He was about to ask what the hell that was supposed to mean.

But he never got the chance.

Three

IN A HELLISH BLUR, Bruno Torenzi whipped his arm around, plunging the scalpel deep into the puffy fold above Marcozza's left eye. With a good butcher's precision and hard speed, he cut clockwise around the orbital socket. Three, six, nine, midnight... The blade moved so fast, the blood didn't have time to bleed.

"ARRRGH!" was a pretty good approximation of the sound Marcozza made.

He screamed in agony as the entire restaurant turned. *Now* everyone noticed Bruno Torenzi. He was the one carving the eye out of that fat man's face—like a pumpkin!

"ARRRRRRGH!"

Torenzi was outweighed by over a hundred

pounds but it didn't matter. He'd positioned himself perfectly, his rigid choke hold keeping Marcozza's head dead still while the rest of his body violently jerked and thrashed. What was premeditated murder if not calculated leverage?

Squish!

Scooped out like a melon ball, Marcozza's left eye fell to the white linen tablecloth and rolled to a stop.

Next came the right eye. *Slice, slice, slice…* Beautiful handiwork, to be sure.

But the right eye didn't pop out like the left one. Instead, it dangled, held by the stubborn red vessel of the optic nerve.

Torenzi smiled and flicked his wrist. He was almost finished here, so hold the applause.

Snip!

Marcozza's right eye, with a gooey tail of flesh and vein, careened off the bread plate and fell to the floor.

Blood, finally catching up to the moment, now gushed from Marcozza's empty eye sockets. In medical terms, his ophthalmic artery had been severed from his internal carotid artery, the high-pressure main line to the brain. In layman's terms, it was just a god-awful, horrifying, and disgusting mess.

A few tables away, a woman wearing everything Chanel fainted, passing out cold, while another threw up all over her tiramisu.

As for Torenzi, he simply tucked the scalpel into the breast pocket of his Zegna suit before heading toward the kitchen to exit through the back door — back into broad daylight.

But before he did, he leaned down again to repeat his message into Marcozza's chubby ear as he lay hunched over the table dying a slow, mean death.

"Justice is blind."

Part One

A JOB TO DIE FOR

Chapter 1

THE WORDS I will never be able to forget were "Hold on tight, because this is going to be one hairy ride." In point of fact, those words not only described the next several minutes, but the next several days of my life.

I had been lying fast asleep under nothing but the high, bright stars of an African night sky with only a frayed, moth-eaten mat separating me from some of the poorest dirt on the planet when suddenly my eyes popped open and my heart immediately skipped a beat. Make that a couple of beats.

Holy shit! Is that what I think it is?

Gunfire?

The answer to my question came the very

next second as Dr. Alan Cole raced over to me in the darkness and grabbed my arm, shaking me hard. We'd been sleeping outside because our pup tents were like saunas.

"Wake up, Nick. Get up! Now!" he said. "We're being attacked. I'm serious, man."

I shot straight up and turned to him as the sound of more gunfire echoed in the air. *Pop! Pop! Pop!*

It was getting closer. Whoever was shooting—*they* were getting closer. And moving quickly.

"Janjaweed—that's who it is, right?" I asked.

"Yeah," said Alan. "I was afraid this could happen. Word got around that we're here."

"So what do we do now?"

"Follow me," he said with a wave of his flashlight. "Quickly, Nick. Keep moving."

I grabbed my pillow—otherwise known as my knapsack. From the corner of my eye I spotted one of my notepads over by the stack of crates that had been functioning as my desk. I took one step toward it when Alan grabbed my arm again, this time to hold me back.

"There's no time, Nick. We've got to get the

hell out of here," he warned. "Otherwise, we're both dead. And that's after they torture us."

Well, when you put it like that . . .

Lickety-split, I fell in line behind Alan as we raced past the few shanties of plywood and corrugated metal that were used as operating rooms at this makeshift hospital on the outskirts of the Zalingei district of Sudan. It dawned on me how in control the doctor seemed, even now. He wasn't screaming or shouting.

Meanwhile, that's all I wanted to do.

For crying out loud, Nick, what's with you and the death wish? Did you really have to take this assignment? You knew this part of Darfur was still too dangerous for journalists! Even Courtney said so when she offered you the assignment.

But that was the whole point of the article I was writing—the reason I knew I had to be here and see it with my own eyes. This part of Darfur was still too dangerous for doctors as well. Obviously. But that didn't stop Dr. Alan Cole from coming here, did it? *No.* The acclaimed thoracic surgeon had left his wife and two beautiful kids back in Maryland to be here for four months with the Humanitarian Relief Corps to save the lives of Sudanese civilians who would otherwise suffer and die without medical care.

Now I was relying on Alan Cole to save my life, too.

Pop! Pop-pop-pop-pop! Pop-pop-pop-pop!

I kept running behind him and the hazy glow of his flashlight, ignoring the sting against my bare feet as I stepped on the sharp rocks and spiny twigs that littered the ground.

Up ahead I could see some movement: the two female Sudanese nurses who worked full-time in the hospital. One was starting up a rickety old Jeep that Alan had pointed out to me when I'd first arrived days earlier.

He'd called it the "getaway car." I thought he was joking.

Ha! Ha! Ha! Think again, Nick.

"Get in!" Alan told me as we reached the Jeep. The nurse in the driver's seat jumped out to let him take over the wheel.

As I practically hurled myself into the shotgun seat I waited for the two nurses to climb in the back. They didn't.

Instead they both whispered the same thing to us. "*Salaam alaikum.*"

I'd already learned what that meant. *Peace be with you.* But I was confused. "Aren't they coming with us?" I asked Alan.

"No," he said, jerking the creaky gearshift out of park. "The Janjaweed don't want them. They want us. Americans. Foreigners. We're interfering here."

With that, he quickly thanked the nurses, telling the two he hoped to see them soon. *"Wa alaikum salaam,"* he added. *And peace upon you.*

Then Alan hit the gas like a sledgehammer, plastering me against the back of my seat.

"Hold on tight," he told me over the rattle and roar of the engine, "because this is going to be one hairy ride."

Chapter 2

A BLAST OF the hot desert air nearly burned my face as we hit the road, or at least what passed for the road in this godforsaken part of the world. There was no pavement, only a beaten track of dirt that was now flying off our tires as we fishtailed back and forth with Alan doing his damnedest to avoid the occasional citrus tree that had managed to survive the wretched heat and droughtlike conditions here.

Did I mention we had our headlights off? *Welcome to the Ray Charles Grand Prix.*

"How we doing?" Alan shouted at the top of his voice. "Do they see us? Can you see *them?*"

He and I were a mere foot apart from each other, but we still had to shout to be heard. I swear, a fighter jet breaking the sound barrier was quieter than this Jeep's engine.

"See us? How can they not *hear* us?" I shouted back. "I don't see anybody yet."

I'd done a good bit of homework on the Janjaweed before arriving from the States. They were the proxy militia of the Arab Muslims in Khartoum, the Sudanese capital, and had long been fighting and killing the African Muslims in the countryside over, among other things, land allocation. The bloodshed had been relentless and mainly one-sided. Hence, the genocide we keep hearing about.

But reading articles and a few books on the Janjaweed from the comfort of my couch in Manhattan was one thing. This was entirely another affair.

I turned to look over my shoulder, the cloud of dirt and dust flying in our wake making it hard to see anything. That's when I felt the air split open around me as a bullet whizzed by my ear. *Jesus Christ, that was close.*

"Faster, Alan!" I said. "We've got to go faster! You can go faster, can't you?"

Alan gave me a quick nod, his eyes squinting

as he struggled to see through the darkness and flying dirt.

As for me, I contemplated my premature death at thirty-three by counting the unchecked boxes on my life's to-do list. Winning a Pulitzer. Learning how to play the saxophone. Driving an Enzo Ferrari along the Pacific Coast Highway.

Oh yeah, and finally having the balls to tell a certain woman back home that I loved her more than I had previously cared to admit—even to myself.

What could I say that one of my half-dozen favorite authors, John Steinbeck, hadn't already figured out? Something about the best-laid plans of mice and men often going awry?

But hold on!

Speaking of plans, the doctor at the wheel apparently had one of his own. "We need something heavy!" declared Alan.

Heavy? "Like what?" I asked him.

"I don't know. Check in the back—the cargo area," he said, handing me his flashlight. "And stay low! I don't want losing you on my conscience."

"No, I don't want that either, Alan!"

Like an added exclamation point, a bullet ricocheted off the metal roll bar. *Ping!*

"Make that *real* low!" Alan added.

I grabbed the thick rubber handle of the flashlight, quickly snaking my way into the cramped quarters of the backseat. Peering into the cargo area I spotted nothing but a few empty water bottles bouncing around like jumping beans.

I was about to tell Alan the bad news when I caught the reflection of something shiny strapped to the side, near the spare tire. It was a lug wrench. *Yes!*

But was it heavy enough? I had no idea, since I didn't know what it was needed for.

I handed it up to Alan, who gave it a shake as if weighing it in his hands. "Good enough," he said. Then he flipped on the Jeep's headlights. "Now hold the wheel steady for me, all right? *Very* steady, Nick!"

I climbed back into the shotgun seat, reaching over for the steering wheel as Alan lifted his left foot and yanked off his running shoe. I could just make out the swoosh of the Nike label.

"I'll be right back," he said.

Right back? Where the hell are you going, doc?
What are you doing now?
Don't leave me, buddy.

Chapter 3

ALAN DOVE BENEATH the steering wheel, the lug wrench held like a baton in one hand, his running shoe in the other.

I tried to see what he was doing. Of course, what I should've been doing was paying attention to what he asked me to do—hold the wheel steady.

Oh, shit! Look out! Look out!

The Jeep suddenly swerved, the two left tires leaping a foot off the ground and nearly flipping us over. I could hear Alan's head slam against the driver's-side door as I struggled to straighten the wheel. *Ouch!*

"Sorry, Alan!" I shouted. "You okay?"

"Yeah, but throw me some light down here. I dropped the damn wrench."

"Sorry, man."

"No, you're doing fine. Just hold that steering wheel steady!"

I flipped the flashlight back on for him. The wrench had fallen behind the brake pedal. With his right foot still on the gas, Alan scooped up the tool and shoved it into his shoe. I still had no idea what he was doing.

Then it hit me.

Alan was weighing down the gas pedal, wasn't he?

Sure enough, as I traded glances between him and the road, I saw Alan replace his foot with his weighted-down shoe. Using the laces like stitches, he looped them around the pedal, quickly tying them tight as he could under the circumstances.

Just as fast he came back up and yanked the belt from his pants, securing the steering wheel to a steel rod beneath his seat.

We were officially on cruise control.

Now what?

Only I didn't really need to ask that question and get an answer. I just didn't want to believe what was happening.

"Are you ready?" Alan asked. "You better be. We're out of here!"

"You're kidding me!"

"No, I'm dead serious. You see that boulder up ahead on the right? There's an embankment right after it," he said.

"How do you know that?"

"I was a Boy Scout, Nick. Always prepared. All we have to do is tuck and roll and they'll never see us! Trust me."

I aimed the flashlight at the speedometer. We were pushing the needle at eighty miles an hour. *What's that, doc? Tuck and roll?*

But there was no time to discuss or argue; that boulder and the embankment were a few seconds away. With another bullet whizzing by us, I took a deep breath and told Alan all he needed to hear.

"Fuckin' A, let's do it!"

I grabbed my knapsack and turned to grab the roll bar. *Ping!* went another bullet. And another: *Ping!* And then dozens of *pop*s and *ping*s.

Gnashing my teeth to build my nerve, I could taste the swirling dirt deep in my mouth. In my four years at Northwestern as a journalism major, not once did I take a class called Tuck and Roll. Wish I had. Would have been much more useful than some of the things I learned about grammar and ethics.

Geronimo!

I jumped into the darkness, then slammed into the soil. Only it didn't feel like soil. It felt like concrete, the pain shooting through my body like an exploding bomb.

I wanted to scream. *Don't scream, Nick! They'll hear you!*

So much for my tucking skills. As for the rolling, I immediately had that down pat—as in, down and down and down the embankment. When I finally stopped, dizzy to the point of vomiting, I turned and looked up.

Continuing in hot pursuit of our Jeep was another Jeep of trigger-happy Janjaweed, surely thinking that they were closer than ever to killing a couple of troublemaking Americans. They'd catch on soon enough—maybe another mile or two—but by then Alan and I would be like two needles in a haystack in the dead of night. They'd never find us. At least I hoped that was the case.

"You okay?" came Alan's voice. He was maybe ten feet away from me.

"Yeah," I said. "You?"

"Never better, man."

I saw a familiar glow coming from Alan's hand. It was an iridium satellite phone. I had the same one somewhere on me.

"Who are you calling?" I asked.

"Domino's Pizza," he joked. "You like pepperoni?"

I laughed. Never did a laugh feel so good.

"No, I'm calling for backup," he said. "It's time you and I got the hell out of Dodge. A dead surgeon and reporter won't do much for world peace and all that good stuff we care so much about, huh, Nick?"

Chapter 4

BRUISED, BATTERED, BANGED UP—but most important, *alive*—Alan and I were airlifted at daybreak by a UN World Food Programme plane to Khartoum. The good doctor decided he'd stay a few more days there in the Sudanese capital to help out at another hospital. What a guy—and I sincerely mean that.

"You're welcome to come with me," he offered, half joking. "I need a muse."

I smiled. "Nah, I think I've had enough wilderness adventure for a while. I think I have more than enough good material to write my article, Alan."

"Don't make me out as a hero," he warned. "I'm not."

"I just write what I see, Alan. If that sounds heroic to some people, so be it."

With that, I thanked him for the twentieth time for saving my life. *"Salaam alaikum,"* I added.

He shook my hand. "And peace upon you," he replied.

Too bad that wouldn't be the case, though. Nosiree.

By that afternoon, I was on a four-hour flight over the Red Sea and Persian Gulf to the United Arab Emirates and the city of Dubai, home of the world's first cloned camel. The place is surreal, if you've never been. If you have, you know what I'm talking about. A few years back, I spent a week there visiting all its "tourist attractions" for a piece I called "Disneyland on Drugs." Needless to say, the Dubai tourism board wasn't too keen on the title, but what did they expect? Their take on Space Mountain is an actual *indoor* ski mountain, Ski Dubai. Then there's the man-made archipelago of three hundred islands created in the shape of a world map stretching thirty-five miles wide. It's a small world after all, indeed.

But I was only passing through this time. In

fact, after a quick nap at the adjacent Dubai International Hotel—by far the cleanest place you'll ever stay that charges by the hour—I was back on a plane en route to Paris to interview one of the European directors of the Humanitarian Relief Corps, my final bit of research for the article I was writing.

At least, I *thought* I was on my way to Paris.

While I was literally on line to board the flight, I felt the vibration of my iridium phone. My editor, Courtney, was calling from New York.

"How are you?" she asked.

"Alive," I answered. It was definitely the word of the day. I quickly told her the story of my Mad Max escape from the Janjaweed militia. She almost couldn't believe it. Hell, I still couldn't either.

"Are you sure you're okay?" she asked. "You sound a little nonplussed—for you."

"All things considered, yes, I'm fine. I even learned something very important—I'm mortal. I'm really, really mortal."

"So where are you off to now?"

"Paris," I said.

"Paris?"

"*Oui.*"

"*Je crois que non,*" said Courtney.

Now, I only had one year of French back at St. Patrick's High School in Newburgh, New York, but I was pretty sure she'd just said, "I don't think so."

"Why not?" I asked.

It was a good question—timely, too, because I was only two people away from handing over my boarding pass and heading to Paris, which is probably my favorite city in the world. Except for the people, of course. Not all of them—just the snots.

"You need to come home," said Courtney.

"Why? What's up?"

"Something good, Nick. Something *really* good. You're going to love this one."

That was enough to get me to take a half step out of line. Courtney Sheppard had a few notable vices, but hyperbole wasn't one of them.

"Okay," I said. "So blow me away."

And sure enough, that's exactly what Courtney did. She almost knocked me right out of my shoes.

Chapter 5

LET ME TIP my hand here—I know it's semi-ridiculous, but I am a huge baseball fan, have been since I was a little kid back in the Hudson Valley, throwing apples at tree trunks for practice.

To continue with the narrative, though. I cupped the phone tight against my ear trying to hear every word as best I could. The airport was absolutely swarming, with most of the noise coming from the next gate over, where there were a hundred men gathered, all with neatly trimmed black beards and crisp white flowing robes, otherwise known as dishdashas.

Then there was me.

A shock of sandy-brown hair on top of my six-foot-one frame dressed in a faded pair of jeans and an even more faded polo shirt. I couldn't stand out more if I were Gene Simmons wearing full Kiss makeup and reading the Koran out loud.

Courtney drew a deep breath. "You remember Dwayne Robinson?" she asked. Of course I did and she knew it.

"You mean, the same Dwayne Robinson who cost the Yankees—*my* Yankees—the World Series? That crazy bastard? That total enigma?"

"Ten years ago and you still hold a nasty grudge? You are *nuts* about baseball, aren't you?"

"Absolutely. It could be a hundred years and I'd still never forget...or forgive." I bristled.

What can I say? I've been a die-hard fan of the Bronx Bombers ever since my father drove us down from Newburgh and took me to my first game when I was five. We sat in the upper deck, about three miles from the field, but I didn't care. Ever since then I've just about bled Yankee pinstripes. And yes, I know it's nuts.

"On second thought, maybe this is a bad idea," said Courtney. "Go to Paris, Nick."

"What do you mean by that? What are you getting at? Why are you pushing me off to Paris now?"

She milked it for a few seconds. "He wants to do an interview with you."

I had this bizarre feeling that that's what she was going to say, but I was still surprised to hear it. Very surprised. Dwayne Robinson had been the J. D. Salinger of the baseball world ever since he got banned from the game in spectacular fashion. His last statement to the working press was "I'll never talk to any of you again." For the past decade, he'd been true to his word.

Lucky for me, things change. This was huge. This would be the story of my career so far. It was also a dream come true.

"Courtney, you miracle worker, how'd you get him to agree to an interview?" I asked.

"I wish I could take some of the credit," she said. "Instead I just answered the phone. I got a call from Robinson's agent yesterday."

"The guy still has an agent? That's amazing in itself."

"I know, go figure. Maybe they're hoping he'll be reinstated. Maybe that's it, what he wants to talk to you about."

"I wouldn't hold my breath," I said. "He's well into his thirties by now. Hasn't pitched in years."

"Still, that would explain his wanting to do the interview, right? He comes clean, sets the story straight... It would be his first step toward a comeback," she said. "Maybe not on the mound, but at least in the public eye, his legacy."

"Yeah, so far it's worked wonders for Pete Rose," I joked. "Still, if that's the case, wouldn't he do a television interview?"

The words were barely out of my mouth when I had the answer. Dwayne Robinson, the "Great Black Hope from Harlem" and onetime ace southpaw of the Yankees pitching staff, suffered from, among many things, acute social anxiety disorder. Although he could take the mound and pitch brilliantly before fifty-five thousand screaming fans, he could barely carry on a conversation one-on-one. Especially in front of a camera.

"I forgot one thing," I said. "The guy was like a walking advertisement for Paxil."

"Bingo," said Courtney. "In fact, Robinson's agent told me that he's afraid his client might change his mind. That's why he's already set up a lunch for you two, Nick. You and Dwayne, Dwayne and you. Cozy, huh?"

"When?" I asked, beginning to get more than a little excited about this.

"Tomorrow," she said. "Lombardo's, twelve thirty."

"Courtney, *I'm in Dubai.*"

"Hopefully not for long, Nick. You have an important lunch tomorrow. In New York."

As if on cue the gate attendant approached me. He looked just like Niles Crane from the show *Frasier.* Weird. "Excuse me, sir, will you be joining us to Paris?" he asked with a slight smirk. "The gate is closing right now."

I looked around. Everyone was on the plane already. Everyone but me, that is.

"Nick, are you there?" asked Courtney. "I need to know if you can do this. Tell me you're in."

Now it was my turn to milk it for a few seconds.

"Nick? Nick? Are you there? Nick? Damn you—stop playing silly games."

"Oh, I'm in," I said finally. "I'm in."

Way over my head, as I'd find out.

"I never had a doubt," said Courtney. "You bleed Yankee pinstripes, isn't that right, Nick?"

Chapter 6

TWO FLIGHTS, eight time zones, and twenty exceedingly long hours later, I was finally wheels down at JFK at a little before eleven the next morning. Walking off the plane I felt like a zombie. I probably looked and smelled like one, too.

There was only one message waiting for me as I ditched the satellite phone for my iPhone. It was Courtney, of course.

"Lombardo's. Twelve thirty," she reminded me. "And don't be late! This is the big one, Nick. You'll probably get a book deal out of it. And a film. So don't blow it, guy."

Thanks, boss...

There are a couple of things I think you need

to know about Courtney Sheppard at this point. First, at the relatively young age of thirty-four, she's the editor in chief of *Citizen* magazine — the same magazine that in only two short years of existence has defied the odds and done what so many other upstarts will never do. *Turn a profit.*

On the heels of editor stints at both *Vanity Fair* and *The Atlantic,* Courtney made a formula for success at *Citizen* by taking those two magazines' seemingly divergent sensibilities and combining them into one. Smart move. But then again, she's a smart woman.

A very pretty one, too. And not particularly impressed with her looks, either.

Which brings me to another thing you need to know about Courtney Sheppard. On second thought, we'll get to that information a little later.

From Kennedy Airport I caught a cab to my apartment on the Upper East Side of Manhattan. I live mostly out of my suitcase, and that's a good thing because my apartment isn't all that much bigger than one.

Clearly I'm not in journalism for the money. Who — besides maybe Thomas Friedman of the *Times* — is? I don't mean that Friedman doesn't love what he does, merely that he makes a lot of change doing it.

Anyway, when I was eleven years old I saw the movie *All the President's Men* with my parents. My father loved it because he despised Richard Nixon. Like Pavlov's dog, he would always blurt out "That crook!" at the mere mention of Nixon's name.

My mother was gung ho on the movie as well, but I'm pretty sure her motivation was a crush on Robert Redford. And maybe the young Dustin Hoffman, too?

My parents had no real intention of having me tag along. I was supposed to stay home under the evil eye of my older sister, Kate. Instead, I smooth-talked them into taking me. "Who knows, maybe I'll grow up and be a famous news reporter one day," I said, pleading my case. "I could be another Woodward, another Bernstein."

Of course, that was a ripe load of bull. I was only in it for the bucket of popcorn, a Mountain Dew, and maybe some Raisinets if my dad was in a chipper mood.

But as I sat there in the theater munching and slurping away, something amazing happened. Magical, almost. Up on the screen were two young guys who were on the biggest treasure hunt of their lives, only they were searching for something more valuable than gold or diamonds, or even the Ark of the Covenant. I was only eleven but I got it—and till this day I've never wanted to let go.

They were searching for the truth.

So even after two flights, eight time zones, and twenty exceedingly long hours, I couldn't wait to travel a few miles more. I quickly grabbed a hot, then cold, shower and changed into some clean clothes.

Then it was out the door and back into a cab heading down to 67th Street and Third Avenue.

At twelve thirty on the dot, I walked into Lombardo's Steakhouse ready to meet one of the best pitchers and most confounding puzzles ever to play the game of baseball.

And if I handled everything just right, I'd have the story that a hundred other writers around New York would kill for. *Dwayne Robinson, what* really *happened that night you were supposed to pitch the seventh game of the World Series? Why didn't you show up at the ballpark?*

How could you break so many hearts, including my own?

Chapter 7

"JUST ONE SECOND, SIR," I was told after giving the hostess at Lombardo's my name. "I'll be right back to help you. One second."

As she disappeared into the dining room, I leaned forward over her podium to catch a glimpse of the reservation book. When you eat out as much as I do, you get pretty good at reading your name upside down.

Sure enough, there was "Robinson/Daniels" on a line for twelve thirty. After it was a star.

The star treatment, perhaps? Not for me, of course. Maybe for *Citizen* magazine?

Seconds later, the hostess returned. "We have a nice quiet table reserved for you, Mr. Daniels. Follow me."

If you insist.

She happened to be a very pretty blonde, and as my father's father, Charles Daniels, used to say right up until his dying day, "If there's one thing I have a weakness for, it's pretty blondes. That's followed very closely by pretty brunettes and pretty redheads."

We arrived at a table along the back wall. "What's your name?" I asked, sitting down.

"Tiffany," she answered.

"Like the pretty blue box?"

She smiled, her eyes shining like gems. "Exactly."

That was for you, Grandpa Charles. Hope you were watching and getting a laugh.

Tiffany turned, leaving me on my own—and that's how I remained for the next ten minutes. Then twenty. Then half an hour. What was this all about?

Thankfully, of all the restaurants in which to be stuck waiting for someone, Lombardo's Steakhouse ranked near the top, thanks to its truly sublime people watching. It was easy to pass the time counting the Botoxed foreheads or, for the truly cynical, playing Hollywood

Hamlet with the tabloid celebrities sprinkled in the mix.

Rehab or not rehab? That is the question.

I guess that's why I had been a little surprised that Dwayne Robinson would agree to meet me here, let alone be the one to actually choose the place.

Sure, he was as famous as they come in the world of sports. Or maybe *infamous* was a better word these days. But even way back when he was the toast of New York—make that *America*—he never would've eaten at Lombardo's. That's how bad his anxiety disorder was.

So maybe he's cured now. Maybe that's one of the hooks of this interview, that he's "going public" in more ways than one.

Or maybe not.

As I glanced at my watch again, I wondered if perhaps nothing had changed about him and my flying halfway around the planet with barely a minute to spare was all for naught. Dwayne Robinson was now an hour late.

What's the deal? Where the hell is he? What an asshole this guy is.

I rang Courtney, who called me right back

after getting in touch with his agent. The agent was equally as baffled, especially since he had confirmed the interview with Dwayne earlier in the morning. Now he couldn't reach him.

"I'm so sorry, Nick," said Courtney.

"You and me both. Well, at least Robinson hasn't lost anything over the years. He's still a no-show. What a chump."

After another fifteen minutes, I finally gave up waiting. Dwayne Robinson was officially MIA—just like when he was scheduled to pitch that seventh and deciding game of the World Series and flat-out disappeared.

All of a sudden I felt like the kid who confronted Shoeless Joe Jackson on the steps of the Chicago courthouse during the Black Sox scandal of 1919.

Say it ain't so, Dwayne.

Say it ain't so…

But…it was so.

And Robinson wasn't the chump—that would be me.

Chapter 8

CALL ME LAZY AND SHIFTLESS, but on the heels of being chased by a gang of bloodthirsty, trigger-happy militiamen, leaping from a speeding Jeep, and flying a gazillion miles for a career-making interview that didn't happen, I decided to play hooky the next day. I didn't trek into my office at *Citizen* magazine nor did I plan to work out of my apartment, something I do from time to time with decent results.

Instead I spent the morning in bed relaxing with some coffee (cream, no sugar), the *New York Times* (Sports section first, then Arts, then News in Review), and one of my favorite Elvis Costello albums (*My Aim Is True*).

And by records I mean, literally, the record.

Nothing against CDs and MP3s, but I've yet to hear anything that quite captures the pure sound of a needle against vinyl. So yeah, I'm afraid I'm one of *those people,* a purist who still swears by his LP collection.

Anyway, at a little past noon I finally ventured out to my go-to neighborhood eatery, the Sunrise Diner, a few blocks south of my apartment. I was just being served my lunch (cheese omelet, sausage, black coffee) when Courtney called.

"Where are you?" she asked in a near panic.

"About to bite into a delish-looking omelet at the Sunrise."

"Don't!" she said. "Step away from those eggs!"

"Why would I do that?"

"Because you're already late."

For what?

I had no idea what she was talking about. Then it suddenly clicked without her saying another word. "You're kidding me," I said.

"No, I'm not. I just got a call from his agent. Dwayne Robinson is sitting inside Lombardo's at this very moment waiting for you."

"He thought our lunch was *today?*"

"I don't know. I didn't exactly hang around

for the excuse," said Courtney. At least I thought that's what she said. I was already clicking off the phone.

"Check, please!"

"Is anything wrong with the omelet, Nick? I'll get you another one, honey."

"No, no, it looks great, Rosa. I just have to run. Sorry."

Luckily I had my shoulder bag with me—the same beat-up brown leather bag I've had since I graduated from Northwestern. Tucked inside as always was the one thing I absolutely needed to conduct the interview: my tape recorder. It's actually a "digital voice recorder," but thanks to that purist streak in me I've yet to get comfortable calling it that. Probably never will.

Bolting out of the Sunrise, I snagged a cab heading south and offered the driver five dollars for every red light he ignored. Eight minutes and twenty-five dollars later, we were screeching to a halt in front of Lombardo's.

For the second day in a row, I was walking into the same bustling steakhouse for lunch. As my favorite Yankee catcher, Yogi Berra, said, "It's déjà vu all over again."

Fittingly, the same hostess — "Tiffany, right?" — was there to greet me. She took the leather jacket I was wearing and led me to the same quiet table in the back.

And there he was, in the flesh. Dwayne Robinson. The legend. The *fallen* legend. And definitely the greatest sports mystery ever.

"I'd just about given up on you," he said.

Right back atcha, buddy.

Chapter 9

I HONESTLY DIDN'T know what to expect next as I sat down across from him. I knew my job was to be objective, but sometimes it's pretty hard, if not impossible, to completely shut off your feelings. There had been a time I had revered Dwayne Robinson, but that was ages ago. Now he was just some guy who had squandered an amazing Hall of Fame talent, and if anything, I resented him for it.

Maybe that's why I was so stunned at my reaction to the man now.

After just one look into his eyes, the same eyes that used to stare down opposing batters without an ounce of fear, I could feel only one thing for him: sorry as hell. Because all I could see in those eyes now was fear.

Cue Paul McCartney and the Beatles: *I'm not half the man I used to be*.

"What are you drinking?" I asked, eyeing the three knuckles' worth of what appeared to be whiskey in front of him.

"Johnnie Walker," he answered. "Black."

"Sounds good to me."

Rumors of Dwayne Robinson's drug use had begun by his third year of twenty-win seasons in the majors. Mind you, this was back when the worry wasn't all about performance-*enhancing* drugs. Supposedly, he was doing cocaine and sometimes heroin. Ironically, when you shoot those two together it's called a "speedball."

But if the persistent rumors were true, the two-time Cy Young Award winner wasn't letting it affect his performance on the field. And whatever erratic behavior he displayed elsewhere was explained away by his social anxiety disorder.

Then came the famous "Break-In."

With the World Series between the Yankees and the Los Angeles Dodgers tied at three games apiece, Dwayne was scheduled to take the mound in the Bronx for the decisive game seven. He had already won two games in the series, allowing only a single run. In other words, he seemed unhittable and therefore unbeatable.

Only this time, he never showed up for the game.

He disappeared for something over seventy-two hours. Hell, it would've been longer had the super in his Manhattan luxury high-rise — a die-hard Yankees fan, no less — not used his master key to enter the star's penthouse apartment. Inside he found Dwayne Robinson lying naked on the floor, barely conscious. According to insider stories the irate super actually kicked the star a couple of times.

From a hospital bed at Mt. Sinai, Dwayne told the police that two men had forced their way into his apartment and drugged him, probably to increase their odds on a huge bet they'd made on the game. So that's why his blood tested positive for a near-lethal dose of heroin. Because of the "Break-In."

Naturally, it became one of the biggest stories in sports — no, make that one of the biggest news stories, period. *After Watergate, it was the second most famous break-in in history,* I quipped at the time, writing for *Esquire.*

Of course, the difference was that Watergate had actually happened.

While Dwayne Robinson had his supporters, the prevailing sentiment was that he was lying — that no matter how vehemently he denied it, the ugly truth was that he had overdosed on his own.

The fact that the two thugs — whose descriptions he provided to the police — were never found didn't exactly bolster his case.

Within a year, Robinson was banned for life from the game of baseball. His wife left him, taking their two young children and eventually winning full custody of them. If you thought about it, and I did, it was the worst bad dream imaginable. Everything he lived for was gone. It had all disappeared. Just like him.

Until now. This very moment. The first interview in a decade.

I reached down and slid my tape recorder out of the brown leather bag on the floor. Placing it in the center of the table, I hit record. My hand was actually shaking a little.

"So how's this work?" asked Dwayne cautiously as he leaned forward in his white button-down shirt, his enormous elbows settling gently on our table. "Where do you want me to begin?"

That part was easy.

What really happened that night, Dwayne? After all these years, are you finally ready to tell a different story? The real story? Solve the mystery for us. Solve it for me.

But before I could ask my first question, I heard a horrific scream, one of the most wretched, guttural, god-awful sounds I'd ever heard.

And it was coming from the next table over. We couldn't have been any closer.

Chapter 10

MY HEAD SNAPPED sharply to the left, my eyes tracing the horrible sound to its source. As soon as I saw what was happening, I wished that I hadn't. But it was too late and I couldn't turn away. I couldn't do anything, actually. It was over so fast, I couldn't even get out of my chair to help.

Two men.

One knife.

Both eyes!

A chorus of shouts and screams flooded the restaurant as the man wielding the knife let go of the other man's head, the blood spouting from his eye sockets as he collapsed onto the table. A little spark was triggered in the back of my brain. *I know him. I recognize him.*

Not the man with the knife, not the killer. He didn't look familiar; he didn't even look human.

He moved lightning fast—and yet there wasn't a trace of emotion coming from him. He coolly tucked away the knife in his jacket, then bent down to whisper something in his victim's ear.

I couldn't hear it…but he definitely whispered in the dying man's ear.

For the first time, I glanced over at Dwayne, who looked exactly as I felt. In complete shock. I could tell he hadn't heard the killer's whisper either.

What came next, though, everyone in Lombardo's clearly heard.

The killer began walking toward the door to the kitchen when a man behind him shouted, "Freeze!"

I turned to see *two* men with guns drawn. Cops? If they were, they were out of uniform.

"I said, *freeze!*" the one repeated.

From twenty feet away they had the killer dead in their sights. At least that's the way it looked.

Plates, silverware, and entire tables went

crashing as people scrambled for their lives to get out of the way of whatever might happen next.

The killer stopped, turning to the two men and their guns. Sunglasses blocked his eyes.

He said nothing. He barely moved.

"Put your hands up slowly!" the second man barked. They certainly sounded like cops.

The killer just smiled. It was a sick, twisted grin that seemed tailor-made to the crime he'd just committed. His hands, however, remained at his sides.

"Put your fuckin' hands up!" came the second warning.

My eyes pinballed back and forth between the killer and the two men. It was a standoff so far. But something had to give. *Or someone.* And everything, including the barrels of two guns, was pointing at the killer.

Suddenly his hands jolted up, but not before first taking a detour. As fast as you can say Travis Bickle, the killer reached into his jacket, removing two guns of his own.

You talkin' to me? Are you talkin' to me?

Who the fuck do you think you're talkin' to?

Dwayne's reflexes were still there, and he dove to the floor. I was right behind him, closing my eyes as sheer pandemonium broke out above our heads. There were countless gunshots. People screaming.

People dying.

Finally, when it all stopped, when all I could hear were the horrified sobs and gasps of everyone down on the floor around me, I opened my eyes again.

And I nearly threw up.

There, in a pool of blood on the polished hardwood floor of the restaurant, was one freshly carved-out eyeball staring up at me.

Chapter 11

MY LEGS WERE rubbery and my stomach rolled as I slowly stood, gazing at a sea of overturned tables and chairs, smashed plates, scattered silverware and food. Shocked and bewildered, everyone was asking everyone else the same question.

"Are you okay?"

The answers were quickly drowned out by the piercing sound of sirens. I barely had time to grab my tape recorder as the New York police descended on the restaurant, blocking off all the exits and corralling us like sheep in the bar area.

Soon, everyone was asking a different question.

"Haven't we been through enough already?"

A few ambitious cops fanned out among us,

quickly trying to get as much information as they could before turning the investigation over to the detectives. What they didn't want to get in return was lip and blowback from a high-class clientele that just wanted to get the hell out of there.

"Tough shit," I actually overheard one officer say to some red-faced stuffed shirt complaining that he had to be at an important board meeting all the way downtown.

The officer's anger made all the more sense as word got around fast that the two men who confronted the killer had indeed been off-duty cops. Their precinct, the nineteenth, was nearby and they had been grabbing a quick beer and hamburger at the bar after working the graveyard shift together.

Now they were dead.

How could that be? I had been there—and it almost hadn't seemed possible. They had had the guy covered like white on rice!

Clearly the killer knew what he was doing, and that was the King Kong of understatements. As fast as lightning he'd taken down two of New York City's finest, and not with lucky shots, either. I'm talking about dead center to their foreheads, twice over. The cops never knew what hit them.

Then—*poof!*—the killer was gone. He had apparently escaped unscathed through the kitchen and out a back door.

All told, he left behind three dead, four wounded, and dozens who were really, *really* shaken up about what they had just—unfortunately—witnessed.

Few more so than Dwayne Robinson, who now stood by my side. I almost felt like his bodyguard at this point. Or his sports agent. Someone there to take care of him.

"Here, drink this," I said, handing him some Johnnie Walker Black that I grabbed from behind the bar. Technically, I was looting. Officially, I didn't care.

"Thanks," Dwayne mumbled, reaching for the glass. That's when I saw that his hands were trembling badly. *Is there a Valium in the house?*

Or maybe it was his anxiety disorder kicking in. He had that look, like the restaurant walls were caving in on him. *Better make that two Valium . . .*

It didn't help matters that people were beginning to recognize him. You didn't need any poker skills, though, to read his body language. It basically screamed, *Back off!*

Unfortunately, one idiot couldn't help himself. He walked right past Donald Trump, Orlando Bloom, and Elisabeth Hasselbeck, heading straight for us.

"Hey, aren't you Dwayne Robinson?" he asked, removing a slip of paper from inside his suit jacket. "Do you think maybe you could sign—"

"Now's not really a good time," I interrupted.

The guy turned to me, raising his tweezed eyebrows. He looked like a real slickster, maybe from Madison Avenue. "Who are you?" he asked.

Good question. Who was I to Dwayne Robinson at this moment? But the answer seemed to come easily. "I'm a friend of his," I answered. Then I channeled my best tough-guy imitation. "And like I said, *now's not really a good time.*"

I must have been convincing enough, because the guy backed off. He even mumbled, "Sorry."

"Thanks," Dwayne said again.

"You're welcome. So what brings you here?" I

said, and grinned so he'd know I was trying a joke to ease the tension. Not a good joke, just a joke.

Dwayne took a big gulp of the Johnnie Walker and finally managed to find his voice. "Man, I don't know if I can do this," he said. "How long do you think they'll keep us here?"

It was another very good question. I was about to tell him I had no idea when some guy with a badge hooked to his belt stood on a chair and introduced himself as Detective Mark Ford. That was followed by a bit of good news, if you could call it that. He and his partner wanted to take statements from people according to how close they had been sitting to the initial murder.

"We'll do this table by table," he said. "As soon as you're done, you can go."

I glanced over at Dwayne, expecting him to be relieved at the news. We'd be among the first to be interviewed.

Except Dwayne wasn't there. He wasn't anywhere. He'd just up and disappeared.

Gone.

Again.

Chapter 12

IT TOOK ANOTHER two hours before I finally got out of Lombardo's. While I was being interviewed by one of the detectives, I kept waiting to be asked about Dwayne's disappearance. The question never came. That probably explained how he was able to escape Lombardo's undetected—there were just too many people for the police to control, too much commotion. It was truly a mob scene.

A prophetic choice of words, as I'd soon discover.

Anyway, the last thing I felt like doing later that night was go to a party, but Courtney wouldn't take no for an answer, not even under the circumstances.

"You're coming, and that's that. You promised me," she told me over the phone. "Besides, you need to get your mind off what happened today. Compartmentalize, Nick. Just stuff it into a box for a little while."

I had to chuckle. Compartmentalize? Stuff it into a box? That was Courtney at her best. And worst, I guess.

Since I first met her ten years ago at the National Magazine Awards banquet, I've yet to meet anyone who could—for lack of a better word—*compartmentalize* better than she could. Like any normal person she was shocked and horrified to hear what had happened at Lombardo's that afternoon. But she was also a born and bred New Yorker and knew the importance of being able to get on with your life, no matter what had happened to you.

It wasn't just talk with Courtney, either. Her younger brother had worked in the South Tower of the World Trade Center. Ninety-seventh floor. And she had really loved him, too.

So at eight o'clock I walked into the white marble splendor that was Astor Hall in the New York Public Library. The party was a benefit for

New York Smarts, a citywide tutoring program for grade-school students. Courtney was one of its board members and had purchased a table for ten on behalf of *Citizen* magazine. Good for her. Even better for the kids. A thousand dollars a plate can buy a lot of tutoring.

"There you are!" I heard over my shoulder. Courtney had found me where you can always find me at these types of events: the bar. "And I see you've discovered the house Scotch," she said.

Indeed I had. It was a Laphroaig 15 Year Old, which happened to be my personal favorite. Courtney obviously had some pull with the event's liquor committee.

"Thank you," I said, tipping my glass. "I definitely needed this."

"You're welcome. Just try to leave a little for the other guests, if you can," she said, deadpanning.

"Okay, but just a little."

Courtney helped herself to one of the flutes of champagne that were being passed around. "Well, so much for being able to take your mind off today," she said.

"Why do you say that?"

"Because Lombardo's is the talk of the party, Nick. Hell, it's the talk of the city."

I was hardly surprised.

The front page of the *New York Post*'s late edition had screamed, "DEATH DU JOUR!" Meanwhile, the local and cable news networks were having a field day. By the time they hit the airwaves with live feeds outside of Lombardo's, they were able to report the identity of the first victim—the guy sitting next to Dwayne and me.

I could've sworn I knew him, and I was right.

His name was Vincent Marcozza, and he was the longtime lawyer—excuse me, *consigliere*—for reputed Brooklyn mob boss Eddie "The Prince" Pinero.

"Everyone's convinced today was payback," said Courtney.

I nodded. "I guess."

Eddie "The Prince" Pinero had been convicted the week before on criminal usury charges, otherwise known as loan-sharking at an interest rate that would make even your credit card company blush.

The case was the first time Vincent Marcozza—a legal heavyweight, in every sense of the word—had failed to spring his biggest client. But hey, even Bruce Cutler didn't win every time on behalf of John Gotti.

But Marcozza's performance in the trial had been heavily criticized by legal pundits. They said he'd been uncharacteristically sloppy and at times seemed ill-prepared. As Jeffrey Toobin told Anderson Cooper on CNN, "Marcozza really took his eyes off the ball this time."

His eyes, huh?

Courtney raised her champagne glass. Then she gave me that big blue-eyed wink of hers. "So here's to you, Nick."

"Me? For what?" I asked.

"For starters, being alive," she said. "I had no idea you were such a magnet for danger these days. A girl could really get in trouble hanging around you."

We clinked glasses, but what followed could only be described as an awkward silence between us. It was all due to the subtext of what she'd just said.

Which brings me back to the second thing you need to know about Courtney Sheppard.

I owe you that one, remember?

Chapter 13

THE PROBLEM BETWEEN us was as clear as the ten-carat diamond on her finger.

Courtney was engaged.

And not just to anybody, but to Thomas Ferramore, one of the wealthiest guys in New York. We're talking loaded here. Super megabucks. A one-man stimulus package, if you will.

Ferramore owned commercial real estate, lots of it. He owned an airline. He owned over a dozen radio stations. Two soccer teams.

Oh yeah, and he owned *Citizen* magazine.

After their yearlong "whirlwind courtship" that rivaled the likes of Lindsay Lohan, Britney Spears, and Brangelina for boldfaced mentions in the gossip pages, the two of them were scheduled to be married this fall at the ultraposh San Sebastian Hotel here in the city. You guessed it. Ferramore owned that, too.

The whole thing promised to be the don't-miss social event of the season. A real storybook wedding. Problem was, there'd been an unexpected chapter written. Only two people knew about it, and Thomas Ferramore wasn't one of them.

The night before I left for Darfur, Courtney and I had slept together.

We immediately agreed that it was a one-time thing, a complete lapse in judgment due to our close working relationship over the years. And our friendship, platonic up until then. Sometimes histrionic, often hilarious.

"We can't pretend it didn't happen, nor do I want to," she said the morning after. "But we have to *act* like it didn't happen, Nick, okay? And that's that."

Compartmentalizing again.

But I suspected it wouldn't be as easy as "that's that."

Sure enough, after her little toast to me, "it" was suddenly the big white elephant in the big

71

white marble room of Astor Hall. We couldn't ignore it, not until we at least had discussed it some more. As much as we might have tried, there was no way to stuff that elephant into a box.

More important, I didn't want to. For better or worse, Courtney needed to know how I felt about her, and maybe it had taken getting shot at in Africa for me to fully understand that.

So I took a swig of my Laphroaig 15 Year Old Scotch, followed by a deep breath. *Here goes, well, everything,* I was thinking.

I turned to her. She was wearing a long black dress with a jewel neckline, her auburn hair elegantly pulled back behind her ears. Beautiful—and so, so sweet.

"Courtney, there's something I need to—"

"Uh-oh," she interrupted.

Uh-oh?

But she wasn't reading tea leaves. This had nothing to do with what I was about to say to her. Instead, Courtney was peering over my right shoulder. She'd seen someone, hadn't she?

"We've got big trouble at twelve o'clock," she announced.

Chapter 14

"HELLO, NICK," I heard coming up behind me.

I turned to see Brenda Evans, the very blond, very attractive on-air stock market analyst for WFN—the World Financial Network—based here in New York. Her nickname, mainly among men, was the "Bull and Bear Babe." I, however, knew Brenda by a different moniker.

My ex-girlfriend.

"Hello, Brenda," I said. Those two words were the first I'd spoken to her since she'd broken up with me a little less than a year ago. My next five words were a complete lie. "It's good to see you."

"You too, Nick," she said. She was probably lying through those brilliantly white teeth of hers, but I couldn't be sure. That's how good she was.

As Brenda and Courtney quickly exchanged air kisses and pretended they liked each other, I realized Brenda wasn't alone. With her was David Sorren, the all-powerful Manhattan district attorney, not to mention one of *People* magazine's "25 Most Eligible Bachelors."

"Hi," he said to me, not waiting for Brenda to introduce us. "I'm David Sorren."

"Of course you are," I said jokingly. Jeez, he had shiny white teeth, too.

Beyond the cover of *People*, I'd seen him on the news at least a hundred times, usually standing on the steps of the Manhattan Criminal Courthouse touting the latest conviction of some bad guy. Now, with any luck, Sorren would be a complete prick in person so I could immediately hate him.

"And you're Nick Daniels," he said as we shook hands firmly. "I'm a big fan of your writing. In fact, I think you got robbed last year on the Pulitzer."

So much for hating the guy.

"Well, as we runners-up say, it was an honor just to be nominated. But thanks," I said.

"Don't let him fool you—he cried for three

days straight," said Courtney, chiming in with one of her patented wisecracks. She began to introduce herself, but it was another case of someone who needed no introduction.

"Yes, hello, Courtney," said Sorren, giving her the extra-friendly two-handed grasp direct from the Bill Clinton playbook. "I've been wanting to meet you for quite some time. I'm glad our paths have finally crossed."

Courtney wasn't born yesterday.

"You're not just saying that so *Citizen* magazine will run a big puff piece on you after you announce your candidacy for mayor next week, right?" she said.

Sorren wasn't born yesterday, either.

"Of course I am. Let me know if it works," he answered with a wink. "In the meantime, congratulations on your recent engagement. Is Mr. Ferramore here?"

"No, he's actually traveling on business," said Courtney. "He's in Europe. Home next week."

Brenda promptly took back the reins of the conversation, another thing she was always good at.

"So, Nick, I understand you had quite the

eventful afternoon," she said. "That must have been terrible. I'm sorry you had to see it."

I was about to ask how she knew I had been at Lombardo's when I remembered that this was Brenda Evans, the dogged reporter. Her sources extended well beyond her Wall Street turf.

"Yes. It was terrible," I said. "I'm sorry I was there, too." I didn't really have anything more I wanted to add. Thankfully, Courtney saved me. She turned to Sorren and instantly made like the investigative reporter she used to be.

"David, I'm sure you've heard all the speculation about Eddie Pinero being responsible for Marcozza's murder, right?" she asked. "What's your take on it?"

As leading questions went, this one was a major gimme. Sorren, like a young Rudy Giuliani—albeit better looking and with a full head of thick hair straight out of a men's shampoo commercial—had made cleaning up organized crime one of his highest priorities as Manhattan DA.

"At this point," said Sorren, "most of my thoughts are with the families of those two officers who were gunned down." He paused and drew a deep breath. "That said, I can assure you of this: We'll nail whoever committed those murders. And if it turns out that Pinero was connected, I'll be swinging the hammer on him myself, and I'll be swinging it hard."

Whoa. Easy there, Popeye...

I could see the veins in Sorren's neck pop through his skin as he finished that last sentence. It was more than mere conviction. It bordered on vengeance.

It also brought the conversation to a screeching halt. All that remained were the obligatory parting pleasantries. *So good to see you again... Yes, we really should try to get together sometime... Blah, blah, blah...*

And that was that.

I was done talking to Brenda and her new boyfriend for the evening. At least, that's what I thought.

Chapter 15

"SO, WHAT WERE you and I saying before we were interrupted by Blond Ambition?" asked Courtney when we were alone again. "You were about to tell me something, no? So tell me, Nick."

Yes. Yes, I was. But timing is…um…uh…everything, and the moment for that heartfelt declaration had come and gone. Along with my having the guts to say the actual words to her.

All the more reason why I suddenly didn't feel like sticking around at the benefit.

"I guess it's jet lag," I explained to Courtney. "I need to catch up on some sleep. You okay with that…boss?"

She probably knew I was making an excuse to leave, but she also knew the only reason I had come in the first place was because she'd asked. Plus, I'd had a rough couple of days, right?

"We'll talk tomorrow," she said, giving me a sweet kiss on the cheek. "As soon as possible we've got to get you back together with Dwayne Robinson. We need that interview, Nick."

I couldn't have agreed more. I definitely wanted this story as much as she did.

A minute or so later I was on the steps outside the New York Public Library—smack between its two landmark lion sculptures, Patience and Fortitude—when I heard someone call out my name.

I turned to see David Sorren catching up to me. He was jogging, actually.

"You got a second?" he asked.

"Sure," I said.

Sorren reached into his jacket, removing a pack of Marlboro Lights. I was surprised to see that he smoked, if only because of his widely known political ambition. Gallup poll: candidate + cigarettes = less trustworthy. Obama didn't go on the patch just for health reasons.

"You want one?" he offered.

"No, thanks."

"Yeah, I know, bad habit. Don't tell the press," he said, lighting up. "Wait a minute, you *are* the press."

I smiled. "I'll consider this off the record. Besides, I'm not much for petty crap."

"Good, because I actually have a favor to ask you." Sorren slid the pack of Marlboro Lights back into his jacket. When I saw his hand again, he was holding something else.

"Here," he said. "Go ahead, take it."

It was his business card. I looked at it as if to ask, *What's this for?*

"Now's not the time, but I was hoping the two of us could maybe talk on Monday about what you witnessed at Lombardo's," he said. "I shouldn't be saying this to you, but I'm convinced Eddie Pinero was behind it. Now I have to figure out some way to prove it. Believe it or not, I am torn up about those two detectives."

"I understand," I said, taking the card. "I'll give you a call. Monday."

"Great—I appreciate it. Because if it's the last thing I do, I'm going to bring that cocksucker Pinero down for good."

I nodded. I mean, I think I nodded. Tell you

the truth, I was still pretty taken aback by the district attorney's intensity. He wanted Pinero bad. Really bad.

Sorren firmly shook my hand again and was halfway back up the steps when he turned around.

"Hey, one other thing," he said. "Brenda told me that the two of you used to be a couple." He let go with a slight chuckle and shake of the head. "Small world, huh?"

"Yeah," I said. "Small world."

Maybe a little too small.

Chapter 16

CUE THE NIGHTMARES.

I knew I'd have trouble sleeping that night. There wasn't enough warm milk and Ambien in the world. As soon as I closed my eyes, it was as if I were back in Lombardo's, living it all over again in a continuous loop. I could hear the screams, the chorus of terror that ripped through the restaurant. I could see the shine of the scalpel in the killer's hand, the dark plum color of the blood that was suddenly spurting everywhere.

At one point it was even *my* eyes being carved out.

Finally, I raised the white flag.

I got out of bed and into the chair behind my

desk. If I couldn't sleep, maybe I could at least get some writing done.

Perhaps that was the only silver lining in my missing the interview with Dwayne Robinson—I could put all my focus into the piece on Dr. Alan Cole and his work in Darfur with the Humanitarian Relief Corps. First things first, I needed to sort through the hours' worth of recordings I had made with him, taking careful notes to string together an outline. *Note to any kids reading this: outline—always!*

The reality is, the longer I do this, the more I understand that there are no shortcuts in journalism. At least not any worth taking.

So I flipped on my laptop and grabbed my tape recorder. I was about to hit the rewind button when my hand suddenly froze. I realized something.

In the horror of those moments at Lombardo's, as well as in the haze and commotion of the aftermath on the killing floor, I'd forgotten that I had already been recording when Vincent Marcozza and those cops were murdered.

I didn't get my interview with Dwayne Robinson.

But what *did* I get?

Part of me almost didn't want to know. After tossing and turning half the night, I didn't particularly want to relive the murders yet again.

But how could I not?

Taking a deep breath first, I braced myself for what I knew was coming. Once more, I'd hear Marcozza crying out in agony. I'd hear the shots that had brought down the two detectives.

But before all of that, there had been something else, something I couldn't believe as I listened to the tape recording now.

Holy shit.

This changes everything.

Chapter 17

MY HEART WAS pounding as I played the tape back three times just to make sure. *Am I really hearing this? Did he really say that?*

Yes. Yes, he did.

It was the voice of the killer before he committed three murders in cold blood. He was speaking to Marcozza, telling him something, something I wasn't supposed to hear, something I shouldn't have been listening to now.

"I have a message from Eddie."

My recorder had barely picked it up and the Italian accent wasn't helping, but there it was — creepy, ominous, and beyond a reasonable doubt.

Evidence.

There was no other Eddie it could be, not since

Vincent Marcozza had worked for Eddie Pinero. The speculation around town was nearly unanimous — Pinero had ordered the hit. Now, word for word, it was more than just speculation.

"I have a message from Eddie."

The killer delivered it, all right. I listened to his words once, twice, three times.

Then I pushed back from my desk, the wheels of my chair carrying me nearly all the way to my bed. On the bench by the footboard were the trousers to the suit I'd worn to the benefit at the public library. I dug through the pockets looking for the business card David Sorren had handed me. I hadn't lost it, had I?

No. There it was, along with my money clip, a half-eaten roll of Cryst-O-Mint Life Savers, and two pieces of Trident bubble gum.

Right below Sorren's office number was another number for his cell. I looked up, checking the clock on my bedside table. It was almost three a.m.

Don't be crazy, Nick. You can't call Sorren now. Wait until morning.

On the fourth ring he answered.

Chapter 18

"HELLO?"

"David, it's Nick Daniels," I said. "Sorry to call so late."

It took him a few seconds to respond. "Oh... hey, Nick," he said in a whisper. "What's up? Is everything okay?"

I knew why he was whispering. He wasn't alone. Sure enough, I heard another whisper in the background.

"Nick Daniels? At this hour?"

It was Brenda.

Don't sweat it, I felt like telling him. *You're in bed with my ex-girlfriend. I get it. You weren't playing Boggle.*

Instead, I pretended I hadn't heard her and

quickly explained why I was calling him in the middle of the night. I'm pretty sure the sound I heard next was his shooting up in bed like a nuclear missile.

"Are you serious?" he asked.

"Dead serious," I answered. "I just listened to the tape several times."

I expected his next question to be a breathless *Can you play it for me over the phone?* Or maybe even *How fast can you meet me?*

Who cared what time it was? This was the guy who only hours before had looked me straight in the face and declared, "If it's the last thing I do, I'm going to bring that cocksucker Pinero down."

Thanks to my tape recorder, I was all but doing it for him. I had what he desperately wanted and needed to drop the hammer on the biggest mobster in New York.

That's why I was so surprised by what David Sorren said next.

Chapter 19

I WALKED INTO the Nineteenth Precinct on East 67th Street at a little after nine the next morning and was greeted by Detective Mark Ford, who led me back to his desk. It sat in the middle of a slew of other desks, in a large open area that reminded me of every police drama I'd ever seen on television, albeit without the ridiculous "extras" of gum-chewing hookers in fishnet stockings and belligerent drunks handcuffed to benches.

Then again, maybe Saturday mornings were just a little slow around here in the real world.

"Have a seat," Detective Ford told me, pointing to a metal chair that rode sidecar to a file cabinet.

"Thanks," I said. My butt was still hanging in the air, though, when he cut straight to the chase.

"So, do you have it?" he asked. "Did you bring it with you, Mr. Daniels?"

What, no small talk first? No chitchatting?

Of course not. From the moment Detective Ford had taken my statement at Lombardo's, I knew that everything about this guy was direct and to the point. His short, cropped gray hair. His rolled-up sleeves. The way his sentences were all about finding the quickest route to either a period or a question mark.

"Yeah, I have it," I said. "But there's something I want to talk to you about first. Something I need to know."

Oh, great, said his expression. It was as if I'd just told him some god-awful, horrible news, such as the TV show *Cop Rock* was returning to the air. All Detective Ford wanted to do was listen to the recording, and here I was telling him, *Not so fast.*

Just like David Sorren had told me.

As happy as the Manhattan DA had been to learn about my recording, he didn't want to hear it himself. At least not yet. Not until certain "protocols" had been met, he had explained.

"I can't be seen playing detective, you know what I mean?" he told me.

I did. Even though that's precisely what he had been doing with me on the steps of the New York Public Library.

So now here I was, sitting in front of Detective Ford, following protocol. There was just one problem.

"So what is it? Tell me," said Detective Ford. "What do you need to know?"

I cleared my throat. Twice, actually. "It's just that...well, I'm a little concerned about—"

He cut me off with a raised palm. "Let me guess—you're scared shitless that Eddie Pinero will want to carve your eyes out, too? That it?"

Maybe "scared shitless" was a touch extreme, but I wasn't about to quibble over semantics. I just would've preferred to slip the recording to David Sorren as an anonymous source and then get far, far away from this murder case, police protocols, and anything else that might eventually pop up.

"Will Eddie Pinero know I'm the guy supplying this?" I asked. "Seriously, detective. I'd like a straight answer."

Ford quickly folded his arms. "Here's the deal. For the time being, Pinero can't even know this recording *exists*. If it is what you say it is, then the first time he'll hear it will be after he's indicted." He shrugged. "Now, can he find out that you're the Good Samaritan who came forward with it? Sure. I won't bullshit you on that. Will he want to kill you because of it? I highly doubt it. Killing you would serve no purpose. How could it?"

I nodded as Detective Ford leaned back, the legs to his chair squeaking loudly as they scraped against the linoleum floor. If I had to guess, that had been the most uninterrupted string of sentences the guy had put together in a long, long time.

"If killing me would serve no purpose, then what was the purpose of killing Vincent Marcozza?" I asked. "It would seem to be no different — simple revenge."

I stared at the detective, waiting for him to alleviate my fears, to give me some great and compelling explanation as to why I had nothing to worry about. But that clearly wasn't his style.

"Look, Mr. Daniels, it's like this," he said.

"Eddie Pinero is a sick and twisted motherfucker who kills with little provocation and even less remorse. Personally, I don't think you have anything to worry about. Then again, Vincent Marcozza probably thought the same thing. So it's your call. *Now, are you going to give me the recording or not?*"

Chapter 20

"OH MAN, oh man, oh man."

Dwayne Robinson sat alone in the darkness of his tiny one-bedroom apartment on the Upper West Side. The place was barely furnished, almost as empty as the bottle of Johnnie Walker Black tipped over by his feet.

He was mumbling to himself, thinking that he missed his kids so much, it felt as if his heart had been carved out of his chest. For years now their mother had Kisha and Jamal out in California, as far away from him as possible. But even if they lived next door he knew he'd probably be too ashamed to see them. He hadn't paid child support for over a year. The last time he did, the check bounced, and he was ashamed about that, too.

There was nothing more to hock. His two Cy Young awards were long gone. So were the old Yankee jerseys. On eBay, the highest bid for one of his signed baseballs was $18.50. His rookie baseball card had no bids at all.

Again, the phone rang.

It had been ringing all afternoon and into the night. Not once did he answer or even check the caller ID. He didn't need to; he knew who it was.

He was sure that writer, Nick Daniels, was a decent guy, and that's what made it worse. Dwayne pleaded with himself, *Just call him back and tell him you're okay.*

Just lie, like you always do.

But he couldn't even do that much. He was too scared. The same fearless pitcher who chose to stay here in New York, even after letting the entire city down, was too scared to talk to some writer.

All he could do was close his eyes and let the darkest of dark thoughts creep into his mind like shadows across the outfield and around the monuments at Yankee Stadium.

Never having to open his eyes again. Not ever. That would be good.

"Goddamn it!" he yelled, swinging his huge clenched fist through the darkness. But the invisible demons were always out of reach.

His eyes popped open as he stood, turned on the light, and began pacing the floor. His fear had turned to rage, the alcohol coursing through his blood no longer dulling the pain. Instead, it was greasing the wheels. Every muscle, every nerve ending, fired at once as he lunged for the empty bottle of Johnnie Walker, scooping it up while cocking his arm.

This would be no curveball.

This was a ninety-eight-mile-an-hour fastball aimed right at the bare wall before him.

Smash!

Shards and splinters of jagged glass scattered across the apartment as he fell hopelessly back into his chair, sobbing into both hands.

Dwayne knew one thing for sure.

He couldn't keep his secret any longer.

He had to talk to that damn reporter, whatshisname—Nick Daniels.

Chapter 21

AFTER RETURNING HOME from the Nineteenth Precinct, where Detective Ford had sweet-talked me into handing over my recording from Lombardo's under the threat of a subpoena, I spent the rest of my day alternating between calls to Dwayne Robinson and contemplating life on the run from Eddie Pinero.

On the plus side, an extended stint in the Witness Protection Program would make for one hell of an article.

I could only pray I was overreacting about Pinero and what he might do to me.

As for getting through to Dwayne Robinson, well, that was getting damn frustrating—and I don't give up easily. Especially not on a story as big as this one could be.

Courtney had given me Dwayne's home number, courtesy of his agent, but if Dwayne was home he sure wasn't picking up. The guy didn't even have an answering machine, so I couldn't leave a message, something like *Call me, you self-centered son of a bitch. It's time to grow up, Dwayne.*

I just kept trying and trying every hour on the hour for the rest of the day. Half the night, too.

I'd like to tell you I had big plans for that evening as a certified, very eligible bachelor living in Manhattan, but I hadn't expected to be home for the weekend, let alone in the country. There were friends I could call but I wasn't really in the mood to do anything.

As for the one person who maybe could've changed my mind about that, she was with her fiancé. Unfortunately, I happened to know that the future Mr. and Mrs. Thomas Ferramore were guests of the mayor and fellow billionaire Mike Bloomberg at his home on the Upper East Side. Clearly my invitation had gotten lost in the mail.

So instead I ordered in a Hawaiian pizza,

popped open a Heineken, and watched some TV. Flipping around the dial, I sampled a few minutes of Larry King and his suspenders, followed by the local ten o'clock news.

Then I landed on the ultimate of ironies.

Staring back at me beneath the brim of his cap pulled tight above those intense, fearless eyes I remembered was none other than Dwayne Robinson. The channel was ESPN Classic, rebroadcasting the game that had first put Dwayne on the map—a twenty-strikeout gem against the Oakland A's on a very hot August night ten years ago.

Given my fruitless attempts that day to reach Robinson, I was tempted to switch the channel if only out of spite. I couldn't, though. It truly was a classic game, and no matter how many times I've seen it, I always have to watch some of it again.

Apparently, I wasn't alone.

Out of the blue, the phone rang next to me on the couch. "Private caller," read the ID.

"Hello?" I answered.

There was no response, but I could tell someone was there, and it was more than just a gut feeling. *Through the phone I could hear the same game I was watching.*

"Dwayne?" I asked. "That you?"

It was my first thought. I mean, if I ever struck out twenty people, I'd be watching a replay of the game, too. Every chance I got!

But if it was Robinson he wasn't answering.

I tried again. "That was an amazing night for you against Oakland. One for the history books. You'll never forget it, right?"

After another silence there finally came a voice. *His* voice.

"Yes," said Dwayne. "It was a special night. Almost seems like it wasn't really me. Or that *this* isn't me. I'm not exactly sure, Mr. Daniels."

I drew a deep breath and exhaled. "It's good to hear from you," I said. "I was a little worried."

"Yeah, I know you were trying to call. I'm sorry I—"

"No apologies necessary. I wanted to make sure you were all right, that's all. You are all right, aren't you?"

He sure didn't sound like it. I could tell he'd been drinking—or doing something—but he wasn't slurring his words. He sounded more depressed than drunk.

He left my question hanging.

"Dwayne, you still there?" I asked.

"I'm here." He paused. It felt like a lifetime. "Listen, there's something I need to talk to you about."

"Sure. Absolutely," I said. "Just tell me where."

"Not now. Tomorrow."

No, not tomorrow, right now! I wanted to yell.

This was no longer about finishing a sports interview, that much was pretty clear. There was something else going on. What the hell was it?

"Where are you now, Dwayne? Are you home? I can be there in ten minutes."

"No, I'm tired, Nick. A little wasted, to tell the truth. I need to get some sleep."

"But—"

"We'll do it tomorrow. I promise. Believe me, I can keep a promise."

I wanted to keep pressing, hopefully change his mind. Instead, I pulled back.

"Okay, how about we meet for breakfast?"

"I've got something to do in the morning. Let's meet for lunch again," he said.

We didn't exactly have a great track record with lunches, but I didn't want to point that out now.

"Sounds good, but on one condition," I said.

"What's that? What's your condition for the interview?" he asked, and chuckled lightly.

It was simple, and it made all the sense in the world. *"I choose the restaurant this time."*

Chapter 22

IT WAS A little before noon when I walked into Jimmy D's Pub three blocks south of my apartment. Any self-respecting writer has a local bar that doubles as his second home. I read that in Pete Hamill's memoir, so it must be true, right?

A couple of doors from Jimmy's I gave a buck to a panhandler I know named Reuben. Reuben's a homeless man, nearly blind, unemployable. A quirk of mine is that I leave the house every morning with ten singles. I give them out on the streets until they're gone. My father used to do the same thing with five singles when we would visit New York together. He didn't think it was a big deal, and neither do I.

"Hey, Nick," I heard from behind the bar as I

grabbed a stool inside Jimmy's. It wasn't quite a chorus of people shouting "Norm!" on *Cheers,* but it was welcome just the same.

"Hey, Jimmy."

Jimmy Dowd was the owner as well as his own daytime bartender. He poured a mean shot and could draw a clean pint of Guinness. I had no idea how his mixed drinks were because I'd never had one, let alone seen him make any. Jimmy's was a pub for those who had only one decision to make with their liquor: straight up or on the rocks?

But I was holding off on either. At least until Dwayne Robinson arrived for our meeting.

Jimmy nodded when I told him as much, and the two of us chatted for a few minutes about the Yankees' upcoming series against the Red Sox at Fenway. "We'll take two of three," predicted Jimmy. "As long as we pitch around Big Papi. Slumping or not, he always kills us!"

There were a lot of reasons why I liked hanging out at Jimmy D's, not the least of which was Jimmy himself. He was a Vietnam vet who had made some money in stocks and decided to fulfill his lifelong dream of owning a pub. There was also the fact that three years ago Jimmy had saved my life one night. But that's a story for another time.

The story now was Dwayne Robinson. I checked my watch—he was due any minute. Knowing that Jimmy, a Bronx native, shared the same passion for the Bombers that I did, I told him who I was waiting on.

"No shit, really?" he said, tossing back his head of jet-black hair with a surprised look. Then he summed up an entire city's feeling with four words. "He broke my heart."

We started comparing favorite Dwayne Robinson pitching performances. With lots to choose from, it wasn't long before I lost track of the time.

"When was he supposed to meet you?" Jimmy finally asked, glancing at his watch.

"Noon," I answered, doing the same.

Shit! It was twelve thirty. *Here we go again!*

I reached for my cell phone and dialed Robinson's apartment. By the sixth ring I was about to hang up. That's when I heard the beep of an incoming call. I hit the flash button to switch over to the other line, not bothering to check caller ID. I was sure it was Dwayne.

It was Courtney.

I dispensed with "Hello" and cut to the chase, my frustration leading the way like a bulldozer. "He didn't show," I said. "Dwayne Robinson screwed me again."

"I know," said Courtney.

I know?

"Are you near a television?" she asked.

I motioned for Jimmy to turn on the TV.

"What channel?" I asked her.

"Take your pick," Courtney said. "I'm watching ESPN."

She didn't say another word.

Chapter 23

"ESPN!" I SHOUTED to Jimmy.

He punched the remote, the picture came up, and within a few seconds my heart sank down into the floorboards.

A reporter was talking, the street scene behind him not giving too much away. I could see a cop car, a bunch of people milling about.

But it was all summed up on the bottom of the screen in plain English.

DWAYNE ROBINSON IS DEAD.

The reporter was rambling on, but it was as if I'd gone deaf. Jimmy said something to me and I couldn't process his words, either. I just kept staring at the TV screen in shock, getting numb all over.

The picture changed as a few words from the reporter finally began to sift into my ears.

Jump... building... apparent suicide... mystery man... now mystery death.

I snapped out of it to watch the TV screen fill with the shaky image from what looked like a handheld recorder. There was a hardwood floor—a hallway—and the pink slippers of the woman running with the camera. She was heading for a sliding-glass door off her living room.

Word for word, I could hear the reporter's voice-over.

"What you're about to see is dramatic home video shot by one of Dwayne Robinson's neighbors right after she apparently heard the crash outside her apartment window. I must warn our viewing audience that this footage is very unsettling."

The handheld camera finally stopped jumping around, the focus tightening from blurry to clear. Dwayne's neighbor was shooting from her terrace high above the street below.

Dwayne Robinson's six-foot-four body was sprawled facedown on the roof of a white van, the impact creating a crater of twisted and bent metal around him.

I went partially deaf again as the shot returned to the reporter standing on what was clearly the same street where Dwayne had lived.

And died.

"Guess he's not coming," Jimmy muttered, sounding as shaken up as I felt. "The poor son of a bitch. He blew us off again, huh, Nick."

Part Two

THE SETUP MAN

Chapter 24

BRUNO TORENZI OPENED the door to his room at the San Sebastian Hotel overlooking Central Park and gave a head-to-toe gaze at the five-foot-ten-inch blonde standing before him in the hallway. She was wearing a shiny red cocktail dress with matching high heels and strands of gold jewelry.

"What's your name?" he asked. "Your real name?"

"Anastasia," she answered. Her Russian accent was almost as thick as his Italian. "What's *your* real name?"

Torenzi ignored the question and simply turned around, walking back inside.

"Nice to meet you," the blonde said, closing

the door behind her. "I'll call you Sebastian, then. Like the hotel?"

"I get the joke," Bruno Torenzi called back to the girl.

Torenzi's preference was for Italian girls, but the ones on this side of the Atlantic were like eating at the Olive Garden: you would never mistake the experience for a home-cooked meal. As for the American girls, they talked too much about themselves. And the Asians were too skinny for him, nothing to grab on to.

Thank God for the Russian girls. Or Polish, or Greek, for that matter.

"Take your clothes off," said Torenzi, grabbing a beer from the minibar. There was no offer of anything for the girl.

"First things first," she shot back. "*Sebastian.*"

"Sure," he mumbled, walking over to an open black duffel bag perched on a round table in the corner. He pulled out a stack of cash. "Two thousand, right?" he asked, removing the rubber band holding the wad together.

"Not including gratuity," said Anastasia, hoping the Italian man, the apparently *rich* Italian man, didn't know the rules of the game.

Torenzi peeled off twenty crisp one-hundred-dollar bills and stuck out his hand. "I wasn't born yesterday...*Anastasia*."

She took the two thousand and thought that would be good—for a start.

Then she nuzzled up to his ear while sliding her hand down to the crotch of his black trousers. Nice material, Italian-made. "You know what *Anastasia* means?" she whispered through lips painted cherry red. "Means 'flower of resurrection.'"

Torenzi took a swig of his beer. "Excellent. Now take off your clothes," he repeated. "Forget about the history lessons."

The big guy liked to be the boss and he was hardly the first, thought Anastasia as she reached for the zipper running down the back of her dress. *Let him enjoy it while he still can.*

The former governor of New York notwithstanding, most men know that two thousand dollars was a pretty good price to pay for a call girl. Meaning she better be pretty and she better be good.

Anastasia didn't disappoint. As the cocktail

dress slipped off her shoulders, her blue eyes and high cheekbones became all but an afterthought to the rest of her. There was no bra, no panties underneath the dress. Just all-natural, gravity-defying talent and beauty.

"You know what, Sebastian," she purred. "I like you."

Torenzi finally laughed and then he unbuttoned his dress shirt. When it came off, along with his white undershirt, Anastasia couldn't help but stare. He was solid muscle, chiseled to perfection. But that wasn't all.

"My God, what happened to you, honey?" she asked. She couldn't help herself.

The better question would've been what *hadn't* happened to Bruno Torenzi. His left shoulder and arm were riddled with the scars of a shotgun blast—black tarlike circles the size of nickels and quarters. Count them all up and you had a buck fifty in change.

His other shoulder bore the scar of a severe burn, a six-inch patch of leathery skin that had the texture of beef jerky left out to bake in the sun for a month.

There was more. On one side of his stomach

were two stab wounds, the scars bubbled up from the flesh. Very hard to look at.

Torenzi glanced down at himself but said nothing. Certainly no explanation. All he did was remove his trousers and underwear and climb onto the bed.

Anastasia didn't press it. As it was, she was beginning to feel sorry for the guy.

"Oh, I get it," she said playfully, the back of her hand gently brushing across the curve of her breasts. "You're one of *those*. A real tough guy, right?"

She had no idea.

Neither did the two men just now stepping off the elevator, heading for the hotel room. Her partners.

For a year, the three of them had had the perfect scam going, but they had overlooked one thing this time.

Even contract killers get horny sometimes.

Chapter 25

THE BELOVA BROTHERS, Viktor and Dmitry, pumped up on adrenaline and blow, arrived at room 1204 of the San Sebastian. They eyed the plush hallway around them to make sure they were alone.

"Our father wouldn't approve," said Dmitry. He always said that before they did a job. Always.

"Fuck him," said Viktor, who thought he was sounding more American every day. "Fuck our father, Dmitry."

A dozen or so times before, they had stood outside expensive hotel rooms all over Manhattan, breathing fast to the point of panting while flipping off the safety switches on their Yarygin PYa semiautomatic pistols. The Yarygin's seventeen-round double-column, single-feed magazine was a major reason why it was the standard Russian military-issue sidearm. But for Viktor and Dmitry it was the ultrasleek stainless-steel barrel that they loved. It felt sturdier than the old-school Makarov pistol, more reliable.

Not that they had ever had to pull the trigger during one of these jobs.

That was the beauty and the brilliance of the scam. Most of the time they caught their victims with their pants down.

More important, the johns were always too embarrassed to go to the police afterward.

These were men of some means, usually high-level executives traveling on business. They had reputations to protect. They had wives and children. Whatever was stolen from them wasn't worth looking an NYPD detective in the eye and explaining, "I just got swindled by a prostitute and her two partners."

And all it had taken was an ad in the back of *212 Magazine* promising the highest-quality escort for the discerning gentleman. "From Russia with Love" read the headline.

It was good enough to entice somewhere

around twelve men to date—not that Viktor and Dmitry were keeping track. They were too busy counting the laptops, gold Rolexes, Kiton suits, and cold hard cash.

The brothers traded quick nods. Everything was good. Anastasia had placed the swath of tape over the lock chamber, same as always. All they had to do was turn the handle and they could stroll right in—no muss, no fuss.

But where was the fun in that?

Instead, the two of them burst into the room like a couple of class 5 hurricanes. They immediately spotted Bruno Torenzi lying buck naked above the covers.

"Don't move, motherfucker!" barked Viktor, taking advantage of one of the design features of New York's better hotels: thick walls.

Torenzi's confusion lasted only a second. He eyed Anastasia standing at the end of the bed. She confirmed what he already knew. It was a setup; she was the bait and he was today's sucker.

Sure enough, she started to put her dress back on. "Duffel bag," she announced. "Jackpot."

Dmitry's eyes moved off Torenzi and he walked over to the black duffel bag on the table in the corner. His smile grew as wide as Red Square at the sight of the cash inside.

Then the smile disappeared. It was gone. Totally gone.

"What the hell is this?"

Chapter 26

DMITRY REACHED DOWN into the duffel bag. He removed a gray rectangular block of C-4 explosive. A detonator wire was hanging from one end like a mouse's tail. Next he pulled out an absolute beast of a handgun, the Model 500 Smith & Wesson Magnum. A box of .50-caliber cartridges followed.

This was one serious duffel bag.

Dmitry's eyes narrowed to a suspicious squint as he looked back over at Torenzi. It was as if he'd just seen the second image in one of those optical illusion drawings.

This guy was naked, with the shiny barrels of two guns aimed directly at him. But he was completely calm and under control. Not a trace of fear.

Who is this guy? Is he connected? And why is it suddenly fucking hot in this room?

Dmitry pulled at the baby-blue silk shirt now sticking to his chest. "Do you work for somebody?" he asked.

Torenzi stared straight back, taking his time to answer. "Not your business."

Dmitry jerked his head at the duffel bag. "What are you doing with this stuff?"

"Not your business."

"I'm making it my business!" he snapped. "I say again, what are you doing with this stuff? You better talk to me."

Torenzi continued to stare at Dmitry, only now he was silent. Then he actually smiled and scratched his balls.

Suddenly Viktor lunged forward, jamming the barrel of his Yarygin into the john's cheek.

"YOU THINK THIS IS FUNNY? SOME KIND OF JOKE? MY BROTHER ASKED YOU A QUESTION!" he yelled.

But Torenzi didn't even look at Viktor. His eyes remained focused on Dmitry, over by the table. There was something else in the duffel bag—a box the Russian hadn't discovered yet.

Viktor pulled back the hammer on his Yarygin. "HEY, I'M TALKING TO YOU. YOU DEAF?"

"For Christ's sake, answer him!" chimed in Anastasia. She was practically pleading with the Italian. "These guys aren't fucking around."

Neither was Bruno Torenzi.

Faster than Viktor's trigger finger, Torenzi swung his hand and knocked away the barrel of the Yarygin pressed against his face. With his other hand he reached underneath the goosedown pillow behind him. He pulled out a Bersa Thunder .380 pistol.

The other box in the duffel bag was the extra ammo for it. Not that it was needed right now.

Bruno Torenzi's first shot caught Dmitry Belova high in the chest. The second split his forehead between the eyes. Only then did Viktor Belova's reflexes kick in. He tried to muscle his gun back toward Torenzi, but it was no use. Torenzi was too strong, too quick, too good at what he did.

He pumped three rounds into Viktor's stomach, causing the Russian to fall backwards onto the carpet. As he lay faceup and spilling blood, Torenzi stood and lodged his gun into Viktor's open mouth. The blast sent his brains shooting out from his skull in a perfect circle.

It was a bad day for the Belova brothers.

Now the only sound in the room was Anastasia crying like a little girl.

She had fallen to her knees, the red cocktail dress still unzipped in the back, hanging off her shoulders. She wanted to run for the door but couldn't. She was in shock, paralyzed, scared to death that she would be next.

"Get on the bed!" Torenzi ordered. "Take off that goddamn red dress."

"Please," she begged, her blond hair covering her face and tears. "Please, don't..." But then she shrugged off the dress. She climbed onto the bed.

"Now, where were we?" said Torenzi. "By the way, Anastasia, my name is Bruno. That is my *real* name."

Hearing that, the girl began to cry even harder. She knew what he meant.

"That's right. You know my name. You know what I look like," he whispered. "You might as well enjoy your last time in the sack."

Chapter 27

DWAYNE ROBINSON'S unspeakably sad funeral unfolded under a rain so heavy that had it been a baseball game, it would've surely been postponed. There was no church service. Instead, we all gathered graveside with a nondenominational minister at the sprawling Woodlawn Cemetery in the Bronx, final resting place for Joseph Pulitzer, Miles Davis, and Fiorello La Guardia among so many others.

The turnout was sparse, although bigger than I thought it might be. Many of Dwayne's ex-teammates were actually there—former Yankees and heroes of mine, whom on any other day I would've been thrilled to see in person.

Just not on this day.

Also on hand was Dwayne's ex-wife, who had left him the same week that he'd been banned from baseball. She was a former Miss Delaware. Alongside her were their two children, now approaching their teens. I remembered reading that she had petitioned for full custody of them during the divorce and won without much of a fight from Dwayne. For a man unaccustomed to losing on the mound, once off it he had clearly known when he'd been beat.

"Let us pray," said the minister at the front of Dwayne's mahogany casket.

Hanging toward the back, hunched under an umbrella like everyone else, I felt strange being there. Technically, I'd only met Dwayne once. Then again, I was one of the last people to speak to him.

Maybe even the very last. Who knew?

Certainly not anyone standing around me. As the service broke, the chatter was all about the "man they once knew." It was as if the poor soul who had reportedly jumped to his death from the terrace of his high-rise apartment had been a complete stranger to just about everyone at his funeral.

"Once he was banned from the game, it's as if Dwayne stopped living," I overheard someone say.

Now he'd just made it official.

What wasn't official yet was the autopsy, but in the intense media frenzy following Dwayne's death, a leaked toxicology report showed he was high on heroin. Space-shuttle high. That probably explained why he hadn't left behind a suicide note.

One mystery down, perhaps.

Another still unresolved.

What the hell had Dwayne wanted to tell me?

Weirdly, I felt as though I was also hiding some kind of secret. Courtney was the only other person who knew about the late phone call Dwayne had made to me the night he killed himself.

But as secrets go, mine was minor league. Dwayne's was a whole lot bigger, and he'd just taken it to the grave.

I walked back to my car, an old Saab 9000 Turbo—my one "extravagance," if you can call it that, in a city dominated by subways, taxis, and crosswalks.

Closing up my umbrella and sliding behind the wheel, I kept replaying that last conversation with Dwayne in my head. I wondered if I was overlooking something, if there was an important clue I wasn't catching.

Nothing came to mind yet. Or maybe my memory was a poor substitute for a tape recorder. What I wouldn't give to have a recording of that last phone call with him.

I was about to turn the key in the ignition when my phone rang.

I glanced at the caller ID.

Now, I'm not a big believer in the notion that nothing happens by accident, but for sheer timing this was stretching the boundaries of coincidence. It was spooky, actually.

The caller ID said "Lombardo's Steakhouse."

Chapter 28

"HI, I'M LOOKING for Tiffany." I said this to the man with the reservation book standing behind the podium at Lombardo's. I thought I recognized him, but it took me a few seconds to be sure.

Of course. He was the manager. I remembered seeing Detective Ford interviewing him on the afternoon of the murders.

"She'll be right back—she's seating someone," he said, barely looking up at me. He was average height and build, his tone sprinkled with an air of superiority that presumably came with the job. "Are you the man with the jacket?" he asked.

Actually, I was the man *without* the jacket.

Although not for long.

Before I could answer, I heard a voice over the

manager's shoulder. "You made it," she said.

She remembered me. I certainly remembered her. "Tiffany," I said, extending my hand. "Like the pretty blue box."

She smiled. Great smile, too. "Hi, Mr. Daniels," she said.

"Please, it's Nick."

I followed Tiffany to the coat-check room opposite the bar area. "Your jacket's over here," she said with a glance back at me. "We kept it nice and safe for you."

I nodded. "Listen, I appreciate your calling me. I didn't even realize I'd left it here."

"Pretty understandable, given the confusion that day." She stopped on a dime, turning to me. "*Confusion.* That word doesn't really capture it, does it?"

"I'm afraid not."

Tiffany shook her head. "You know, I was going to quit this job the next day. Go back to Indiana where I'm from. I even discussed it with Jason."

"Jason?"

"The guy you talked to at the desk. The manager."

"What did he tell you?"

"That this was New York, and I should just suck it up, and I would if I belonged here."

"What a sweetheart."

"I know, tell me about it," she said. "Then again, look around at the crowd of ghouls. I don't know whether to be amazed or really depressed."

I could see what she meant. Lombardo's Steakhouse was even more crowded than usual, if that was possible. Call it the perverse logic of hipness, especially in Manhattan and, I would guess, LA. After serving as the backdrop to three vicious murders, the joint actually *gained* in popularity.

Tiffany continued on to the coat-check room, grabbing my jacket. "Here you go," she said. "It is yours, right?"

"Yep, that's it, all right." A leather car coat I had gotten for a near steal years back at a Barneys outlet sale.

As I folded it over my forearm, something occurred to me. "Tiffany, how did you know this was mine?" It was a good question, I thought. It's not as if I had my name sewn inside the collar like some kid at summer camp.

"I went through the pockets. Hope you don't mind," she answered. "I found one of those e-tickets for a flight you recently took to Paris. It had your name and a phone number listed. That's how I—"

She stopped.

"What is it?" I asked.

Tiffany's jaw dropped. I could practically see the wheels churning behind her dark brown eyes.

"Oh my God!" she blurted. "You were here with the baseball pitcher that day, weren't you? The poor man who just killed himself?"

"Yes, Dwayne Robinson," I said. It still hurt just to say his name. "I just came from his funeral, actually. Very sad."

She shook her head slowly. "I couldn't believe it when I saw it on the news."

"You remember him, huh? From when he was here that day?" I asked.

"Yes," she said. "And from the day before, too."

I looked at her sideways as her last sentence knocked around in my head.

The day before?

133

Chapter 29

IT DIDN'T MAKE SENSE, none at all. Dwayne Robinson hadn't been at Lombardo's that first day. He had stood me up.

But he *had* been here. At least according to Tiffany.

"When?" I asked. "What time was it? Sorry to bother you, but it's important to me. I was supposed to do a story on Dwayne. For *Citizen* magazine."

"I'm not sure exactly. It was on the early side. Noonish, maybe."

That had been before I'd arrived, about a half hour before Dwayne and I were supposed to meet. Odd. Crazy.

"You're sure it was him?" I asked.

"Yes," she said. "Of course, I didn't think anything of it at the time. I remembered seeing him only after they showed his picture on TV. I'm not a big baseball fan. I didn't know who he was until then."

"Did you seat him?" I asked.

"No. I didn't even talk to him."

"What was he doing? Did you happen to notice? Anything at all?"

"I don't know. I was busy with other customers. I just remember seeing him at one point. He was looking around."

For me?

Had he thought we were meeting at noon instead of twelve thirty?

I stood there utterly perplexed, trying to think this new mystery through. All I knew for sure was that Dwayne had been at the restaurant the following day at twelve thirty. Courtney had said she'd never bothered to ask his agent why he had stood me up. Could Dwayne have thought I had stood him up? But then why would he have gone to the trouble to meet with me the next day?

For the past dozen years, asking questions

has been second nature to me. It's how I do my job. I ask questions, I get answers, I find out what I need to know. *Boom, boom, boom.* Simple as that. Especially when I'm really into a story.

But this was different. The more questions I asked Tiffany, the less I understood about what had happened.

"I'm sorry to keep pressing, but is there anything else you can remember?" I asked. "Anything at all?"

She turned her head away, thinking for a moment. "Not really. Except…"

"Except what?"

"Well, he did seem *really* nervous."

"You mean, like, he was pacing?"

"Nothing quite so obvious," she said. "It was more his eyes. He was a big guy, but he looked almost…scared to be here."

I literally smacked my forehead as a Latin expression from my school days at St. Pat's came rushing back to me. *"Entia non sunt multiplicanda praeter necessitatem."*

I was always so-so at Latin, yet this mouthful I've somehow never forgotten. It's the basis for what's commonly referred to as Occam's razor.

Translated, the phrase roughly means "entities should not be multiplied more than necessary." In other words, all things being equal, the simplest solution is the best.

And what was I *simply* forgetting about Dwayne Robinson?

His anxiety disorder. Of course.

It made total sense now. He had arrived early to meet me for lunch that first time. He looked scared, according to Tiffany. That's because he was. He was nervous about doing the interview and perhaps just nervous to be in the crowded restaurant, period. People could see him; some of them would definitely recognize Dwayne Robinson.

So he got cold feet and left.

I thanked Tiffany for my jacket and her time and help. I thought she'd thrown me a curveball about Dwayne Robinson, but as I walked out of Lombardo's, I was convinced I had it all figured out. *"Entia non sunt multiplicanda praeter necessitatem."*

Unfortunately, what I didn't know at the time—what I couldn't know—was that I actually had it all wrong. Because as theories go,

Occam's razor isn't foolproof. Sometimes, the simplest solution *isn't* the best.

Like I said, I wasn't terribly good at Latin. Downright *horribilis,* to tell the truth.

Chapter 30

DAVID SORREN JUST loved one-way mirrors. To him, they represented the heart and soul of his job as Manhattan DA, a literal metaphor for his success.

I've always got my eye on you.

And I never blink.

Ever since he'd been a rising-star prosecutor out of NYU Law, he'd been standing behind these one-way mirrors, his arms crossed, tie loosened—watching, gauging, sizing up hundreds and hundreds of criminals. Occasionally there'd be an innocent person thrown into the mix, but they were few and far between.

The simple truth was, if you ever found yourself in a police station, on the wrong side of a one-way mirror, the overwhelming odds were that you had something to hide.

And David Sorren's job—no, his *mission*—was to find out what it was.

Then nail you to the wall for it and throw the proverbial book at you.

"I say we play the recording for this douche bag bastard and watch him squirm," came a voice over Sorren's shoulder. "Make 'im squirm, make 'im turn."

As in, turning state's evidence.

Sorren heard every word of what his assistant DA Kimberly Joe Green was saying, but his eyes remained locked on Eddie "The Prince" Pinero on the other side of the glass.

Dressed in a natty gray-pinstriped suit with his trademark black handkerchief stuffed into his lapel pocket, Pinero was seated with his attorney—his *new* attorney—in the second-floor interrogation room of the Nineteenth Precinct.

No stranger to these rooms, Pinero clearly knew he was being both watched and recorded. He wasn't saying a word to his attorney, and he was staring straight into the one-way mirror with a smile on his handsome, ruddy face that declared, *Here I am, folks. Stare at me all you like!*

"Yeah, play him the tape," came a second voice behind Sorren in the observation room. It was Detective Mark Ford. "Pinero's about to return for sentencing. If there was ever a deal to be made, the time is now. Hate to admit it, but I'm with Kimberly Joe on this one."

Ford, a first-grade detective, and Green had an openly contentious relationship, to put it mildly, having endured numerous run-ins over the years. That said, they both knew how good the other was at their job. Respect, even when it came begrudgingly, trumped just about everything in law enforcement.

Finally, Sorren turned around to face Green and Ford. He could feel the heat rising to his head.

"A deal? Fuck, no," he said. "There's no way I'm ever giving that son of a bitch immunity."

"But—"

Sorren cut Green off. "The hit on Marcozza got two detectives killed. Two good guys with wives and children, seven kids between them.

No, there's only one way I want Pinero, and that's with his head on a plate," he said.

But even more than the words, it was the way he said them.

Teeth clenched.

Eyes unblinking.

As if the life of everyone in the room depended on it.

"Christ, did I say immunity? What was I thinking?" joked Green, dialing up her deadpan sense of humor. As an assistant DA she was smart enough to know when to fall in line behind her boss. "Okay, so let's wait on playing the tape. Who knows? Maybe Pinero will dig his own grave."

Sorren's scowl crept up slowly into a satisfied smile.

"Exactly," he said. "Now let's go give the prick a shovel."

Chapter 31

EDDIE PINERO GAVE a quick tug on the starched French cuff of his Armani spread collar shirt as he watched the three people enter the interrogation room. *Look who it is, the Three Stooges!*

If he could whack each one of them and get away with it, he would. In a heartbeat. He'd pull the trigger himself, smile while he did it.

Especially when it came to Sorren, that Eliot Ness wannabe!

Pinero was sure that if it weren't for the DA's hard-on for organized crime, he wouldn't be on his way to serving two to four years upstate. Of course, his former lawyer, Marcozza, hadn't exactly helped the situation. Pinero still couldn't understand how his consigliere had allowed him to take the fall for some trumped-up loan-sharking charges. At the trial it had been as if Marcozza had been phoning it in.

Pinero had a new attorney now, Conrad Hagey, called the "White-Collar Knight" among New York defense attorneys. His usual clientele were Wall Street and CEO bigwigs, mostly WASPs. In fact, Hagey had originally turned down Pinero's request to represent him because he hadn't wanted to sully his image.

That's when Pinero had taken out his check-book and a diamond-encrusted Montblanc pen. A half-dozen zeroes later, the tall and lean Hagey had had a sudden change of heart. Funny how that happens.

"Gentlemen," began Hagey. "I'd like to reiterate for the record that my client has come here voluntarily and will certainly leave here voluntarily. It's further understood that the sole purpose of this meeting is to ask him about the death of his—"

"The murder," interrupted Sorren.

"Excuse me?" said Hagey.

"Vincent Marcozza was *murdered*. As were

two New York City police officers. All three of them were *murdered*."

"And my heart goes out to all of their families," said Pinero, inserting himself into the conversation.

"I'll bet," said Sorren with a sneer. "You're just all beat up over it, aren't you?"

Hagey resumed his preamble only to have Pinero raise a palm to him. "Let's get to the questions," he said before turning to Sorren. "Sound good to you, *Mr. Mayor?*"

Sorren smiled at the jab but gave away nothing more. He wanted to tangle with Pinero but not about his own political aspirations. Indeed. *Let's get to the questions.*

"Do you have any idea who might have wanted Vincent Marcozza dead?" asked Sorren for starters. "That is, besides you?"

"I loved Vincent," Pinero shot back. "We were very close, for a lot of years."

"Even after he completely botched your trial? I mean, that was a real butcher job he did. Why am I telling you—you were *there*."

Pinero turned to Kimberly Joe Green, the assistant DA. Green had prosecuted the case.

"Your boss sure doesn't give you much credit, does he?"

Green didn't take the bait. She simply waited for Sorren to continue—and he did.

"Here's the thing, Mr. Pinero. If Marcozza was so close to you, who would have been crazy enough to kill him—and disappoint you so greatly?" asked Sorren.

"That's a damn good question. I guess I'll have to keep watching the news to find out," answered Pinero. "Which reminds me, how's that little news reporter of yours, Brenda Evans, doing? Nice little piece you've got there, if I do say so myself." He leaned forward on the metal table, his arms crossed. "Listen, do you really think I'd be stupid enough to whack my own lawyer?"

Sorren shrugged indifference. "Stupid enough? I don't know about that. Angry enough? Perhaps." He turned to Hagey. "Better watch your back with this guy, counselor. Either that or just make sure you never lose a case of his. Like this one."

"Don't you worry," said Hagey, an ex-forward on the Princeton basketball team. He'd taken more than his share of hard elbows while delivering a few in return. "All I've heard here so far is a lot of talk and zero evidence. You do remember what evidence is, don't you, Mr. Sorren?"

"As a matter of fact, I do," said Sorren. "Not only do I remember it, I have it."

Pinero immediately broke into laughter. It was loud and from the gut, like he was in the front row at Caroline's comedy club. He kept laughing until everyone in the interrogation room had to stop to watch him.

This was the very last thing Sorren would ever have expected him to do, and Pinero knew it. Or maybe it was the second to last thing.

The *very* last thing was what happened next.

"So, is this when you play us the recording from Lombardo's?" asked Pinero. "Gee, I can hardly wait."

Sorren's face said it all. He couldn't hide it. *How the hell does he know about the recording?*

Pinero tugged on the cuff of his shirt again, leaning back in his chair with a self-satisfied grin that stretched straight back to his porcelain-capped molars.

"What's the matter now, Sorren?" he asked. "Cat got your tongue?"

Chapter 32

"I'LL TAKE ONE dog with the works," I said. Culinary snobs will tell you that ordering a hot dog on the streets of New York is like playing Russian roulette with your gastrointestinal tract. Maybe so. But what better way to find out if you can stomach this city or not?

I've never gotten sick once. Well, maybe once. But that was on the Staten Island Ferry.

It was a little past noon now and I'd just come from the *Daily News* headquarters on West 33rd Street, where I was picking up my latest fix of Yankees tickets from my buddy Ira at the paper. Years back I had helped him get a job there as a sports reporter. Ever since, he's been regularly landing me in the first row behind the Yankees dugout right near where Rudy Giuliani always sits. *That's my kind of quid pro quo.*

"Here you go," said my hot dog man from behind his cart. Clearly he took pride in his work, as he bestowed upon me a perfectly layered masterpiece of onions, ketchup, mustard, and sauerkraut. I took it on faith that somewhere beneath it all was the actual hot dog.

Not that it really mattered by this point. I was starving, having worked straight through breakfast. This was my first bite of food all day, and as I began walking east on 33rd Street, I couldn't wait to dig in.

That's when I heard a guy's voice over my shoulder. "Hey, aren't you Nick Daniels?"

It's pretty rare that I get recognized out on the street. It happens maybe once or twice a year, mainly because my picture appears every week in the Contributing Writers section of *Citizen* magazine.

I'd be lying if I said these little encounters didn't stroke my ego a tad, but unfortunately this guy's timing couldn't have been worse.

I spun around, hot dog in hand, praying that

whoever the guy was, he didn't want to talk my ear off about some article I'd written.

Turns out, he barely wanted to talk at all.

Standing before me was a stone wall of a guy wearing dark wraparound sunglasses and a New York Knicks sweatshirt. At least I thought it was the Knicks—the orange and blue logo had faded more than the team itself during these past few years, ever since that James Dolan guy took over and ruined everything.

"Yeah, I'm Nick Daniels," I said to the guy. "How you doing? What's up?"

"Get the fuck in the car!" was his response.

Huh? What?

He jerked his head at a beat-up black van parked alongside the curb. The side door was already open. As if to give me a little encouragement, he lifted the side of his sweatshirt to reveal a pistol tucked between his jeans and a bulging gut.

I froze. *Is this really happening? Right here in broad daylight?*

Hell, yes, it really was.

In case there was any doubt, the guy swiped the hot dog out of my hand. The onions, ketchup, mustard, and sauerkraut landed *splat!* on the sidewalk.

And just like that there was one more ugly, sticky mess in the middle of Manhattan.

Me.

I was "going for a ride."

Chapter 33

SO THIS IS IT, I couldn't help thinking. *This is how I die. What a joke.*

Not while fleeing an attack by the Janjaweed militia in Darfur, or by catching typhoid fever, as I did a couple of years back in India while doing a piece on the prime minister, Manmohan Singh.

No, I go down in my own backyard, New York City. All because of a recording I had never intended to make.

Christ, how did Eddie Pinero find out about me so fast? Then again, am I really that surprised? He probably has more people on his payroll than the NYPD.

"Where are you taking me?" I asked from the

back of the windowless van. I was sitting on the metal floor. There were no seats.

There were also no answers forthcoming from my captors.

My escort in the Knicks sweatshirt was sitting sideways up front, riding shotgun. His dark sunglasses were fixed on me, and his mouth was shut tight. After he had demanded my cell phone—which I had reluctantly handed over—he hadn't said another word.

Same for the driver, who was big and baby-faced, at least from his profile. He looked barely twenty-one. On his right arm was a large, seemingly new tattoo of a Harley-Davidson logo. The orange color was so bright, it made the ink look as if it were still wet.

Again I asked where we were going, and in their continued silence I realized that there might be something scarier than being told you were going to die.

Not being told.

For twenty minutes, I sat idle with only my thoughts, a panic beginning to feast on me. From the floor of the van I couldn't see the windshield, but I could tell we were out of the city; we were going too fast. The van was old, the suspension shot. I could feel every bump, every pothole.

We're going to some out-of-the-way, deserted landfill, aren't we?

That's where they were taking me, I was almost sure of it. Out to Brooklyn. Out to the middle of nowhere. I could almost smell it— some godforsaken dump with a stench so thick it hung like fog.

"On your knees!" one of them would order me. I could hear the words in my head, cold and without mercy.

Would they have me turn away, face the opposite direction?

Hell, no, not these sick bastards. Not if they worked for Eddie Pinero. They'd shoot me straight on, a bullet to the brain. Probably stare right into my eyes, too.

Oh, God. My eyes! Were they going to carve my eyes out?

I was sweating now, shaking a little, scared shitless a lot. Most of all, I was convinced I had to do something to try to get away from these two gorillas.

But what? They had my cell phone, and at

least one of them was carrying a gun. So what could I do?

That's what, I realized.

Tuck and roll! The sequel to the desert.

The handle to the sliding door of the van was there in front of me. If I could reach it before Mr. Knicks could stop me, I could jump for it, maybe outrun them and survive to write another day.

Of course, I had to survive the jump first. And this time I wouldn't be landing on desert sand in Darfur.

Still, those odds had to be better than staying in the van, right? Those odds sucked. But I couldn't make myself jump out of a speeding van, could I?

Yes—I had to do it.

So this is it.

This is how I don't *die...*

I swallowed a deep breath and pushed the air down into my lungs, past my heart, which was beating so loud it was scary in itself.

Slowly, casually, I shifted my right foot so I could launch myself toward the sliding door. There would be no do overs, no second chances. I had to time this just right.

On three, Nick, okay? You can do this. You've done it before...

I counted backwards to myself, the adrenaline pumping through every vein in my body.

Three...

Two...

One...

Chapter 34

STOP!

The van suddenly made a sharp hairpin turn, the tires screeching and then skidding on what sounded like a slipstream of gravel.

Mr. Harley-Davidson at the wheel didn't just hit the brakes, he pummeled them into submission. Newton's third law of motion did the rest. I tumbled face forward in the back of the van, my head smacking the metal floor.

But instead of twinkling stars and Tweety Birds, it was a blast of sunshine I encountered next, as the sliding door of the van opened with a rusty grind.

Then out of the sunshine he stepped, a greeting party of one.

Eddie "The Prince" Pinero.

He motioned for me to exit the van. As I did, he extended a hand to help. *A helping hand? That doesn't mesh. What's going on here?*

The "here," as I quickly saw, was the driveway of what I presumed to be his home. Check that. *Estate* was more like it. With its lush gardens and a water view contained behind wrought-iron fencing, monstrous stone walls, and a show of armed guards, the property reminded me of a cross between the Kennedy and Corleone compounds.

"Thanks for making the trip out to see me, Mr. Daniels," said Pinero. "I appreciate it."

"You say that like I had a choice," I said, immediately regretting it.

But Pinero actually seemed amused. He smiled, anyway. "Hope I didn't give you the wrong impression. I just wanted to speak with you in private," he said. "Can I get you a drink? A Laphroaig, perhaps? Fifteen year?"

He knew what I drank. What else did he know about me?

"Okay, sure," I said. "Laphroaig would be good."

Pinero nodded at Mr. Knicks, who disappeared

inside the enormous Tudor home that boasted a magnificent wraparound porch. A few minutes later, I was sipping a generous pour of Laphroaig from an etched crystal tumbler initialed *EP*.

For the first time since I got into the van, I allowed myself to think that I might actually live to see tomorrow. Still, I was far from comfortable. I wasn't here with Pinero to discuss the weather or the series finale of *The Sopranos*. *Did Tony get whacked or not? What do you think?*

"Come, Nick, let's walk. Bring your drink," said Pinero. "I need to talk with you. Don't worry, you're not going to get hurt. You're with me. You're perfectly safe now."

Chapter 35

I TOOK ANOTHER sip of Scotch only to notice that Pinero hadn't joined me in a drink. I also noticed he wasn't wearing one of his natty suits with the trademark black handkerchief. As for what he was wearing, it was impossible *not* to notice that. I followed Pinero, in his royal blue Fila tracksuit, to the water's edge, the choppy waves of the Rockaway Inlet lapping against the breakwater of his property. He lit a cigarette and pulled a deep drag. Slowly, he exhaled into the breeze.

"So, Nick, that must have been some frightening scene that day at Lombardo's," he began with a slight nod. "It's not every man who witnesses murder that close. Unnerving, isn't it?"

"That's definitely a good word for it," I said.

"*A good word?* I'll take that as a compliment, you being a big-time writer. So you were there to interview Dwayne Robinson?"

"Yes."

He shook his head ruefully. "Sad story. All that talent, wasted. What a shame."

I didn't say anything to that. I was too consumed with trying to figure out where this conversation was heading. Pinero was obviously aware of the recording and how it implicated him. Instead of serving a little time for loan-sharking, he was looking at a murder conviction. So what did he want to talk to me about?

That's when I decided to try to cut through the bullshit and just ask him. "Mr. Pinero, exactly why am I here?"

The man they called "The Prince" took another long drag off his cigarette, his eyes never leaving mine. I don't even think he blinked. Then he calmly explained.

He didn't want to kill me. He wanted to help me.

Or at least warn me.

"Nick, I've been set up," he said. "And that

means you've been set up, too. I would like you to help me figure out who screwed us both. Let's help each other, Nick."

Chapter 36

MY FIRST LOGICAL assumption was that slick Eddie Pinero was full of good old-fashioned Grade A bullshit. He was, after all, the high-profile head of an organized crime family, not exactly a poster boy for the straight and narrow. Clearly he was appealing to my journalistic instincts, hoping that he might pique my interest so I'd dig a whole lot deeper into what had happened at Lombardo's. If he couldn't prove his own innocence, maybe I could.

All in all it was incredibly transparent. The problem was, it worked on me. Or, at the very least, it got me thinking. The guy had his goons basically kidnap me, but I wasn't heading straight to the police. What was I going to do, *press charges?*

Instead, like metal to a magnet, I found myself right back at Lombardo's Steakhouse later that same day.

I still hadn't eaten, but a nice porterhouse was the last thing on my mind.

No, the rumbling in my gut was the feeling that something wasn't quite right about my originally being there to interview Dwayne Robinson. Or, I should say, everything was *too* right.

Too convenient.

That's why I'd come back to see my new good friend—Tiffany.

As it happened, I caught her with one foot out the door. It was half past three; lunch was over. The dining room was all but empty.

"You got a second?" I asked. "I'm really sorry to bother you again. I'm relentless, I know.

"Sure, what is it?"

Only there was nothing "sure" about her response. She seemed anxious at the sight of me, even glancing over her shoulder to see if anyone was looking at us.

"Hey, are you okay?" I asked her.

"Huh?" she said, turning back to me. "Oh ... um, yeah, I'm fine."

I wasn't exactly sold on that. But I pressed on.

"I was hoping you could check something for me," I said. "You mentioned that the day before Vincent Marcozza was murdered, Dwayne Robinson came in but never sat down. I was wondering—did Marcozza eat lunch here that day?"

"Probably," she answered quickly. "He practically ate lunch here every day. Sometimes dinner, too. Mr. Marcozza was a *big* customer."

"Is there a way you can check for sure? About the day before the shootings? Maybe in your reservation book?"

Again, she seemed distracted. It was as if the question had caught her off guard. *What gives, Tiffany?* After another glance over her shoulder, she motioned for me to follow her.

We walked over to the reservation book. "That was Thursday, right?" she asked.

I nodded and watched as she flipped back a few pages, the ruby-red nail polish on her index finger scrolling down the list of reservations for that day. Putting my upside-down reading skills to use, I kept looking for Marcozza's name.

But I didn't see it. Neither did Tiffany.

"Hmmm. I guess he wasn't here that day," she said. "That's unusual for him."

"*Who* wasn't here *what* day?" came a sharp voice over Tiffany's shoulder.

Chapter 37

IT WAS THE manager of Lombardo's. Jack, was it? No, Jason, I thought. Given his tone, though, his name might as well have been Mr. Royally Pissed Off. Tiffany froze at the reservation stand, like a deer in xenon headlights.

I took that as my cue to help out. "My fault. I was just checking to see if Vincent Marcozza had eaten here the day before he was murdered. That's all. Nothing sinister."

I was expecting the guy to ask me why I wanted to know that. He didn't. Instead, he said, "Reservations made by our guests are considered private. It's restaurant policy, Mr. Daniels."

Jason knew my name. That was a little strange.

We hadn't officially met. Or exchanged business cards.

"Then my apologies," I said. "I didn't know."

"Yes, but Tiffany did," he said, turning to her.

She raised her palms apologetically. "Jason, I know you told me—"

He cut her off. "I don't want to hear it."

"But—"

"Shut up!" he barked at the poor girl. "You're fired."

Fired? You've got to be kidding.

"What are you doing? She was only trying to help me," I said, dumbfounded. "I was a customer here, too. Actually, I *am* a customer. I was about to have a steak."

My new best friend, Jason, gave me a drop-dead stare. "Was I talking to you?"

"You are now," I said.

He took two steps forward, getting right smack in my face. He was so close I could tell what flavor gum he was chewing. Wintergreen.

"In that case," he said, pushing the words through his clenched teeth, "I want you to listen to me real closely, okay? *Get the fuck out of my restaurant.* Don't come back."

So much for the customer always being right...or even tolerated.

"What are you going to do?" I asked. "Call the cops?"

"I won't if you won't," he fired back at me.

I wasn't exactly the technical adviser on the movie *Fight Club*, but I'd been in enough scuffles to more than catch his drift. This prick was challenging me.

Keep your cool, Nick. Diplomacy first.

"Listen, there's no reason this thing needs to get out of hand," I said.

No sooner had I said it, though, than he suddenly grabbed the lapels of my jacket, pushing me backwards. "I don't think you heard me," he said.

Oh, I heard you all right...

Screw diplomacy!

I dug my heels hard into the floor and gave Jason the shove back he so richly deserved. Then he raised his fists. Suddenly, this might as well have been a Rangers hockey game down at Madison Square Garden.

The gloves were coming off, whether I wanted this to happen or not.

Smack!

He threw a right-handed jab, tagging my cheek. It was a sucker punch, completely uncalled for. So I let fly with one of my own — only to catch nothing but air. Jason wasn't big but he was quick. Too quick to go toe-to-toe.

Time to improvise.

"Nick, be careful," Tiffany called from the sidelines. Well, that was my plan for sure.

Dropping my head, I charged him straight on and wrapped my arms around his waist. We went hurtling into the dining room, his feet barely skimming the floor as I kept pushing and pushing him like a football tackling sled.

Then, *crash!*

Table for two, please!

Make that two tables. We upended the first and kept right on going, landing squarely on the table behind it. Plates and silverware went flying above our heads as we hit the floor, barrel-rolling back and forth while trading punches.

I gave a whole lot better than I got now, too. A good right to Jason's jaw. Another right on the cleft of his chin. "You asked for this," I yelled in his face. "You wouldn't let it go."

Don't Blink

Hey, this was even better than a hockey fight. If we were on the ice, the refs would've broken it up by now.

But no.

Jason and I were just getting warmed up.

Chapter 38

"BOY, YOU'RE HAVING some kind of week," said Courtney, gently dabbing at the dried blood below my nose with a damp paper towel. "Keep this up and they'll have to name an action figure after you."

We were sitting together on the couch in my office at *Citizen* magazine. Me, the patient. Courtney, the concerned, and quite beautiful, nurse. With a surprisingly soft touch, too. And she was wearing Chanel.

As it turned out, some referees did break up the fight. The sous-chef and a dishwasher heard all the commotion and came running out of the kitchen. Otherwise, I'm fairly sure I would've won big-time on points.

That's my story and I'm sticking to it!

At least for the guys at Jimmy D's Pub. Courtney was another deal. There was no way I'd jeopardize this sudden warm and affectionate outpouring of sympathy. I'm not *that* stupid. Besides, I'm in love with her. Deeply and hopelessly, I suppose.

"I guess I've always been more of a lover than a fighter," I said with an eye roll.

"Oh, you poor thing," she cooed, playing the same game on me. "Why would the manager pick a fight with you like that?"

"I'm not sure yet," I said. "It's very strange— everything is, Courtney. Mystery on top of mystery."

I couldn't help but suspect that Jason was under some kind of orders. Someone didn't want me snooping around. But who?

That was just one question I had. There were so many others in the aftermath of my recording from Lombardo's.

But as I laid my head back and closed my eyes, all I could really focus on was how amazing Courtney was. She was sitting so close to me, her hair grazing my shoulder. Finally I couldn't help myself.

"I love you," I blurted out.

I just said it—*boom!*—like that. I didn't know what I was thinking. Actually, that was it. I *wasn't* thinking.

For a second, there was some hope that she would answer, "I love you, too." But in the next second, that hope was beaten down—worse than Jason at the restaurant.

It was as if I had suddenly become contagious with Ebola or the swine flu.

Courtney sprang up from the couch, practically darting to the other side of my office. She was shaking her head. "No, no, no," she said. "Don't say that, Nick. I wish you hadn't said that. I really wish you hadn't."

"Why, Courtney? Tell me why."

"Oh, for heaven's sake, Nick, *because I'm engaged!*"

"But you don't love him."

"You're wrong, Nick. I do love him. I love Tom very much. I do."

It hurt to hear her say that—worse than any of the punches I'd just taken—but I wasn't about to stop now. She meant too much to me. If I hadn't known that before, I sure did now.

"I don't believe you," I said. "I'm sorry, but I don't, Courtney."

"You need to, Nick."

"No. You may want to believe that you love him."

I looked at her. That's all I had to do. The big white elephant was back in the room. I hadn't meant for it to happen; neither had she. But it had happened. Courtney and I had slept together. We had made love. Not just lust—which had been part of it, I'll admit—but love. We'd been intimate with each other. Very much so. We had talked until dawn.

"I told you, that was a mistake," she said.

"It didn't feel like a mistake. Not to me, any-way."

"Nick, it did to me."

I got up from the couch. That one hurt, too.

"Do you really mean that?" I asked her. I was trying desperately not to let my eyes plead.

"Yes," she said again.

"Are you sure?" I asked, taking a step toward her.

She raised her hand. "Stop," she said. *"Don't."*

I took another step toward her. She didn't say

Stop this time. She didn't say *Don't*. She didn't say anything. All she did was stare at me with those amazing blue eyes.

But before I could take another step, the door to my office suddenly swung open.

"There you are!" said Thomas Ferramore, Courtney's fiancé, the man she said she loved.

Chapter 39

I GUESS I couldn't blame him for not knocking or, for that matter, acting as if he owned the room the moment he stepped foot in my office. Thomas Ferramore literally *did* own the room. The entire building, in fact. What better way to cut down on rent for his *Citizen* magazine than to buy the building that housed it?

I stood and watched as Ferramore, with his salt and pepper hair and perennial tan, strode over to Courtney, planting a kiss on her lips. It seemed to last for a couple of eternities, and probably would've had Courtney not finally pulled back.

"Tom, what are you doing here?" she asked. Very good question. Didn't Ferramore realize that Courtney and I were falling in love now?

"What else would I be doing here? I've come to see the most beautiful woman in the world."

"You know what I mean," she said, rolling her eyes playfully. (*Ugh.*) "You told me you were coming home tomorrow."

"Change of plans," said Ferramore. "Aren't you happy to see me, Courtney?"

"Of course I am," she said. "Why wouldn't I be? Even here at work."

He was still supposed to be in Paris making his latest acquisition. For all I knew he was buying the Eiffel Tower.

Now here he was in my office. *You do know this is my office, Mr. Ferramore, right? Or that I'm standing here, too?*

Apparently not.

Not until Courtney shot me the world's most uncomfortable glance. She didn't say a word, but I could read her mind like the first line of an eye chart. *Did my fiancé just walk in on another man professing his love for me?*

Yeah, he sure as hell did.

"Sorry, Nick, I didn't see you standing there," said Ferramore before his eyes immediately collapsed into a squint. "Holy shit, what happened to your face?"

"You should see the other guy," I said, dusting off the old joke, which happened to be accurate in this case.

Ferramore humored me with a quiet chuckle, but as he resumed his full attention on Courtney, it was clear he couldn't care less what actually had happened to me or my face.

He reached out, taking both of Courtney's hands in his. (*Ugh again.*) "Actually, sweetheart, there is something I need to discuss with you."

I took that as my cue. (*Shit.*)

"Why don't I leave the two of you alone," I said with a step toward the door.

"Nonsense. This is your office, Nick," said Courtney. "Come, Tom, we'll go to mine. Nick has a lot of work to do."

Before Ferramore could even nod in agreement, though, my office filled with the sound of Courtney's cell phone. Instinctively, she reached into the pocket of her Chanel suit to check the caller ID.

Out of the blue, Ferramore's entire personality changed. He looked anxious and concerned.

Now what was going on? Was it about me? Or Courtney and me?

"Who is it?" he asked Courtney.

She seemed momentarily baffled that he would want to know, let alone ask her outright. "It's Harold Clark," she finally answered him.

Clark was a seasoned reporter with the Associated Press. His nickname was "Baskin," short for Baskin-Robbins. In other words, he was known for his scoops.

"Don't answer it!" Ferramore practically shouted at her.

"Why not?" asked Courtney. "What's going on, Tom?"

"That's what I need to talk to you about, sweetheart."

Chapter 40

"MORE COFFEE, NICK?" asked the waitress behind the counter at the Sunrise Diner near my apartment the following morning. She had the glass pot hovering and ready to pour as she waited for my answer.

"Absolutely," I told her. "Thank you, Rosa." I was going to need the extra caffeine today.

There was no way I could've known what Courtney and Ferramore had discussed once they'd left my office. Even if I had been so nosy as to approach Courtney about it afterward, there was still no way I could've known.

That's because I couldn't find her.

Courtney had basically disappeared—*poof!* —for the remainder of the day. Her terrific assistant, M.J., said she'd stormed out of the office without saying a word. That night she didn't answer her phone at home.

But then came the morning. And now *I understood everything.*

So did the rest of Manhattan, if not the world.

Someone had posted a video on YouTube. It starred the French supermodel Marbella, backstage a few days earlier at the Hermès fashion show in Paris. The stunning brunette had a cigarillo in one hand, a glass of champagne in the other—and next season's must-have Jimmy Choo shoe planted firmly in her mouth.

A voice off camera asked the supermodel who the richest man she'd ever slept with was.

After a sip of the champagne and a puff of the cigarillo—removing the shoe from her mouth first—she looked straight into the camera and answered with her French accent. "Thomas Ferramore. Far and away, him!"

"When was that?" the off-camera voice asked.

She giggled and whispered, "Last night."

Whoops.

I hadn't actually seen the video, but news of it was splashed all over the papers, especially the

New York Post that was opened on the diner counter in front of me as I gobbled up my fried eggs over easy and a stack of wheat toast. How do I stay at my current weight of 175? A very good gene pool. There's no other possible answer.

Anyway. Of course I felt horrible for Courtney that she would have to endure such a public humiliation, but at the same time I couldn't help selfishly hoping that this would change everything between her and Ferramore.

"Excuse me, is this your phone?" I suddenly heard to my left.

I turned to see a man sitting on the stool next to me. He must have just sat down, because I hadn't noticed him. He was pointing at my iPhone on the counter between us.

"I'm sorry," I said, moving it closer to me.

"No, it's fine, it wasn't in my way. I only wanted to make sure it was yours and not the person who was sitting here before me."

"Oh," I said. "Thanks. It's mine, all right."

I was about to turn back to my newspaper when he motioned to the article about Ferramore.

"That's pretty amazing," he said, "don't you think?"

"Yep, it sure is," I said, if only to be polite. I knew diner counters were prone to communal chitchat, but I really just wanted to finish eating and reading in peace, then get off to work and whatever else awaited me at *Citizen* that morning.

But the stranger wasn't finished with his spiel. "That's the thing about gossip. Everybody loves to stick their nose into other people's business," he said. "Then again, how much sympathy can you have for an engaged billionaire who sticks his prick in some Euro-trash supermodel's business, right?"

I said nothing. I didn't want to encourage the guy too much.

Not that it mattered.

"Isn't that right, *Nick?*" he asked again.

Huh?

Not only did he not need any more encouraging, he clearly didn't need an introduction.

"Do I know you?" I asked.

"No, Nick, you don't. But I know you," he said with a dead stare. "I also know you're in a shitload of danger. The two of us should talk."

Chapter 41

OKAY, YOU'VE OFFICIALLY got my attention. Now let's rewind the tape a bit. Who the hell are you?

"What's your name?" I asked.

"It doesn't matter," he said.

"It does to me. Especially if you want this conversation to continue."

He smiled, a real shit-eating New Yorker's grin. He was enjoying this. "You can call me... *Doug.* Don't you want to hear why you're in danger, Nick?"

"I don't know yet," I said. "But for sure the cops sitting at the other end of the counter might. Would you like me to call them over?"

I have to admit I felt pretty smug pointing out the two policemen in uniform saddled up to the counter with their coffees about a dozen stools away.

But the stranger—Doug?—didn't even bother to look. He kept his eyes trained on mine.

"The last time you were in a restaurant with two cops—that didn't work out too well, did it? I don't think so."

I suddenly didn't feel so smug, or protected, either.

"What do you want?" I asked. "Why did you follow me here?"

He casually pulled back the lapel of his sport coat to show me his holster. It sure wasn't empty, and I was getting tired of seeing guns lately.

"What I want is for you to ask me nicely why it is that you're in danger, Nick Daniels," he said. "Say *please*. Better yet, say *pretty please*."

I glanced at all the people around me. The Sunrise was packed for breakfast as usual, just like Lombardo's was for lunch.

I could literally feel the sweat beginning to seep out from my pores. Not so good.

"Please tell me why I'm in danger," I said, my voice nearly cracking. The stranger stared at me, saying nothing. He was waiting.

"Pretty please," I added.

He leaned in close.

"You see, that's what's so intriguing," he whispered. "Because I think you already know the answer, Nick."

He tilted his head, inspecting the bruises around my eyes and mouth. They were now ripening to a soft purple. "In fact, you might say it's written all over your face."

"Who do you work for?" I asked.

"What makes you think I work for someone?"

It was actually a pretty good question, because he certainly didn't come across as the "for hire" type. Unless, that is, IBM was doing the hiring. This guy was clean-cut, straightlaced. He didn't look scary at all. Actually, he looked like a "Doug."

And that was scaring me even more.

"You obviously know a lot about me," I said. "What is it that you want me to do? Tell me what you want."

"Now we're making some progress. *Finally,*" he said with a satisfied nod. "What I want you to do is *nothing.* Whatever you're planning on doing, whatever you're even thinking of doing, I don't want you to do it. Do you follow what I'm saying?"

"I think so."

"Good. Because if you do nothing, maybe—just maybe—you'll live to see another sunrise. Hey, make that another Sunrise *Diner*."

With that wisecrack, he stood and walked away. Out the door, and out of the diner.

Gone.

But definitely not forgotten.

Chapter 42

TWENTY MINUTES LATER, I was marching very quickly into One Hogan Place, otherwise known as the New York County District Attorney's Office. Or David Sorren's home away from home.

"Hi, Nick Daniels to see Mr. Sorren," I said to his secretary, a young woman with big hair and an attitude to match. She acted as if I'd just interrupted her wedding ceremony.

"Who are you?" she asked.

"Nick Daniels," I repeated my introduction of myself. "I'm here to see David Sorren."

"That's what you think."

"Excuse me?"

"Do you have an appointment to see Mr. Sorren?"

189

"No."

"Is he expecting you?"

"No."

"Yeah, like I said, that's what you think."

Cute, very cute. But in case you haven't noticed yet, I'm in no mood for cute today. I'm a man with a mission, a man on fire.

I stormed right by her.

"Hey!" she shouted. "Come back here!"

But she was a little too slow on the draw. By the time she scrambled out of her evil little chair on wheels, I'd already opened the door to Sorren's office. The funny thing was, he barely batted an eyelash as he looked up from a file he was reading.

"Hey, Nick, have a seat," he said. Almost as if he actually *was* expecting me. "It's all right, Molly."

"Yeah, it's all right, Molly," I echoed him. "We're good."

I winked at his secretary, who shot me the royal stink eye as she closed the door on her way out. Then I did exactly what Sorren had invited me to do. I took a seat facing his big wooden desk.

Frankly, I didn't know where to start. The threatening guy I'd just "met" at the Sunrise Diner? My bout with the manager of Lombardo's? Or perhaps what I had learned from the hostess there?

Turns out, Sorren decided for me. As I began to apologize for barging in on him, he interrupted my train of thought with one of his own.

"So, how was your visit with Eddie Pinero?" he asked. "That's quite a spread he's got out there in Sheepshead Bay, huh? Crime does pay after all. Boy, does it ever."

My jaw dropped. How did he know I'd been there? Quickly, it occurred to me. "You've got his place staked out? There's surveillance on Pinero?"

Sorren leaned back in his chair with an easy chuckle. "Hell, no. That would require way too many man-hours, too much overtime pay," he said. He pointed his finger in the air. "There's a much cheaper way."

"Satellites?"

Sorren brought his finger down, tapping his nose. *Bingo.*

"It's kind of ironic, actually," he said. "These

capos love to talk outside to make sure we're not listening. Little do they know we can practically read their lips now. That's how well we can see 'em."

He did a double take, squinting at the bruises on my face. "Though I don't recall seeing any punches thrown during your visit."

"There weren't any punches. At least not there," I explained. Then I told Sorren everything else — the whole shebang, what I'd learned since I'd first called him about my recording from Lombardo's.

As clear as those satellites were, he'd see why I was concerned. *Right?*

"So let me get this straight," he said with a befuddled look. "You think we've got the wrong man? You think Eddie Pinero had nothing to do with Marcozza's murder? Or the two cops? Is that your conclusion, Nick?"

"I don't know anything for certain. All I'm saying is that I have my doubts."

Sorren swung his black wingtips up onto his desk, the perfect heels landing against the wood with a jarring thud. He'd been cool and easy-breezy up until this point. Now that same intensity I'd first encountered was bubbling up to the surface.

"I don't get you," he said finally, shaking his head. "You come forward with that terrifically useful recording, what amounts to a smoking gun, and here you are now trying to make me forget about it. What gives, Nick?"

"I'm not trying to make you forget about anything, David. I simply want you to rethink it, that's all."

"Rethink it? What's there to rethink?" he asked, his voice booming. "There's a reason the only currency we trade in around here is cold, hard evidence. Because evidence speaks for itself, clear and simple—just like the killer's voice on your recording. Remember? *I have a message from Eddie.*"

Before I could even respond, the intercom on Sorren's phone beeped. It was his secretary, Ms. Stink Eye. "Excuse me, Mr. Sorren, but they're waiting for you downstairs."

"Thank you, Molly. I'm done here." He shot me a look that said, *We're done, Nick. For now.*

Then Sorren jumped up, grabbing his suit jacket from behind his chair. He swirled it through the air like a matador's cape as he put it on.

"Now, if you'll excuse me, I've got a press conference to give," he said. "Big one, too. You might want to stick around for it. This morning, Eddie 'The Prince' Pinero was arrested for ordering the murder of Vincent Marcozza."

Chapter 43

I WOULD HAVE sooner volunteered for a double root canal than stuck around for Sorren's press conference that morning.

Still, there was no escaping it later that night on the news. It was everywhere on the dial—not that I was too surprised by that. Americans have always loved a good mob story.

But was David Sorren telling the public the right story? Was it the truth?

With practically every flip of the channel there was a clip of Pinero in handcuffs followed by another clip of Sorren facing the hordes of media on the steps of his building. And to watch and listen to Sorren was to make no mistake:

the New York County DA's Office was *his* building.

For now, anyway.

As I continued to watch him address the cameras without a single hair out of place, it was easy to picture him making the move to a new building. Like City Hall. If timing is everything, then Pinero's arrest would be the perfect lead-in for Sorren to announce his candidacy for mayor.

So don't screw it up, I was about to be told in no uncertain terms.

Out of the blue, or at least out of *my* blue, the doorbell rang. Whoever it was had made it past the night doorman unannounced. Then again, what else was new? Newborn babies dozed off less than the guy manning our front door.

Looking through the peephole, I blinked with disbelief. It was really her, though.

Brenda.

Bumping into her at the New York Library benefit was one thing, but now here she was at my apartment.

"Wow, twice in one week," I said as I opened the door. "Just like old times."

"Twice too many," Brenda shot back, zipping

right by me into my narrow foyer. She turned to face me, her hands planted sternly on her hips. "Just what the hell do you think you're doing?"

"Excuse me? Can I have a little hint here?"

"Don't play dumb, Nick," she said. "I really hate it when you play dumb. That was another of our problems."

Fair enough. "Did Sorren put you up to this?" I asked. "He's worried about me, isn't he?"

"David doesn't even know I'm here. He would never ask me to intervene on his behalf. Never happen."

Again, it was so hard to tell when Brenda was lying, telling the truth, whatever.

"He obviously told you I went to see him today, though, right?" I asked.

"Yes," she answered. "David and I are a couple, Nick. Couples tell each other things."

"Don't remind me," I said.

She knew exactly what I meant by that. It was ostensibly the reason we broke up.

Long, painful story made short, I had done an important interview with Bill Gates in which he went on record for the first time about his planned retirement from Microsoft. That night I told Brenda. I mean, everyone knows that pillow talk never leaves the bedroom, right? Especially when both of you have made promises to that effect.

Apparently Brenda had had her fingers crossed. The very next day, she reported it on air. "According to a reliable source," she began the story. It was a real coup for her at the network, a feather in her cap.

And a dagger right through my heart.

I knew right then and there that I could never trust Brenda Evans again. Not that she would ever give me the satisfaction of telling her that. No chance. Ten minutes after her broadcast I received a Dear John e-mail from her. That's right, *she* was breaking up with *me*. With an *e-mail*. Her reason why? I wasn't as driven as her and she needed someone who was. And that was that.

"Are you doing this because of what happened between us?" she was asking me now. "Because if you're trying to get even, it's not fair to David."

"What is it exactly you think I'm doing?" I felt compelled to ask.

"I know you, Nick. I know how you play your hunches. You're relentless even when you're dead wrong, not even warm."

"I think what I discussed with your new boyfriend was a little more than a hunch. I may very well be right. There's evidence, and it's mounting."

"But what if you're wrong? Have you considered for one second how making waves about Pinero's guilt would reflect on David and his political future?"

I shook my head and smirked. "Wow, you've already got your dress picked out for the inauguration, don't you?"

If looks could kill, this story would end right here. Fortunately, they can't.

"This isn't about me, Nick."

"That's where you're a hundred percent wrong. It's always about you, Brenda, and it always will be."

That touched a nerve, to put it mildly. Her face immediately flushed bright red, her hands balling into fists. Apparently it was time for her to wake the neighbors.

"Fuck you!" she yelled. "Do you hear me? FUCK YOU! You're such a loser, Nick."

She then marched out of my apartment, making a beeline for the elevator. She hit the down button so hard, I was sure she broke a nail.

"Does this mean I'm not getting a Christmas card?" I asked from my doorway.

It was a glib comment, but I couldn't help it. She was bringing out the worst in me, as she always did.

The elevator opened and Brenda stepped inside—but not before having the last word, a proverbial kick to the groin. She really did know how to hurt a guy, especially me.

"By the way," she said. "My new boyfriend? He's way better than you in bed!"

Ouch.

Chapter 44

I WALKED INTO the cavernous Main Concourse of Grand Central Station the next morning, weaving my way through the buzzing crowd of tourists and visiting weekend suburbanites. I must say that I love this building and can't thank Jacqueline Onassis enough for saving it once upon a time.

Out of nowhere I bumped shoulders with a young man who had a knapsack strung over one shoulder. As we traded polite, if not clipped, apologies and went our separate ways, I couldn't help noticing his T-shirt. In big block lettering it read, "SAVE DARFUR."

Naturally, I couldn't help thinking of Dr. Alan Cole and wondering how he was doing—and where he might be doing it. Hopefully, he'd soon be back home safely.

Of course, that would make only one of us. With everything that's happened since I returned home from Darfur, I almost longed for the relative peace and quiet of being chased and shot at by the Janjaweed militia . . .

Maybe that's why I was so looking forward to this day and what I would be doing soon.

Pure and simple, there'd be no talk of murder, no mention of the mob, no discussion of the mysterious stranger who'd told me to mind my own business and do nothing.

That would all take a backseat to a pair of box seats at Yankee Stadium. Myself in one, and the center of my current universe in the other. That would be my niece, Elizabeth.

Her passport says she's fourteen, but you'd never know it. Bright and articulate beyond her years, she also happens to be the bravest kid I know.

No, scratch that. She's the bravest *anybody* I know.

Elizabeth's train hissed to a stop right on time at platform forty, the long row of doors opening in perfect unison. While the mad dash to exit was nowhere near your typical weekday morning rush hour, there was still enough of a crowd that I couldn't spot her right away.

That's when I heard her, the familiar sound that always accompanies her arrival on any scene.

Immediately, I smiled. I could see her now. But she couldn't see me.

Elizabeth couldn't see anything.

She's been blind since the age of five.

"You forgot your mitt again, didn't you?" I said as she got a little closer.

She smiled an amazing smile before scrunching her freckled nose. "And you're wearing too much cologne again. I could just about smell you on the train coming in."

I gave her a hug, squeezing her tightly in my arms. "I think Jeter's going to hit one today," I whispered. "I can feel it in my bones."

"I think he's going to hit two," she whispered back. "Let's go and see."

Then she did what she always did. She broke away from my grasp so she could walk on her own, her foldout white cane leading the way.

Tap-tap-tap . . .

That's my niece, Elizabeth.

The bravest anybody I know.

The perfect antidote for everything that had happened this week.

Chapter 45

YOU MIGHT WONDER—WASN'T I afraid I might be putting Elizabeth in harm's way? I had thought about it and briefly considered canceling our day together, but that would have broken her heart—*and* the Mafia had always put women and children out of bounds. That was the code.

So it was Elizabeth and me—and we were already drawing some attention, as we always do.

I understood the double takes. I could even put up with the excessive staring. After all, whoever heard of bringing a blind girl to a baseball game?

But they didn't get it, not any of them. It was as if they were the ones who were blind.

Don't you see? Anybody?

Baseball is the crack of the bat and the roar of the crowd, the smell of cut grass and hot dogs, the crunch of peanut shells at your feet.

Elizabeth couldn't see the game with her eyes, but she enjoyed it no less than those who could. Perhaps she even enjoyed it more. Because while others merely watched it, she *felt* it.

And the gushing smile on her face was all I needed to see to be assured of that.

"So, how is Courtney?" Elizabeth asked after the top of the first. Between innings was when we did most of our talking. My niece had met Courtney half a dozen times and they adored each other.

"Courtney told me to say hello," I said, which was the truth. "How's your mom?" I asked then, quickly changing the subject.

"Mom's lonely, that's how she is," answered Elizabeth. "But she's tough, too."

As often as I spoke to my older sister, Kate, I never felt as if she completely leveled with me. Elizabeth, on the other hand, always told it like it was.

"Lonely, huh? Like, *sad* lonely?" I asked.

"Is there any other kind?"

"Good point."

"She needs to meet someone," said Elizabeth. "Isn't Courtney getting married?"

"She is, and to a very impressive guy. Your mom's been going on a few dates, hasn't she?"

"Yeah, few and far between."

I laughed out loud. "It takes time, Lizzy."

"Okay, but it's been, like, four years since he died, Nick. That's enough time."

Four and a half, to be exact. That's when my sister's husband, Carl, had suffered a fatal heart attack while on business in London. He had been only forty-two. *How on earth does that happen? Why? On whose orders?*

Kate had called me to break the news. She'd also asked that I come out to their home in Weston, Connecticut, so I could help break the news to Elizabeth. She couldn't bear to do it alone. The girl was nine years old and blind, and suddenly she was also fatherless, and her mom had a huge hole in her heart.

I'll never forget what Elizabeth asked me that hot August afternoon as I held her hand on their living room couch. She was wearing a yellow sundress, her frazzled blond hair tucked back in rows of barrettes. "Will I be able to see my daddy in heaven?" she wanted to know.

My eyes welled up. I could barely hold back the tears.

"Yes," I told her. "You'll see him every day."

"Do you promise?"

"I do."

I squeezed her little hand and she squeezed back, and all I could remember thinking was one thing.

If there is indeed a God up there, he better not make a liar out of me.

"So anyway, Uncle Nick," Elizabeth said after a quick sip of soda, "tell me all about Courtney and this impressive fiancé of hers."

"Okay, okay—I'm heartbroken," I finally admitted.

"I knew you were," she said. "I could tell in your voice, just in the way you say her name. You truly are heartbroken. And I'm heartbroken for you."

Part Three

IN TOO DEEP, WAY TOO DEEP

Chapter 46

COURTNEY HAD APPARENTLY been holed up in her large Upper West Side apartment through the weekend. When she finally returned one of my many phone calls that Sunday evening, I convinced her to let me come over.

When she opened the door, she was dressed in baggy sweats, she wasn't wearing a touch of makeup, and her eyes were so red from all the crying that she could have been the "before" picture in an allergy medication ad.

But to me, she never looked more beautiful. I just wanted to hold her. But I didn't. I wouldn't even try under the circumstances.

We hung out in her kitchen and opened up a bottle of Bordeaux. It was a 2003 Branaire-

Ducru, her favorite. I couldn't help wondering if Thomas Ferramore knew that. Did he know any of her favorite things? Maybe he did. Maybe he loved her like I did. *Screw Ferramore. Of course he doesn't.*

After a few sips in complete silence, she took the deepest of deep breaths and exhaled. "Go ahead," she said, "ask the sixty-four-thousand-dollar question."

Given Ferramore's bank account it was more like the sixty-four-million-dollar question, but that was a bad joke I wasn't about to crack. I was also going to do my best to avoid the word *supermodel*.

Still, I asked the question she wanted—make that *needed*—me to ask. "Is it true?"

"Tom swears that it isn't. He even said he'd be able to prove it to me."

"Do you believe him?" *Don't, Courtney. He's a super-rich super-scumbag.*

Courtney stared down at the wineglass cradled in her hands, the plum red of the Bordeaux reflecting off her ten-carat diamond ring. She was still wearing it.

"I don't know," she answered finally.

That was that.

She didn't ask my opinion. She didn't want to know what I thought she should do. Perhaps that's because she already knew. She is *that* smart.

"Let's focus on work," she said. "I've got a magazine to run and you might have the biggest story in your life to write. Correct so far?"

I had to smile. She was proving it once again. If Arnold Schwarzenegger was the Terminator, Courtney Sheppard was the Compartmentalizer.

"The police have arrested the wrong man for the murder of Vincent Marcozza," she continued. "And you're the only one who can prove it."

"They *maybe* arrested the wrong man," I corrected her. "As for my proving it, I'm nowhere near doing that."

"Not yet, you're not. But tomorrow's another day," she said. "Tomorrow's always another day."

I shot her a look. "What are you up to?" I asked.

There was something about the way she'd said *tomorrow*, like she had something tricky up her sleeve.

And sure enough, Courtney definitely did.

Chapter 47

"C'MON IN," said Derrick Phalen of the Organized Crime Task Force, greeting me with an easy smile and a firm handshake at the door of his office in White Plains, New York. As he walked back to his desk, he motioned to an old, beat-up gray chair in front of it that looked to be one fat guy away from total collapse. "Have a seat, if you dare," he joked, though given the chair's condition, it wasn't all that funny.

"Thanks," I said, gingerly settling in. Then I reported, "Made it okay."

Quickly glancing around the young prosecutor's modest office, I came to an equally quick conclusion. This guy *worked* for a living. His desk was absolutely covered in paperwork while files as thick as phone books surrounded him like a moat.

But it was the little yellow stickies of notes and phone numbers that really caught my eye. They were stuck to every conceivable surface—his computer, desk lamp, stapler, coffee mug, even the framed diploma from the Fordham School of Law hanging on the wall.

"So how do you know Courtney?" I asked. "She didn't tell me all the details."

"I was roommates with her brother, Mike, at Middlebury College," he said.

I immediately felt as if I'd put my foot in my mouth, even though I knew I really hadn't. "Oh" was all I could manage.

"Yeah," he said. "I know. We're coming up on ten years since Mike died, and I still can't believe he's gone." He rubbed his chin, reflecting. "He was a helluva guy. In fact, I was actually in Manhattan that morning and we were supposed to have lunch together. He even left a message on my cell phone to confirm twenty minutes before the first plane hit." Phalen paused for a moment. "I still listen to it from time to time."

"Jesus, I'm sorry," I said.

"Hey, no, *I'm* sorry—I didn't mean to be a downer on our first date." He sat up in his chair, snapping his shoulders straight. "So tell me, what can I do for you? And for Courtney."

To tell you the truth, Derrick Phalen, I'm not sure. That's what I'm here to find out.

"Did Courtney give you any of the background?" I asked. "Anything at all?"

"Only that you wanted to talk to me about Eddie Pinero," he said. "I assume it's for an article you're writing for *Citizen*. Right so far?"

"Yes, hopefully," I said. Instinctively, I reached into my leather bag to retrieve my tape recorder. I placed it on his desk.

Immediately, Phalen looked at it like Superman does kryptonite.

"I'm sorry, Nick," he said. "As I told Courtney, I'm happy to talk to you, but I can't go on record—or for that matter be recorded—when it comes to anyone this office has investigated. Them's the rules."

"I'm sorry, I didn't realize," I said. It was the first and only time I wasn't a hundred percent on the level with the guy. He'd soon know why.

"No worries," he said. "It's just that when you

work for the Organized Crime Task Force, you try to limit how much your name appears in print."

"I can certainly appreciate that," I said. I then held up my tape recorder, giving it the same kryptonite look Phalen had. "Actually, this thing has been nothing but trouble for me lately."

"What do you mean?" asked Phalen.

Bingo, there it is. My opening.

A week ago I was worried that word about my recording of Vincent Marcozza's killer would leak. Now here I was about to leak it myself.

"You might say I'm the reason Eddie Pinero is in jail for murder right now," I said. "How's that for an opening line?"

Phalen leaned back in his chair, a knowing smile filling his lean face. "Holy shit, it was you. All I'd heard was that someone had accidentally recorded Vincent Marcozza's killer at Lombardo's."

"Yeah, well, that's what I wanted to talk to you about," I said. "Because I don't think it was an accident."

I expected Phalen to immediately ask me what I meant by that. He didn't.

Instead he stood up and asked me a question I never would've guessed in a million years.

Chapter 48

"DO YOU LIKE pasta fagioli?" asked Phalen.

Huh? Come again? Bizarre soup segues for a thousand, Alex?

Phalen didn't wait for my answer. "I know this place right across the street that serves the best pasta fagioli you'll ever have. Best in White Plains, anyway. C'mon, we'll get a bowl, have some lunch."

The next thing I knew, I was following the guy out of his office and to the elevator bank on his floor. *What's going on?* I was thinking as we walked—kind of fast, actually.

I was no psychic, but this much I could figure out: Derrick Phalen didn't want to be in his office when we discussed Eddie Pinero's involvement—or rather, noninvolvement—in Vincent Marcozza's murder.

He had his reasons, I'm sure. Hopefully he'd explain them to me over lunch. Bring on the pasta fagioli!

Not quite yet, though. No sooner did the elevator arrive than we were stopped by a man's voice coming from down the hall. He was calling out Phalen's name.

Immediately, Phalen muttered something under his breath.

"What did you say?" I asked.

"Huh? Oh, nothing," he answered. "I was just saying we'll catch the next elevator."

But I was almost positive that wasn't what he'd said. In fact, I was pretty sure he'd muttered only two words. *Holy shit.*

As if he couldn't believe something. Like what? This bruiser coming down the hall?

"Oh, hey, Ian," said Phalen as the man caught up to us at the elevator. "How are you?"

"I'm good," he said. "You got a minute?"

The two of them started to talk shop for a bit—at least, I think that's what they were doing. I tuned out mostly, my ears giving way to my eyes and how different these two guys were physically. Derrick Phalen was a lean, compact man with short-cropped brown hair and a square jaw. Ian LaGrange was much taller and considerably wider. To be blunt, the word *fat* came to mind. So did the all-you-can-eat buffet at Caesars Palace in Vegas.

Of course, I didn't even know then that Ian LaGrange was, well, Ian LaGrange.

"Oh, I'm sorry," said Phalen, suddenly realizing he hadn't introduced me. "Ian, this is Nick Daniels."

"Nice to meet you, Nick," said LaGrange as we shook hands.

Phalen turned to me. "Ian's the deputy attorney general in charge of the Organized Crime Task Force. Or, as I like to call him, the God-father."

"It does have a nice ring to it, I have to admit," LaGrange said, smiling through his scruffy beard. "So where are you guys heading?"

"We're getting a quick bite to eat," said Phalen. "Just across the street."

LaGrange glanced down. "You're wearing your vest?" he asked. "Derrick?"

"We're only going *across the street*," Phalen repeated.

"Yeah, and Lincoln was just going to the theater. Go put it on."

Phalen shot LaGrange an exasperated look that reminded me of a teenage son catching heat from his father.

"Vest?" I asked.

"Bulletproof vest," said Phalen before turning around for his office. "I'll be right back."

Wait a minute. The guy needed a bulletproof vest to go out in public? More important, where was mine?

"Hey, we could always order in!" I called after him. It sounded funny but I wasn't really joking.

"Don't worry, it's just office policy," said LaGrange, trying to reassure me. "There's never been an attempt on anyone working for the OCTF."

I was going to make some crack about there always being a first time for everything, but I bit my tongue. I'd only just met this guy. I didn't know his sense of humor or for that matter anything else about him. Except his size.

"So what line of work are you in, Nick?" he asked. Very cool and casual-like.

Uh-oh. Careful, now.

"I'm a writer," I said.

"No kidding. What do you write?"

"Articles, mostly. I work for *Citizen* magazine. You heard of it?"

"Sure have. Is that why you're here to see Derrick?" he asked. "To do an article?"

There was no outright concern in his voice, but I knew subtext when I heard it. No way he was asking just to make idle conversation in the hallway.

And I wasn't about to give an answer that could get Phalen in any kind of trouble.

"No. Derrick's actually helping me out with some background on a novel I'm writing," I said. "Verisimilitude and all that."

"No kidding. We help out on the Alex Cross books sometimes."

"Never read them," I said.

I watched closely as LaGrange nodded, relieved when he quickly changed the subject. He asked which restaurant we were going to.

"Actually, I don't know," I told him.

He seemed to believe me. And as far as I could tell, LaGrange didn't know that I was lying about why I was in his building to see Phalen.

He had bought the novel line.

At least that's what I thought.

Only it turned out Ian LaGrange knew exactly what I was up to. The real surprise, however, was *how* the big man knew.

As Phalen had said himself . . .

Holy shit.

And then some.

Chapter 49

DERRICK PHALEN RETURNED to his office after lunch with Nick Daniels and did very little but stare up at the grid of white ceiling tiles above his desk. He stared at the ceiling for a good twenty minutes straight. The prosecutor had a lot to digest and it certainly wasn't the pasta fagioli. It wasn't even the very interesting story he'd just heard from Nick Daniels.

"Knock, knock," came a voice at his door.

Instinctively Phalen looked to see who it was, but he really didn't need to. He knew it was Ian LaGrange, and not because of his boss's all-too-familiar baritone.

No, he expected the Godfather to be dropping by sooner or later. Probably sooner.

"Hey, Ian, what's up?"

"Not much," said LaGrange. "How was your lunch with the writer—the novelist?"

Phalen rolled his eyes up toward the ceiling tiles. "*Don't ask*. All I can say is, that's the last time I do a favor for a friend."

"Why? What do you mean?"

"That guy I introduced you to at the elevator is a writer for *Citizen* magazine. As a favor to his editor I agreed to give him some research, a little help for a novel he's working on. Only it turns out there's no novel."

"I don't follow," said LaGrange. "What was he here for, then?"

"It was a ruse," said Phalen. "What the guy actually wanted to do was sell me on this crazy idea that it wasn't Eddie Pinero who ordered the hit on Vincent Marcozza. What kind of bullshit is that?"

"You're kidding me."

"I wish I were. The guy's a real conspiracy nut. It was like having lunch with Oliver Stone."

LaGrange laughed. "So if Eddie Pinero didn't order the hit on Marcozza, who did? In his opinion?"

"That's the thing. He didn't know."

"Gee, and let me guess, he wanted your help in finding out."

"Exactly," said Phalen.

"So what did you tell him?"

"A polite version of *Go sell your crazy somewhere else, you nutbag.* What else could I do?"

"Thatta boy," said LaGrange, tipping an imaginary cap at Phalen. "Keep your distance from the guy, okay? Writers like that, all they can spell is trouble for everybody concerned."

"Consider it done."

As LaGrange strolled off, Phalen leaned back in his chair, his eyes finding their way back up to the white ceiling tiles. Slowly, he exhaled.

He'd been holding his breath the entire time, hoping that LaGrange would believe him.

It hadn't been easy.

Hell, no. Ian LaGrange—the Godfather—hadn't gotten to where he was by being anybody's fool. Bluffing him was like tap dancing to ZZ Top on a tightrope.

But it was nothing compared to what Phalen was going to do next.

Chapter 50

"I CAN'T FREAKIN' believe I'm doing this," Phalen muttered to himself as he slowly walked down the deserted and dark hallway of the OCTF offices at close to midnight that same evening.

But of course he *could* believe he was doing this. He even knew why.

If he'd learned anything in his nearly three years with the Task Force, it was that his family of fellow prosecutors actually shared one major similarity with the Mafia families they were trying to take down: the motto Never Trust Anyone.

Including the Godfather.

Granted, it was impossible to work for the OCTF without succumbing to a little paranoia.

Phalen didn't have to look any further than the standard-issue bulletproof vest.

But worrying about your enemies in the mob was one thing. Worrying about the people who worked for you—that they weren't loyal or, worse, they were out to get you—was entirely another.

Enter: Ian LaGrange.

Were it not for a spilled cup of coffee, Phalen may never have found the bug planted beneath the enter key of his computer's keyboard. When he did, though, he had no question who had planted it.

He just had no proof.

So he left the bug alone.

Phalen went about his business, knowing that LaGrange could hear everything in his office at any time. For others, that might have been an awful burden—always having to choose your words carefully, always acting like the good soldier.

For Phalen, however, it was like being given the answers to a test in advance.

He always knew the smart thing to say in every situation. He always had a heads-up.

Right up until that afternoon, when he had asked Nick Daniels if he liked pasta fagioli so they could get out of his office and talk in private.

That's when the big surprise had come.

The six-foot-four Ian LaGrange had come bounding down the hallway from his office almost like a linebacker for the New York Giants. Right then and there Phalen had known this seemingly coincidental meeting at the elevator was no coincidence.

LaGrange was very interested in Nick Daniels and what he had to say about Eddie Pinero and Vincent Marcozza. A little *too* interested, in fact.

Something wasn't right about this. It stunk to high heaven already.

That's why Phalen was about to return the favor to LaGrange.

Patiently, he waited in his office until everyone else had gone home for the night. He even waited out the cleaning crew until they'd emptied every last can and mop pail.

Now it was just him and a little birdie.

A Flex-8 "F-Bird," to be exact. The latest, most sophisticated digital recording device used by none other than the OCTF itself. Battery powered, smaller than a quarter, and on its way to a brand-new home.

The Godfather's office.

Phalen slowly turned the doorknob at the end of the hall and stepped inside, quiet as a mouse.

Or a bug.

Here's listening to you, Ian.

Chapter 51

I HAD TO ADMIT, Derrick Phalen knew his pasta fagioli. It was good stuff, very good. Reminded me of my favorite Italian restaurant in the world, Il Cena'Colo, back in my hometown of Newburgh.

But even better than Phalen's pasta fagioli was what came with it—and I'm not talking about a piece of Italian bread. It was my next move.

Thanks for the jump start, Courtney.

Phalen had listened calmly to everything I said at lunch, asking a logical question here and there, but mostly listening. He wasn't about to print up any "Free Eddie Pinero" T-shirts, but he didn't look at me as if I were crazy, either.

What he did do was take a pen from his pocket and write a phone number on a napkin.

"I know a guy out in Greenwich who might be able to help you," he said, pushing the napkin toward me. "Call him and make an appointment."

"What's his name?" I asked.

"Hoodie Brown."

"Hoodie?"

"You'll see when you meet him. Tell him you're a friend of mine. That's all."

"What does he do?"

"You'll see," Phalen said again.

I shrugged my shoulders. *Okeydokey.*

The following afternoon I was on a Metro-North train out to Greenwich, Connecticut, for a two o'clock appointment with someone named Hoodie Brown. When I'd told him on the phone "Derrick Phalen sent me," it was as if I'd delivered the secret password at the door of an underground nightclub. I was in.

"Follow me," said the receptionist at his office.

Greenwich was the capital of the hedge fund world, but what I was doing in the lobby of one such company I had no idea. D.A.C. Investments? Why would Phalen send me to a trader?

He hadn't. The receptionist, a tall, slender brunette who looked as if she'd stepped off the set of a *Vogue* magazine shoot, led me past a long, bustling trading floor to a quiet office tucked away in the back of the building. That's where I met Hoodie Brown.

The name made sense immediately.

Not only was the man who shook my hand wearing a hooded sweatshirt—gray, with the Caltech insignia—he actually had the hood pulled over his head à la the Unabomber. Hell, this guy even looked a little like the Unabomber.

"So, who's the P.I.Q.?" he asked, settling in behind his desk. I noticed there was no place for me to sit. No chair, no couch. Nada for visitors.

"P.I.Q.?" I asked.

"Person in question," he explained. "Who are we investigating?"

Oh. "Dwayne Robinson," I said. "The pitcher for—"

"I know who he is," said Hoodie. "Or was."

"Specifically, I'm looking to see if he has any ties to organized crime," I added.

Hoodie nodded and began tapping away on one of the three keyboards lined up on his desk. At least twice as many computer screens stared back at him.

"Are you a private investigator?" I asked.

He didn't answer. He didn't even acknowledge that I'd asked him a question.

"We'll pull up all domestic bank statements and any police records to start," he said barely above a whisper. "Then we'll see if he has an FBI file. It shouldn't take too long."

My jaw literally dropped. *An FBI file? It shouldn't take too long?*

"How are you able to do this?" I asked incredulously.

"One-hundred-and-twenty-gigabyte fiber-optic connection speeds," he answered.

"No, I mean—"

"I know what you meant, friend. The answer is, you don't want to know. You may think you do, but trust me, you don't."

If you say so, Hoodie ... whoever you are.

I suddenly felt like a little kid swimming into the deep end for the very first time. Maybe I'd be fine.

Or maybe I was in way, way over my head.

And to be honest, I knew the answer to that one. Worse, I still wasn't wearing a bulletproof vest like Derrick Phalen had.

Chapter 52

I STOOD THERE quietly in Hoodie Brown's office, watching and waiting, respectful. Nearly shivering, too. The damn room felt like a meat locker, it was kept so cold. Hoodie, of course, was dressed appropriately. I sure wasn't.

Thankfully, the guy was right and the wait wasn't too long. After another few minutes, Hoodie looked up from his slew of computers for the first time.

"Do you know a Sam Tagaletto?" he asked.

The name didn't mean anything to me. "No," I said. "Never heard of him."

"Apparently Dwayne Robinson did. About a month ago, he wrote him two checks over the span of a week. Both were for fifty grand."

"I didn't think Dwayne had that kind of money anymore. I'm almost sure of it."

"He didn't," said Hoodie. "Both checks bounced."

Red flag, anyone?

"So who's Sam Tagaletto?" I asked.

"Definitely not a Boy Scout, that's for sure. He's been arrested twice for illegal bookmaking, among other things, once in Florida and most recently here in New York," he said.

"How recent?"

"A year ago. He got six months' probation."

"Anything about his having ties to the mob?" I asked.

Hoodie cocked his head in my direction. "You mean other than his being a *bookie*?"

"Yeah, I know, but I'm looking for actual names. Maybe somebody I *have* heard of."

"Give me another minute on that," said Hoodie.

He went back to the keyboard, his fingers tapping away almost as fast as my mind was racing.

Think, Nick. What does all this mean? What could it mean?

Dwayne Robinson had owed a bookie a big

chunk of change and couldn't pay it off. He hadn't bounced just one check to this guy, Sam Tagaletto, he'd bounced *two*.

Maybe that's why Dwayne had killed himself. Or had gotten thrown out of a window by somebody. Because he'd owed money to a bookie and had showed disrespect.

But there had to be more to it than that. It was now officially impossible to believe that my being at the table next to Vincent Marcozza had been a coincidence.

But if it indeed had been a setup like Pinero told me, then *who* had set it up?

Dwayne Robinson? I doubted it. Dwayne had been a former major league pitcher, not a former brain surgeon.

Or had it been someone else and that's what Dwayne had wanted to tell me?

All I knew was that it was time to get to know a certain Sam Tagaletto a little better. Presuming I could find him.

"Do you have a current address for this guy?" I finally asked Hoodie. "Tagaletto?"

He was already two steps ahead of me. I'd no sooner finished the question than the purr of a printer filled the room. Hoodie handed me not only Tagaletto's last known address but also his latest mug shots.

"Anything else I can do for you?" he asked.

Yeah, you can tell me what the hell you're doing working for a hedge fund firm. On second thought, never mind. I probably don't want to know that, either.

"No, that's more than enough," I answered. "Thanks a lot, man."

I shook Hoodie's hand, thanked him again, and was about to show myself out the door.

"Oh, one more thing," he said. "It goes without saying but I'll say it anyway. This meeting never took place."

I nodded. "What meeting?"

Chapter 53

I WAS NEVER one to keep secrets from Courtney, personally or professionally. Nonetheless, I felt I owed it to Hoodie Brown—not to mention Derrick Phalen—to keep mum on the meeting that had supposedly never happened.

What I did plan to tell Courtney was that Phalen had promised to try to help me out, albeit on the down low. That wasn't a lie; it just wasn't the entire truth. A sin of omission, as they say. Or, as one of my journalism professors at Northwestern used to put it, "The truth may set you free, but it's the little white lie that will save your ass."

Now if Courtney would only return my call.

There was no answer on her cell, and when I

rang her secretary, M.J. told me Courtney had left the office without saying where she was going.

Of course, the last time Courtney did that, Thomas Ferramore had stopped by the office with news of a certain supermodel's YouTube video.

Why was I suddenly getting a weird feeling again?

The answer came soon enough as I stepped off the train back from Greenwich. Walking through Grand Central Station I passed a newsstand just as a guy was stacking the late edition of the *New York Post*.

Voilà! There she was again, the French supermodel Marbella, on the cover with yet another glass of champagne in her hand and a mischievous smile.

"JUST KIDDING!" read the headline.

Fifty cents later I was standing off to the side, my head buried among the pages.

Apparently Marbella had given an interview to a French television station claiming—*au contraire*—that she'd never actually slept with Thomas Ferramore. It had all been a bad joke, she insisted, and she deeply regretted any problems it may have caused the billionaire or his "lovely fiancée" in America.

Yeah, right. *Color me sold, sweetheart.*

But there was more.

And on the believability scale, it was actually a bit more convincing, or at least creative.

The CEO of ParisJet, the company in France that Ferramore was negotiating to buy, had told the French business magazine *Les Echos* that Ferramore had been in talks with him day and night for his entire trip.

"Trust me, Mr. Ferramore had no time for any funny business or hanky-panky business," read the money quote.

I closed the *Post* and tucked it beneath my arm, walking toward the Lexington Avenue exit to hail a taxi. I could feel the whoosh of commuters rushing by me for their trains and the vibration of their footsteps against the wide marble floor.

But what I really felt was numb, confused, and more than a little lost.

For sure, Courtney hadn't been scooped by the *Post*. She had to be up to speed on this latest twist and turn in her marital saga. Ferramore probably even made sure of it. Why wouldn't he? It was alibi city.

But was she buying it?

The verdict rang in my pocket no more than a minute later. Courtney was finally calling me back.

"I saw the story. Do you know what you're going to do now?" I asked her.

"I do," she answered.

Chapter 54

IT WASN'T THE words themselves but the way Courtney said them. As if she were already standing at the altar with Thomas Ferramore.

"I do."

I immediately fell silent on the phone. There was no need for Courtney to officially break the news. It was broken. Just like my heart.

"I need you to understand, Nick," she said. "I'm marrying Tom, but I need you to be there for me."

"I *was* there for you," I said.

"I know you were. Promise me you won't stop now. Do you promise?"

What could I say? As much as I loved her, she had always been my friend first, before anything else.

"Please," she said, pressing me. "Do you promise? I need to hear the actual words, Nick."

I took a deep breath and swallowed it along with my pride.

"I do," I said.

Of course, little did I know how fast I'd have to make good on that promise.

A few hours later, with the sun setting over Manhattan, I arrived downtown at the North Cove Marina to climb aboard *Sweet Revenge,* Thomas Ferramore's 180-foot Trinity mega-yacht. I've seen much smaller houses. Actually, I grew up in one.

In a word? *Wow.*

At the bow stood the bar, and at the stern was the live jazz band, a really good combo. In between was a veritable who's who of publishing, fashion, and what remained of the decimated ranks of the banking and Wall Street elite.

You get one guess as to where I headed first, and it wasn't to shake Thomas Ferramore's hand.

"I'll have a Laphroaig Fifteen Year Old," I said to the rent-a-bartender, who barely looked old enough to drive, let alone serve drinks.

The young man looked at me as if I'd just

spoken Swahili to him. "A what?" he asked.

"A Laphroaig Fifteen Year Old," came a voice over my shoulder.

It was Courtney, and in her hand was an entire bottle of my favorite Scotch whisky.

"Here," she said, handing the bottle to the bartender. "Please keep this behind the bar for Mr. Daniels, and *Mr. Daniels only*."

"Yes, ma'am," he said, quickly pouring me a double. "Laphroaig Fifteen Year Old."

Courtney took my arm as we moved away from the bar. "Thanks so much for coming," she said. "It means the world to me. You're the best."

Apparently not, but I took a big swig of excellent whisky and winked at her. "What are friends for?" I said.

She gave me a huge smile and leaned in to tell me something, when the music suddenly stopped. It was replaced by the sound of a knife tapping on crystal. Oh boy, Thomas Ferramore wanted to make a toast.

Once again he had come between Courtney and me. I guessed I'd better get used to it.

"C'mon up here, sweetheart!" he bellowed, standing up straight and proud on the captain's deck. He was wearing a faux white naval jacket replete with shoulder boards and a sleeve insignia. Two blond women flanked him, both very pretty, and I figured they were his PR team. Was this guy for real? I couldn't understand what Courtney saw in him. Not even when I tried extra hard.

As she made her way to join him, Ferramore thanked everyone for coming on such short notice "to this wonderful celebration of love." That brought a rousing cheer from the entire crowd. Minus me, of course. I had one hand in my pocket and I was wiggling my middle finger at him.

Ferramore took no offense and continued: "Courtney and I wanted to make it very clear this evening that no rumor, no unfounded gossip, no nonsense whatsoever, will ever get the better of us. We can ride out any storm that comes our way!"

Ferramore turned to face Courtney, pulling her tightly into his arms. As the two of them kissed, he thrust his hand high in triumph. An even louder cheer erupted from the crowd of his friends, or whoever these hordes of overdressed people were.

Right on cue the first firework exploded in the night air, a beautiful collage of rainbow colors mixing with a sea of stars. It was an amazing spectacle, actually.

But the real spectacle that night was yet to come, and of course, I would be part of it.

Chapter 55

I'D SPENT THE afternoon with Hoodie.

Now here I was with Houdini.

Thomas Ferramore had just pulled off the impossible, a trick for the ages. He had escaped the seemingly inescapable bind he'd been in, and he'd made it look easy.

Deep down, Courtney may have still had some suspicions, but there on his yacht, for all of Manhattan's glitterati to see, Ferramore still had his prize. That's all that mattered to him.

And me.

I should've stolen a page from Courtney's playbook and put everything into a box.

Instead, I put it all into a glass...and drank it.

After about an.hour at the party, and after the youthful rent-a-bartender decided that my drinking two-thirds of a bottle of whisky was clearly one-third too many, I decided I would tell Thomas Ferramore exactly what I thought of his marrying Courtney.

Only I couldn't find him. So I did the next worst thing.

I told Courtney.

Cornering her along the starboard railing, I slurred the truth to her in a voice somewhat louder than it should have been. "You can't marry him! You're making a mistake! Don't you see what a mistake this is? You're smart—so *act* smart, Courtney."

Her eyes filled with tears as everyone within earshot turned to gawk at the scene I was making. Courtney was so upset, she could barely get the words out.

"All I see is someone drunk who just broke his promise to me," she said.

She walked away then, leaving me alone— unless, of course, you count all the lookie-loos still watching. That's when I really gave them their money's worth. All that whisky in my otherwise empty stomach churned and sloshed its way up past my heartache and back out through its original port of entry. Right there over the starboard railing, with an ear-wrenching heave-ho, I power-fed the fishes.

I should've been embarrassed to death, but that's the temporary beauty of being drunk: complete lack of self-awareness. Still, I did manage one decent decision—to go find a bathroom to wash up so I could hail a cab home without scaring off the driver.

Parting the deck crowd like Moses with the measles, I babbled while stumbling and bumbling off. "A bathroom...a bathroom...my kingdom for a bathroom."

No one laughed, and I guess I couldn't blame them for that. I had let myself become a complete horse's ass on Courtney's special night. I had let my best friend down.

I entered the main galley and immediately began twisting every doorknob in sight down a long hallway. It figured that every room was locked.

Finally one door opened. As I groped for a light switch, all I could think was, *Please, Lord, let this be a bathroom!*

But as the room lit up, I couldn't believe my eyes. "You've got to be kidding me!" I blurted out. "This can't be for real!".

Chapter 56

IT WAS LIKE the game of Clue, only the sex-addict edition. *Thomas Ferramore...in the supply room...with his pants down around his ankles.*

In front of him was a young and very pretty blonde on her knees. Needless to say, she wasn't praying. I wasn't sure, but I thought she was one of the PR ladies who had been with him on the deck.

Panic flashed across Ferramore's face, but amazingly, it vanished almost as fast as it had arrived. Apparently you don't get to be a billionaire without being able to think quickly on your feet, even with your dick hanging out.

"Get up, honey," he said calmly to the young blonde. "Go enjoy the rest of the party."

She quickly buttoned her white blouse, dabbed at her lips, and hurried out the door. I suppose I couldn't blame her, but not once did she look at me.

Meanwhile, that's all Ferramore could do. His dark eyes bored straight into mine. He was staring, unblinking. And of all goddamn things, he started to smile.

"So, you caught me," he said, the second we were alone. "Now what are you going to do about it? You have a plan of action yet?"

The son of a bitch hadn't even bothered to pull up his pants.

"What do you *think* I'm going to do about it?" I shot back. "At your own engagement party? After what you said to Courtney up there?"

He shook his head and laughed some more. "It's your word against mine and your word is pretty drunk, isn't it?"

"Not so drunk that I'm blind, pal. I saw what I saw."

In fact, I suddenly felt as if I'd downed a dozen cups of coffee. Not quite sober as a judge, but the thoughts and words were forming just fine.

"Do you even love Courtney?" I asked.

"Does that even matter?"

"It does to me."

He laughed again. "Yes, I know it does," he said. "You love her madly, right? That's probably why you felt it was okay to fuck her when you knew she was engaged to me."

That stopped me cold. How did he know that?

"She told you?" I asked in disbelief.

His laugh grew louder, a booming cackle now, and it dawned on me that there was another explanation.

"Christ, you had her followed."

"I always look after my investments, Nick—force of habit. In a way, all it proves is that Courtney and I are meant for each other. In fact, for your sake, you should feel lucky I was okay with it."

"Tell you what, then," I said. "Since you know about Courtney and me, why don't we go tell her about what I just walked in on and she can decide for herself."

"You do that and you can kiss your sweet job at *Citizen* magazine good-bye."

"Yeah, but I'd sure be going out with a bang."

"Yes, you sure would. Too bad about Courtney, though. She'd be out of a job, too. You understand that, of course."

Checkmate! And he knew it, too. *Citizen* was Courtney's baby, the joy of her life.

Ferramore finally reached down and pulled up his trousers. "To show you there are no hard feelings, though, how about I cut you a check and we forget this whole thing ever happened."

Was this prick really trying to buy me off? That was the worst insult yet.

"That depends," I said. "What does your being caught getting a blow job go for these days?"

"That's a very good question," came a trembling voice over my shoulder. "What *does* it go for, Tom?"

Chapter 57

I SPUN AROUND to see Courtney leaning against the doorway, her arms folded tightly, as if she was hugging herself for comfort. Her eyes were shooting so many sharpened daggers at Ferramore, I practically had to duck.

No one had to ask how long she'd been standing there or how much she'd heard.

She'd obviously heard enough.

But there were no tears like she had had with me out on the deck. She wasn't sad now, she was angry—mad as hell at Ferramore and even more pissed off at herself. I thought I knew what she was thinking: *How could I have been so stupid?*

"So tell me, Tom, what did you have to pay your little French supermodel to change her story? How much was *that* check?" she demanded to know.

I expected Ferramore to show at least a little remorse here. Maybe even a little class.

Boy, was I ever wrong. The rich have such incredibly high opinions of themselves.

The prick smirked. "Hell, she was cheap compared with that CEO of ParisJet. I actually had to buy his company."

All at once, Courtney yanked off her ten-carat diamond ring and threw a fastball at Ferramore's chest.

"C'mon, Nick, let's go," she said.

It was the four most beautiful words she, or anybody, had ever said to me.

"I hope you two are extremely happy together," chirped Ferramore as he buckled his trousers. "Oh, and by the way, you're both fired! Good luck finding new jobs."

"Don't worry, we will," Courtney shot back. "You see, I get to start over. But you? You'll always be a scumbag!"

Brava, Courtney!

She turned and walked off, and I was about to follow in her steps, but I just couldn't help myself.

The moment was too good; I wasn't quite ready to leave yet.

"By the way, Ferramore," I said, glancing down at his ridiculous white jacket, "Captain Stubing from *The Love Boat* called. He wants his uniform back."

Chapter 58

IN THE MOVIES, Courtney and I would have made mad, passionate love all night long to the tune of a saxophone soundtrack. Then we would've blissfully woken up in each other's arms without a single hair out of place.

So much for the movies, which don't seem to get it right very often anyway.

I didn't have Courtney in my arms or anywhere else in my apartment the next morning. What I did have, however, was a terrific hangover and a severe case of bed head that would've scared Lyle Lovett.

As upset as Courtney had been as she'd stormed off Ferramore's yacht, she'd known better than to engage in any "Sweet Revenge" scenarios with me. And as drunk as I had been, I really hadn't been looking for anything more than a kiss on the cheek. *Maybe*. After all, I had been beyond obnoxious at the party, and I'd broken my promise to her.

"We'll be making two stops," Courtney had told the cab driver. "First his apartment, and then mine." But she held my hand for the entire ride and indeed gave me that kiss on the cheek when we rolled up to my place. And that's how the night ended.

At least, I'm fairly sure that's how it ended. It was all still fuzzy in the a.m. In fact, it wasn't until I'd taken in some hot, über-strong coffee and a cold shower that I managed my first lucid thought.

According to Thomas Ferramore I was no longer employed by *Citizen* magazine. Just like that, I was suddenly out of a great job, probably the best one I'd ever had. Pink-slipped. Canned for doing the right thing.

But I still had work to do. I had my mission impossible to try to accomplish.

Armed with an address and some ugly mug shot photos courtesy of Hoodie Brown, I headed out to the South Bronx in search of Sam Tagaletto. Ironically, he lived less than six blocks from Yankee Stadium. Was that how he'd first met Dwayne?

Tagaletto's home was on the second floor of a decrepit corner brownstone, the bricks of which looked to be literally crumbling when not outright missing. This guy apparently didn't care much about curb appeal.

Or, for that matter, who wandered into his building off the street.

Not only was there no buzzer system, the front door was actually propped open with— what else?—one of the bricks from the building's façade.

My plan once inside was fairly simple. So simple, in fact, any eight-year-old could have done it and probably had. *Ring and run!*

After climbing the stairs, I rapped my knuckles hard against the door of apartment 2-B before dashing up to the third floor. I needed a glimpse of Tagaletto to make sure it was really him— assuming he was home.

He was.

After the sharp *snap!* of a turning dead bolt,

the door to his apartment opened as wide as its chain lock would let it. That's when I saw him—tall, skinny, and with a narrow, mottled face not even a mother could love. Hell, this guy looked *worse* in real life than in his terrible mug shots.

I stole another peek down through the third-floor railing as Tagaletto glanced left and right with his dark, deep-set eyes. Then, like a turtle, he retreated back into his apartment.

I settled in for the wait.

Hopefully, the guy would soon have places to go and people to see, any one of which could be the break I was looking for. I needed to get lucky. Then again, with my luck the guy would turn out to be a hermit. Sam Tagaletto, the agoraphobic bookie of the South Bronx . . .

Great, just great.

Less than half an hour later, though, I heard it once again—the sound of a turning dead bolt.

Yes! Sam Tagaletto was leaving his apartment. Now, where was he going? And could I follow him without being spotted and getting the shit kicked out of me?

Chapter 59

I COULD COUNT on one hand how many times in my life I'd ever "tailed" someone. And I'd still have five fingers left over.

This was a new feeling, all right, including the relentless pounding of my heart as I fell in line behind Tagaletto out on the street. *How close is too close?*

Best not to find out, I decided. I kept a safe distance for the first few blocks, nearly losing him once when he turned a corner at a busy intersection. In fact, were it not for Tagaletto's nicotine habit I would've lost him for sure along the crowded sidewalk. All I had to do was keep my eye on the gray cloud hovering over his head. The guy smoked more than a chimney in the wintertime.

Lean and scraggly, Tagaletto wasn't exactly the physically imposing type. But somehow, some way, he still managed to look menacing. Maybe it was the "don't fuck with me" walk. He definitely had that down pat.

For another few blocks I kept right in line behind him. Until, finally, he made another turn, disappearing from view in a maze of storefronts.

Immediately I began to sprint. Tagaletto had gone down a narrow alley next to a pizza parlor, its red neon sign glowing in the window: SLICE OF HEAVEN.

"Shit, where is he?" I mumbled, reaching the alley and peering around the corner. Out of breath, all I could see were piles of garbage lining both sides and no one in between. Slowly, I started to walk. Where the hell did he go?

I saw the most probable answer halfway down. It was a metallic door, the only one. If I had to bet, it led into the kitchen of Slice of Heaven, but that's as close as I wanted to get. My nose was telling me this was a bad place to be, and it had nothing to do with the smell of pepperoni and onions in the air.

I was about to turn around and get the hell

out of there, when I heard the door in the alley begin to open, the sound of rusted hinges ricocheting off the walls. I quickly moved behind a Dumpster that reeked so badly I put my sleeve over my nose.

There were maybe two inches of daylight between the piled garbage and the wall, just enough to catch a glimpse of Tagaletto stepping back outside.

He was lighting a cigarette. And he wasn't alone.

Holy shit.

I recognized the other guy right away. How could I not? He was Carmine Zambratta, a.k.a. the Zamboni.

There was never a more fitting nickname for a mob guy. Zambratta not only looked like a Zamboni—the machine that smooths the ice at hockey rinks—he acted like one. From what I knew, he was a fixer, the kind of guy used when there was a "rough patch" that needed smoothing over. All of New York knew his face. Countless times his mug had graced the covers of the city's tabloids—and each time the headline was a variation on the same theme. *Not guilty!*

Zambratta's ability to escape conviction was rivaled by only one other mob figure. That would be Eddie "The Prince" Pinero.

So why was I so surprised to see Zambratta?

Possibly because he didn't report to Eddie Pinero. Just the opposite. The Zamboni worked for a rival boss by the name of Joseph D'zorio.

It took me a few seconds to do anything besides stare at the two mob guys. Then I reached for my pocket. Looking down, I searched for the camera application on my iPhone. Raising the phone, I eyed the screen to center Tagaletto and Zambratta in the picture I was about to take.

Shit. Now what had happened?

Zambratta was gone. Where the hell had he disappeared to?

"I'm right here, cocksucker," I suddenly heard as the nose of a gun hit my cheek.

Chapter 60

"DO I KNOW YOU?" Zambratta asked, his tone already anticipating my expected answer.

"No," I said, trying not to shake. God only knows what my tone sounded like. Scared shitless, probably. Out of my league, out of my element, out of my mind?

"You're right, I don't know you," he said. "So how do you know me?"

"I don't."

Zambratta cocked his gun, the *click!* echoing in my ear. "Don't bullshit me," he said. "Everybody knows me. I'm a legend."

I tried to breathe normally but it was becoming next to impossible. "I know who you are," I corrected myself. "What I meant was, I didn't know you'd be here." What the hell was that supposed to mean?

I turned slightly, my eyes meeting his for a split second. He was very intense and focused, and I saw enough to know that he was trying to decide what to do with me.

"Sam!" he called out.

Tagaletto walked over to the Dumpster, his latest cigarette dangling from his thin lips. "What a stink," he said. Then he shrugged. "Who is he?"

"You tell me," said Zambratta. "You're the one brought him here."

"I've never seen him before. No idea who this idiot is."

"You sure?"

"Of course I'm sure."

"What's your name?" Zambratta asked me.

My first thought was to make one up. Thankfully, my second, somewhat more rational thought prevailed. "Nick Daniels," I answered.

"Turn and face the wall, Nick," said Zambratta, backing up a few steps. I'd barely heard the words before Tagaletto stepped in and gave me some help—courtesy of a hard shove.

As soon as my palms slammed against the bricks, he frisked me.

Out came my wallet.

"*Hey,*" I said instinctively, but then I shut myself up.

"Turn back around," ordered Zambratta. "But keep your hands nice and high."

When I did, I saw Tagaletto checking my driver's license. He gave Zambratta a nod. I was telling the truth. Did that count for something with mob guys? Probably not.

"So who the hell are you, Nick Daniels?"

"I'm a journalist."

"Ahhh. So were you following Sam?"

So much for the truth. It was time to lie. *C'mon, Nick, think fast!*

Faster!

"I'm doing a story," I answered. "It's about bookies. Actually, it's about New Yorkers who are ruined by their gambling habits." That was pretty good, under the circumstances.

"You expect me to believe that total crock of shit?"

I nodded at Tagaletto. "He's a bookie, isn't he?"

"So what does that make me?" asked

Zambratta. "Am I going to be in your story now, too?"

"Absolutely not," I said. "In fact, I'm pretty sure this was a bad idea for a story. A really bad idea, I now realize. So I'm out of here. All right if I slowly lower my hands?"

Zambratta chuckled. I'd become his court jester and that was fine by me. Just so long as I wasn't his next victim.

"What should we do with him, Sam?" asked Zambratta. "Any brilliant ideas?"

Tagaletto shrugged again, flicking the butt of his cigarette against the wall. "The guy obviously knows some things he shouldn't," he said.

"You're saying we should kill him?"

"It's your call. But I would."

Zambratta nodded. "So go ahead," he said, tossing Tagaletto his gun. *Kill him.*

Chapter 61

I SWEAR THE gun traveled in slow motion from Zambratta to Tagaletto. That's how it felt, at least. A stub-nose piece of metal floating through the air, and my life hanging in the balance.

I watched as the bookie fumbled, then nearly dropped the gun. He did drop his cigarette. His hands were clearly as surprised as the rest of him. *Are you serious?* said the look on his face.

Zambratta seemed pretty damn serious to me.

"Please," I said. "Don't do this!" *I'm in love with a terrific woman, and I need to work it out before I die.*

"Shut up!" barked Zambratta.

I stared back at Tagaletto with a whole lot

of irony cruising around in my brain. He was holding a gun, but there was no longer anything menacing about him. The truth was, he looked nervous, almost as scared as I was, and he wasn't the one with the death sentence here.

He can't do it! He doesn't have it in him!

"What's the matter, Sam? What are you waiting for?" asked Zambratta. "Kill him."

Tagaletto didn't say a word. He couldn't even look at Zambratta. Or me. His head was down, his eyes trained on the filthy ground of the alley.

"There's no need to do this," I tried again. "I'm no threat to either of you. You let me leave and it's like this never happened."

"I said, SHUT UP!" barked Zambratta again, the veins in his tree stump of a neck bulging above the collar of his brown leather jacket.

Then he turned back to Tagaletto. "We don't have all day here, Sam. If you don't have the stones for this, let me know."

Christ! Zambratta was goading him to commit murder — my murder!

I watched in horror as Tagaletto started to look up from the ground. His eyes stared directly into mine. Next he raised his arm, the gun aimed straight for my chest.

Do something, Nick! Lunge for him! Anything!

I saw that Tagaletto's hand was beginning to tremble. He steadied it with his other hand. He was steeling his nerve. This was his first time, wasn't it?

"Don't do this," I told him.

Then he pulled the trigger.

The air exploded around me, the blistering sound of the shot piercing my ears.

But no pain right away.

I looked down at myself. There was no blood visible. No wound that I could see.

Did Tagaletto just miss me from six feet away?

That's when I finally looked at Tagaletto. Except he was no longer standing there. He was lying on the ground in a pool of his own blood.

"Lucky for you I always carry a spare," said Zambratta. He returned the second pistol to a holster inside his jacket.

I couldn't move and I felt paralyzed. The question I wanted to ask was, why was Tagaletto dead and not me? But I couldn't speak.

Zambratta answered anyway. "Sam was a

careless motherfucker, always has been," he sneered. "Today, it's a reporter like you. Tomorrow, it's a Fed."

He slid my driver's license into his pocket and tossed my wallet to the ground. Then he *really* fucked with me.

"I'm not supposed to kill you yet," he said.

Chapter 62

ALL THE WAY back to my apartment, Zambratta's last line echoed in my head like the sound of the gunshot that had killed Sam Tagaletto. What's more, he knew who I was even before he saw my driver's license.

Because he worked for Joseph D'zorio.

Everything was coming together in a way I could never have imagined. And that wasn't a good thing. People whom I didn't know, whom I'd never even met before, knew exactly who I was and wanted me dead. Just not quite yet.

It was all the more reason for me to run—*don't walk!*—straight to the police. But I didn't. I decided not to.

Just not quite yet. I was too consumed with the

chase for the truth by this point. The same kid who had stared up in awe at the screen at Woodward and Bernstein in *All the President's Men* was now too preoccupied with piecing together what had really brought me and Dwayne Robinson together that bloody day at Lombardo's. Or, rather, *who* had brought us together.

If I had it right so far, it had all begun when Dwayne Robinson made some bad bets and lost money he didn't have. He owed Sam Tagaletto, but Tagaletto was just a middleman. The person Dwayne really owed was Joseph D'zorio. After Dwayne bounced two checks, D'zorio could've broken his arms or sunk him to the bottom of the Hudson River.

But D'zorio didn't become a mob boss by using muscle alone. He was smart and he was cunning. Played chess, not checkers. So he came up with a better way for Dwayne to pay off his debt. All the former ace southpaw had to do was break his long-standing silence with the media and consent to an interview in a seemingly random steakhouse with a credible journalist who would eat up the potential story.

Let the tape recorder roll.

"I have a message from Eddie."

Just like that, D'zorio had set up Eddie Pinero. He had used Dwayne and me. But most of all, he had used the fact that Pinero would have a motive to want his longtime attorney dead.

It was a pretty damn perfect plan. Right down to my coming across the Pinero reference on my recorder. *Of course* I would have done that. In fact, had I not left my jacket at Lombardo's and talked to the hostess, Tiffany, I never would've become the least bit suspicious.

That's when D'zorio's plan became a little *too* perfect. At least for me.

The question now was whether I could prove my theory to anyone, or at least anyone who mattered in police circles. And whether I would live long enough to do it.

The second I walked into my apartment I grabbed Derrick Phalen's business card. It was only a little past two o'clock. Odds were he was in his office. Still, he had asked that I call him only on his cell.

Phalen picked up quick, only one ring, but then said he'd have to call me back in a couple of minutes. When he did call back, I could hear street sounds in the background. He'd obviously gone outside to speak to me. Was he being extremely paranoid or just smart as hell?

"We've got a lot to talk about," I told him. "This is going to blow your mind."

"You don't know the half of it," he came back. "What I found out last night will blow *your* mind."

Chapter 63

PHALEN SAID HE couldn't get into his news right now and he didn't want to discuss it over the phone. "Nick, can you come by my apartment tonight?" he asked.

Are you kidding me? Yeah, like anything could stop me.

I called Courtney on the way over to Derrick's that night. She was quiet and reserved, so I didn't bring up Thomas Ferramore, and I also didn't get into what had happened in the Bronx today. I did tell her I was seeing Phalen, and she told me, "Be careful, Nick. I don't want to lose you."

At a few minutes past eight, I exited the Henry Hudson Parkway in the heart of the Riverdale section of the Bronx. Phalen's street was a few blocks east and was lined with pre-war brown-stones. If I didn't know better, I'd swear I was on the Upper East Side of Manhattan.

Save for one difference: available parking. I found a spot probably less than fifty feet from Phalen's address.

As I grabbed my shoulder bag and hit the sidewalk, I was reminded of a joke my uncle Leo had once told me. I had been nine or ten years old.

"How do you keep a turkey in suspense?" he asked.

"I don't know. How?"

Uncle Leo smiled. "I'll tell you later. Turkey."

I could barely wait to hear what Phalen had for me. I was actually speed-walking toward his brownstone and my heart was going pretty good. With one foot on the front stoop, however, I stopped.

Did I lock my car?

I couldn't remember.

I reached into my pocket, my thumb searching for the lock button on my electronic key fob. I gave it a click and watched for the taillights on my Saab to blink—only they didn't.

I clicked again.

No luck.

I cursed under my breath and started walking back, thinking I was out of range. The entire key chain was out of my pocket and aimed squarely at the dash. I was definitely close enough now.

But the taillights still weren't blinking.

C'mon, already!

I shook the key fob, pressing the lock button hard a few more times. Was the little battery inside the thing dead?

No, it wasn't. But I sure as hell was supposed to be.

BOOM! went my Saab.

Chapter 64

MY CAR ROSE in the air a good three feet as an orange fireball raced toward me, then knocked me down, my body slamming so hard against the sidewalk that I actually blacked out for a few seconds.

When I came to, the sound of the explosion was still pummeling my ears. All at once I could hear the shattering of glass, the twisting of metal, my car being blown to smithereens!

Slowly I got up, but the heat from the flames was so intense I had to step back. *Am I okay? Am I hurt more than I think I am? Am I still among the living?*

I looked down at my charred clothing and got part of the answer. Smoke literally was rising from my sweater. I was dizzy and scared to death, but most of all I was relieved to be alive.

Okay, Nick. You're okay.

Then came another awful scene—and the kind of screaming that raised every little hair on the back of my neck.

My head whipped left and right until I spotted a chocolate Lab dragging a leash on the opposite sidewalk. The dog was spinning in circles, barking like it had gone crazy.

Then I saw why.

Dashing across the street, I practically ripped the sweater off my own body. By the time I reached the curb, I was already flying through the air.

The dog's owner, a college-aged kid, was on the ground in flames and screaming in agony. I landed on him sweater first, trying to smother the fire. "Help me!" he was pleading now. "PLEASE HELP ME!"

I was smothering the kid with my body and sweater. But the flames were stubborn and I needed help.

Thank God, it came. *Whoosh!* I felt the freezing cold spray of white powder against my skin. It was like an avalanche, and just in time.

I coughed and sputtered, barely able to catch

my breath. Someone had rushed forward with a
fire extinguisher, emptying what seemed to be
the entire canister. That was fine by me. *Really*
fine by the guy who was no longer on fire underneath me.

"You okay?" I asked as I finally rolled off him.

"I don't know," was all he could manage.

By now the entire street was filling with
people from the brownstones. Anyone within
earshot of the explosion had come out to see
what had happened. They didn't understand, but
I did, and it chilled me like the spray of dozens of
fire extinguishers.

Someone had just tried to kill me.

The next thing I knew, I was being helped to
my feet by some good people in the crowd. "Are
you hurt?" one man asked. "You okay, mister?"

I heard the question but didn't respond. All I
could do was look around at all the concerned,
frightened faces. With each face I didn't recognize, I became more afraid. "Oh, no!" I suddenly
cried out. "Oh God, no."

Then I was running away from the crowd.
Fast, as fast as I could go on rubbery legs.

Like someone's life depended on it.

Chapter 65

I WAS NOW the designated madman on the street, the guy covered in white powder, with smoldering clothes and charred skin, with singed hair and desperate eyes.

With each frantic step I kept looking around me, hoping that I'd spot Phalen.

Was that Derrick over there by the fire hydrant?

No.

Was that him on the stoop?

Dammit! No again.

I kept banging into people, forcing my way across the street. It was a block party of lookie-loos, my burning car at the center of it, *me* as the other story of interest.

I reached the front of Phalen's brownstone and bounded up the steps, my arms pumping. The front door was locked — *shit!* — so I turned to the column of buzzers off to the side. I dug into my pocket for his apartment number. I remembered I'd written it on the back of his business card.

3C!

I pounded my fist against the buzzer. The seconds took forever as I waited for a response. Plausible scenarios zoomed through my head. Derrick was in the shower. Taking a nap. Not home yet. Anything but what I feared.

I kept stabbing the buzzer, when the front door suddenly opened. A man in a bathrobe was coming to see about the commotion on the street.

"Hey, what's your problem?" he said as I nearly knocked him over to get inside.

The stairwell was straight ahead. Two by two I took the steps, turning the corner to the second floor, then the third. The man in the bathrobe was still yelling at me, threatening to call the cops.

I scanned the doors. 3C was down the hall, at the front of the building.

It was locked. Of course it was.

I hammered on the door, calling out Derrick's name. *Please be there!*

The more I pounded, the less hope I had, though.

I turned around, searching for something to help break down the damn door. Then I figured out what I needed. Hell, I was practically wearing the answer.

But there was no fire extinguisher in the hallway on Derrick's floor.

I dashed up to the fourth floor. *Yes!* Near the top of the stairs was a large canister, polished red and silver. I ripped it from the wall. Then I raced back downstairs to Phalen's door, smashing it as hard as I could over and over, definitely looking like a madman now.

Finally the door splintered. I was able to get at the locks. Then the door flew open. I was just about to call out Derrick's name.

Instead I fell to my knees. I was staring into what had once been Derrick Phalen's eyes.

Part Four

BURDEN OF PROOF

Chapter 66

I FOUND MYSELF back down on the street again, talking to detectives from the local precinct, when I spotted somebody arriving on the scene, somebody who I really didn't want to talk to right now, or even see.

Officially, the Manhattan DA was out of his jurisdiction up here in the Riverdale section of the Bronx. Unofficially, he didn't seem to care.

Nor did the two detectives who were interviewing me. Receiving nothing more than a nod from Sorren, they both backed away.

Sorren lit a cigarette and gave me a quick head to toe. First things first: "You okay?" he asked.

"Yeah," I said. "I think so."

In that case . . .

Sorren took a step forward, getting in my face. "Then what were you thinking?"

I rose from the bumper of the ambulance to stand closer to him, toe to toe. I'd never felt more drained and upset, but I wasn't about to be pushed around by him, or anybody else at the crime scene. I was one of the victims here, wasn't I? Sure I was.

"I told you what I was thinking in your office. Remember? You told me I had no evidence. You insinuated I should try and find some."

Sorren swatted his hand in the air incredulously. "So you go to the OCTF and bullshit a prosecutor about your writing an article?"

"How'd you hear that?" I asked.

"I spoke to Phalen's boss, a man named Ian LaGrange, on the way over here. He said you lied to both of them."

"He's right, I did lie. That's why Phalen wanted nothing to do with me," I said. "I was here to try and change his mind. That's all."

Sorren smirked. I'm sure he knew that probably wasn't true—not with Phalen murdered and me narrowly escaping the same fate. "Listen to me, Nick," he said, his tone sharpening to an edge. "The time to protect Phalen was when he was still alive."

Whoa. That stung. I was already beating myself up over getting Derrick involved in this mess. The self-inflicted guilt was bad enough. The *Sorren*-inflicted guilt just made it that much worse.

But he was right. Suddenly I was reminded that Sorren was a very bright guy and that I needed him, possibly just to stay alive.

"Derrick Phalen was helping me," I admitted. "He told me he'd discovered something big and that it would blow my mind."

"All right. That's good. So what was it?"

"He was supposed to share it with me tonight. That's why I came here. I'm telling the truth, David. I'm totally leveling with you."

"You have no idea what it might be?" asked Sorren. "Don't try and have it both ways, Nick."

"I'm not," I said. "I have no idea. None."

"Fuck."

"You've got that right."

Sorren took a last desperate drag off his cigarette, throwing it at the ground. I watched as he gave it an angry twist with his heel.

Of course, if I'd been looking up instead of down, I would've seen the man who was charging straight for me, his fist cocked, his nose just about blowing steam.

But it was like everything else that had happened that terrible night.

I never saw it coming.

Chapter 67

MY RIGHT CHEEK imploded, the pain so quick and fierce I thought I'd been hit by a crosstown bus.

In a way I had. Ian LaGrange, all six feet four inches and nearly three hundred pounds of him, had stormed right past Sorren to sucker punch me square in the face, and as I fell helplessly back against the ambulance behind me, I could hear him screaming at the top of his fire-breathing lungs.

"LOOK WHAT YOU'VE DONE, YOU SON OF A BITCH! LOOK WHAT YOU'VE DONE!"

And he was far from done himself.

He lunged for me again, his long and powerful arms flailing in the air. Were it not for Sorren stepping in to block him, he would've probably knocked me out cold, then smashed my face into pieces. As it was, I was seeing stars and a variety of bright colors that weren't in my usual palette.

"Stop it! Calm down!" barked Sorren, pushing him back—or at least trying to. LaGrange outweighed Sorren by a hundred pounds easy, and he wasn't about to be denied another crack at me.

That is, until Sorren tried a different tact. While LaGrange continued shouting about me being the reason Derrick Phalen had been murdered, Sorren reminded the guy that we weren't alone.

Uh, hello? Did you not see the news vans?

"Look around you, LaGrange!" said Sorren through clenched teeth. "This isn't the place."

That did the trick for some reason or another. LaGrange's rage was trumped only by his desire not to be fodder for every news outlet in the city, not to mention his becoming the latest sensation on YouTube. With reporters and their cameramen literally sprinting toward us, LaGrange immediately backed off.

"Nothing to see here, folks!" announced Sorren

to the reporters. "We'll have a statement for you in a few minutes. Just be a little patient."

Reluctantly, they took his word for it.

Sorren waited *impatiently* until it was just the three of us again. He turned to LaGrange.

"Do me a favor, Ian," he said calmly. "I need you to give the detectives whatever personal information you can on Phalen — next of kin, exact title with the Task Force, et cetera.... Nothing that they can run with."

LaGrange nodded. He knew Sorren merely wanted him separated from me. That's probably why he couldn't help himself as he turned to walk away.

"I don't care what anybody says," said LaGrange, jabbing his thick forefinger at me. "You got Derrick killed."

"I'm sorry," I said. It was all I could think of.

No, worse than that, actually.

It was all I had.

Chapter 68

"HE'S AN ASSHOLE. Don't let him get to you," said Sorren as LaGrange headed over to talk to the detectives.

"Too late. He already did," I said, rubbing my jaw, which was already swollen from the guy's roundhouse punch. "I think he loosened a tooth."

"Yeah, that was way out of line." Sorren shifted his feet uncomfortably. "I know it's well within your right, but if you're thinking about pressing charges—"

"Do I look like the type to take him to court for that?"

"No, I suppose you don't," said Sorren, flashing some relief. "Thanks, Nick."

"Sure. And now you owe me one, right?"

"We'll see about that later. Listen, after Ian's done I'll let you finish up with the detectives so you can finally get the hell out of here. Just so you know, though, you're going to need around-the-clock police protection after tonight."

"Is that necessary? Wait, that didn't come out right. I mean, will it help any?"

"I don't know. You tell me," he said with a glance at the scorched and smoking carcass that used to be my car. "It's probably safe to say that whoever wanted you dead still does."

I nodded. "But it's not Pinero."

"So you've been telling me," replied Sorren, reaching for a cigarette. It was like he was only half listening to me.

"It was Joseph D'zorio," I said.

That got his attention.

Suddenly his next smoke could wait. Sorren was all ears. "How do you know that? Who's your source? Talk to me, Daniels."

"I can't give you all the details, but Dwayne Robinson owed him money that he didn't have. So—"

Sorren raised his palms. Smart guy—he saw where I was going. "Wait a minute," he said incredulously. "You're telling me that your being at Lombardo's that day was a setup?"

"It was all a setup. D'zorio knew I'd have a recorder going to catch every word of Robinson's. He knew he could frame Pinero."

"I guess. But how do *you* know all this?"

"I can't reveal my source."

"Then don't. But if you want my help, you've got to give me more than a gut feeling."

I spread my arms wide. *Take a look around!* "Does all this look like a gut feeling? D'zorio knew Phalen and I were onto him."

"Maybe that's true; maybe you've solved this thing. But it's a nonstarter if I can't connect the dots."

"What about Pinero?" I asked.

"What about him?"

"He's been charged with first-degree murder."

"Yes. That's what happens when all the dots connect," said Sorren.

"What if you're wrong?"

"That's exactly why I need to talk to your source."

"There is someone else you could talk to," I said. "The manager at Lombardo's."

"Why would I want to do that?"

"Because Dwayne Robinson didn't just seat himself. If he was supposed to sit next to Marcozza that day, it would have to have been arranged. The question is, who did the arranging? Who's the man with the plan?"

Sorren resumed reaching for his next cigarette, sliding it into his mouth. Out came a Zippo lighter. I could practically see the wheels spinning in his head as he lit up and took a deep puff. Jesus, these cops and robbers really liked their nicotine fixes. First Sam Tagaletto, now Sorren. I moved a half step away from him, upwind. Both of my parents had smoked like chimneys, and both had died of cancer.

"Let me sleep on it," he said. "In the meantime, whether it was Pinero, D'zorio, or the tooth fairy, you still need police protection, Nick. We need to keep you alive. Is that okay with you?"

He extended his hand to shake mine. With his other hand he was returning the lighter to his pocket — only he missed. It fell to the ground, skipping off the asphalt and landing at my feet.

"I got it," I said, bending down.

That's when I got my head blown off.

Chapter 69

JESUS CHRIST! What now? What the hell just happened? Not my head—but damn close!

The back window of the ambulance had just shattered, shards of glass falling on me like jagged rain. A split second earlier and that window would've been my head, a bullet right between the eyes.

"Move! Move! Move!" I heard. It was Sorren, and he was shouting at me.

Tucked in a low crouch, he began pushing me toward the front of the ambulance as the booming echo of the gunshot was drowned out by the collective scream of the street. The neighborhood crowd was scattering everywhere at once. It was pure pandemonium. *Run for your lives!*

"Whoever wanted you dead still does," Sorren had just said to me.

You ain't kidding...

A second shot pierced the side of the ambulance about a foot from my chest, the blast from it ripping through the air. My guess was that the shooter didn't have the right angle yet.

Not *yet*.

The shooter, wherever he was, was obviously using a long-range rifle.

Then came a completely different sound. *Pop! Pop-pop-pop! Pop! Pop-pop-pop!*

Those were handguns—and aimed in the opposite direction. It was return fire. *That's what you get, asshole, for shooting up a street filled with cops!*

I peeled around to the front of the ambulance, the small of my back practically glued to the bumper. Sorren followed right behind me.

"You okay?" he asked, out of breath.

I was gasping for air, too. "Yeah, I'm all right. You?"

"Peachy. Just great, Nick. All in one piece. I don't think I like hanging out with you, though."

Then, as quickly as it had started, it was over,

no more fireworks. All the screaming and confusion gave way to an eerie silence.

No one was standing up yet, though. No one wanted to come out into the open.

Twenty feet away I locked eyes with a woman who'd been ducking behind the crimson bricks of a stoop. Her expression said it all. *Is it really over?*

"Maybe for you, lady," I could have told her.

Not for me.

David Sorren gripped my arm. "Stay here," he said. "Do not move."

"Where are you going?"

"To see if they got the shooter."

Sorren came up out of his crouch, peeking over the hood of the ambulance.

"Hey, be careful," I said.

He nodded before cracking a slight smile. "Still think that police protection isn't necessary?"

I'm sure Sorren thought it was the most rhetorical question he'd ever asked, but as he dashed off I couldn't help wondering if the answer was so clear. I'd just been *surrounded* by cops, and I'd come dangerously close to getting nailed by two separate gunshots. The policemen were New York's finest, but as to how much they'd be able to protect me, I wasn't so sure.

That's when something off in the distance caught my eye. It was a bright block of yellow at the far end of the street. There was a white light on top of it, and I could swear it was calling my name. *C'mon, Nick, let's get lost.... Let's get the hell out of here.*

Chapter 70

I HAD THOUGHT about going to Courtney's apartment, but that was somewhere they might come looking for me. So I went someplace else, someplace safer.

"*How* much did the taxi cost?" asked my sister, Kate, cradling her mug of chamomile tea at the head of her kitchen table. At one a.m., it was the only decaf she had had in the cupboard.

"One hundred and seventy-six dollars," I told her. "Plus tip."

Kate shook her head in disbelief. "You know, you could've negotiated a flat fee with the driver up front. Saved yourself some money, Nicky."

I started to laugh. It felt good, but only for a moment.

"What's so funny?" Kate asked. Then it occurred to her. "Oh yeah, you're right. Given the night you've had, maybe the money wasn't so important."

"No, that's not it," I said. "I still can't get used to you being the frugal one in the family."

Of course, truth be told, I wasn't surprised in the least. When Kate's husband had been alive, they'd had lots of money, thanks to his job as an oil trader. After he died, she had even more from his insurance policy. But gone forever was her sense of security. In its place was a newfound appreciation for the value of everything, starting with life itself. Somewhere down the list was the true meaning of a dollar.

Kate took a sip of her tea. "Life is just one big curveball, isn't it?"

"Yes, it is," I said.

A sleepy voice suddenly chimed in from the door to the kitchen. "You can say that again. Life is one big, nasty curveball."

We both turned to see Elizabeth standing there in her pink pajamas.

"What are you doing up, young lady?" asked Kate. "You have school."

Elizabeth flashed her great smile, the one she'd inherited from her mother and father. "The blind have a heightened sense of hearing, remember?"

"How are you, sweetheart?" I said.

"I knew it was you, Uncle Nick."

"Let me guess... was it my cologne?"

She laughed. "What are you doing here in the middle of the night?"

"It's a long story."

"I've got time."

"No, you don't. You've got *school* tomorrow," said her mother again. "You need to get to bed."

"Actually, that makes two of us," I said, standing up from the table. "Walk me to the guest room, Lizzy, okay?"

"Certainly. Be my pleasure."

I followed my niece toward the stairs to the second floor, marveling at how she had every step, every corner, every piece of furniture, mapped out perfectly in her mind. She didn't need to reach out for anything, including my hand.

"Will you be here tomorrow when I get home from school?" she asked, halfway up the steps.

"I don't know," I answered.

She stopped, turning back to me. "Wow," she said. "When most people say 'I don't know' to a question like that, they usually do know. But I can tell in your voice. You really *don't* know."

Elizabeth was spot-on as usual. I had no idea what the next day would bring, or where it would even bring me. I was running from the police, albeit their protection, choosing instead an out-of-the-way home in the woods of Weston, Connecticut. "The pizza delivery guy can hardly find it," Kate always joked. "Or even FedEx."

Still, just to make sure, I had had the taxi driver circle around a bit before pulling into the driveway. All quiet on the Weston front. There was no one following us.

For one night at least, I was safe.

Tomorrow—probably all hell would break loose again.

Chapter 71

I PULLED THE freshly cleaned and starched sheets, the blanket, the duvet—everything—over my head in Kate's very comfortable guest room bed at the end of the hall. For some reason I thought that would help me sleep. It didn't exactly work out that way.

All I could see when I closed my eyes was Derrick Phalen, and no matter how much I tossed and turned, I couldn't shake the image of him. His missing eyes.

Would I ever? I doubted it.

I was exhausted, tired beyond all belief, and yet I still couldn't sleep a wink. Back in Manhattan I would have tried listening to certain street sounds, something I did when I needed to clear my mind. Basically, I'd count car horns instead of sheep.

Out here in the woods of Connecticut, however, there was nothing but silence. And it was deafening—at least tonight it was.

Frustrated, I pushed back the covers and reached blindly for my iPhone on the nightstand.

I'd turned it off in the backseat of the taxi after it had started to ring like crazy. Needless to say, some people were a little curious as to where I was, not the least of whom was surely a very ticked-off David Sorren.

But it was only Courtney I felt bad about. Really bad. Although I had texted her to let her know I was all right, I hadn't responded when she'd written back "Where R U?" Better that she not have to lie on my behalf. Also, better that she didn't get any more involved in my problems than she already was.

I turned on my iPhone again now. 3:04 a.m., announced the home screen.

Sure enough, there were a half-dozen messages from Sorren and even more from Courtney. I'd continue to ignore Sorren's messages until morning, but I thought I'd at least listen to one from Courtney. I knew she had to be incredibly shaken up by Derrick Phalen's murder. After all, she had been the one to send me to him and he had been her friend.

"Nick, it's me again," began her message. "Please call me back. Please, Nick."

I reached for the volume because I could barely hear her, when suddenly the phone began to vibrate.

Shit! What had I pressed?

Nothing. Someone was actually calling me at three in the morning.

I was so worried I would wake up Kate and Elizabeth that I didn't even bother to check the caller ID.

"Hello?" I whispered.

"Hello, Nick."

"Who is this?"

I immediately knew I'd heard the voice before, but I couldn't place it. Right away, he placed it for me.

"I warned you at the diner, Nick, but you didn't listen," he said. "You should've listened."

I shot straight up and turned on the light beside the bed.

Jesus. It was the guy from the Sunrise Diner, the one with the gun. The one who'd told me I was in a shitload of danger.

"Do you know what time it is?" I asked.

"I sure do," he said. "I also know what room you're in, Nick. It's the only one in the house with the light on."

In the middle of the night, he was *here*.

Chapter 72

I RACED OVER to the small window facing the front of the house. Tearing back the closed curtain, I pressed my nose up against the glass. I didn't care if he could see me — could I see him?

Was he really out there? It sure sounded like it. And it looked like it, too.

Even with the reflection from the light in the room, I couldn't miss the shining headlights on the car parked outside in the driveway. But that's all I could see. *Where are you, you son of a bitch?*

It was as if he could read my mind and was playing with me. The next second, he stepped out of the darkness, a creepy-as-hell silhouette right in front of his car. His elbow was bent, the phone to his ear.

"You didn't think anyone could find you out here, huh?" he asked. Only it wasn't a question. It was a boast. I guess he was impressed with his own skills.

"I'm calling the police," I said.

"Yeah, just like you did at the diner."

"This is different."

"Why? Because you're not alone in this nice house out here in Disturbia?"

The mere suggestion of Kate and Elizabeth sent a jolt up my spine. All at once my worst fears collided with sheer rage. My body was spilling over with adrenaline. Whoever this guy was, he was royally pissing me off.

"You listen to me," I said, changing my grip on the phone. I squeezed it so tight I thought it would break in my hand.

"No, you listen to me," he shot back, cutting me off. "You're in so far over your head, you don't know which way is up. You can't deny that, can you, Nick?"

"Who the hell are you?"

"At three in the morning, I'd say I'm your worst fucking nightmare. Agree or disagree?"

Then he stepped away from the headlights, slipping back into the darkness.

Shit! Where is he? I thought.

And — the far scarier thought — *where is he heading?*

Chapter 73

SPRINTING OUT OF the guest room, I called to Kate and Elizabeth. With one hand I was dialing 911; with the other I was groping for a light switch in the hallway.

Kate beat me to it. *Flick!*

The hallway lit up brightly as my eyes locked onto hers. She'd come rushing out of her bedroom like her house was on fire. Sweats, T-shirt, panicked expression.

"What's wrong?" she asked. "Nick, what's going on?"

"Yeah, what is it?" asked Elizabeth, emerging from her room at the same time.

They both got their answer as the voice of the 911 operator suddenly chimed in on my phone. It was a woman. Very calm and sure of herself, thank goodness. An emergency professional.

Like that speed talker in those old FedEx commercials, I gave her the address. "There's a man outside the house," I said next. "I think he's about to break in. He's armed."

Like a bolt, Kate ran over to Elizabeth, grabbing her hand. "Come with me," she said. "Right now."

She led Elizabeth to the stairs heading up to the third floor, the attic.

"Wait, I want to stay with you guys," Elizabeth pleaded.

"No," insisted Kate. "You go up into that attic and lock the door behind you. No matter what you hear, *you do not open that door*. Do you understand?"

Elizabeth nodded, fighting back tears. She reached out for the railing, only to stop and turn around. Suddenly, she dashed down the hall. Just from my voice she knew exactly where I was.

"Be careful, Uncle Nick," she said, plastering me with a hug. Then she dashed back to the attic stairs, climbing them so fast I almost forgot she couldn't see the steps.

Meanwhile, Kate had disappeared into her bedroom. I was about to call out to her when she returned.

"What the hell is that?" I asked.

But I could see it plain as day. She was holding a handgun.

My sister!

The Northeast liberal who once referred to the NRA as the Nincompoop Republican Army.

"Things change," she said. "Here, take it."

I didn't merely take it, I grabbed it. "Thanks."

"It's loaded," she added.

"I hope so. It's not much good if it isn't."

She rolled her eyes and for a moment we were kid brother and big sister back in Newburgh. But only for a moment.

"What do we do now?" she asked.

"We listen. We wait for the police to get here." *If they can find the house . . .*

Edging to the top of the stairs, I peered down to the first floor. Would he smash a window? Shoot the lock off the door at point-blank range?

I stared at Kate, raising my index finger to my mouth. *Shhh.*

We both held our breath. For a second I thought I heard Elizabeth upstairs in the attic. God, how frightened she must have been.

"What do you think?" whispered Kate after a minute or so went by. "Is he gone or what?"

I was about to answer when we heard it. Only it wasn't exactly the sound I expected. It was a car's engine.

Were the police here?

I rushed back to the window in the guest bedroom, staring out at the driveway. No, the police weren't there.

Neither was anyone else.

The driveway was empty, his car gone. Mr. Sunrise Diner, whoever he was, had scared the living bejesus out of us.

But nothing more.

Why?

Who the hell was that bastard?

What did he want from me?

Chapter 74

OKAY, MAYBE POLICE protection isn't such a bad idea after all…

Besides, it was a little hard to say no to it after I was the guy calling 911 in the middle of the night. By morning, as David Sorren put it, I had "seen the light." Yeah, he was pissed at me, but he was also very relieved that I'd called him, if for no other reason than they hadn't caught the guy who'd been shooting at me.

"He was on a rooftop that connected in the back to a brownstone on the next block," explained Sorren. "We never had a chance to get him."

"Do you think it was the same guy who killed Derrick?" I asked.

"Does it really make a difference? I mean, c'mon, Nick, it's time to get real."

Good point. "Either way, I'm still a target, right?"

"Exactly. Which is why I'm sending the first two-man shift of patrolmen assigned to you out to Connecticut right away. They'll bring you back to your apartment," he said. "And Nick?"

"Yeah? I'm here. I'm listening to every word, David."

"Don't even think about taking off again. You got that?"

"Got it."

Fair enough. I deserved that. I also deserved the incredibly sick feeling I had in my stomach for having put Kate and Elizabeth in danger. What the hell had I been thinking? That the Mafia had an honest-to-God moral code against hurting women and children?

In the back of the police car that came and got me, I had plenty of time to mull that over. I also made a promise to myself to keep Courtney out of this. If she would listen to me, that is.

"Okay, here's how it works, Mr. Daniels," said

Officer Kevin O'Shea, one of the two cops who had driven me back into Manhattan. We were in my apartment, although not before he and his partner, Sam Brison, had first scoped it out with their guns drawn.

"You wear this on your body at all times. At the first sign of trouble, any trouble, you press this panic button."

O'Shea handed me a necklace fashioned from a sneaker shoelace and what looked like a cheap, plastic garage-door opener. James Bond and Q, this wasn't.

I put the device on, glancing down. The panic button, appropriately bright red, was the size of a quarter and hung right smack in the middle of my chest.

"It looks more like a target, if you ask me," I joked. Apparently I wasn't the first.

"Yeah, we get that a lot," said Brison.

He went on to explain how one officer would always be posted outside my door while the other would be in the lobby after securing any and all doors in the basement. If I had a visitor — the kind that didn't want to kill me — the doormen had been instructed to clear the person with the cops first, then with me. There would be no exceptions.

"Any questions, Mr. Daniels?"

"What if I want to go out?"

"Like where?" asked O'Shea with a squint of his eyes.

"I don't know," I said. "Like, the movies or something."

"The movies? Did you just say the movies? I don't think you're catching on to what's happening to you."

"It was just an example."

He shook his head. "No, you don't go to the movies or anywhere else. For the time being, this is where you need to stay. Safe and sound in your apartment."

"Okay then, I have one more question. How long is 'for the time being'?"

"Until you're told otherwise."

Well, that clears everything up...

The two officers started to leave. There was really nothing more to say. Still, I couldn't help myself.

"Be careful, guys, okay?" I said.

I meant it, too. But I could understand how it

must have sounded strange to the two of them. They exchanged odd glances before looking back at me.

"We will," said Brison casually.

"No, I'm serious," I said. "People have an awful way of dying around me."

Chapter 75

HAD I EVER wondered what it felt like to be under house arrest, I now had my answer. Problem was, I'd never wondered.

And for good reason.

This.

Sucks.

After a few hours, my cramped shoe box of an apartment was beginning to feel more like a matchbox. I swear the walls were creeping in on me.

I'd been staring at my MacBook screen straight into the afternoon. Courtney was right: I was literally living the story of a lifetime. Now I had to start writing it.

So why couldn't I?

Maybe because I didn't know if I'd live long enough to finish it.

Ten years ago, I'd done a long piece on Salman Rushdie when he'd still been the target of a fatwa against his life. I had asked him what it had felt like to know there were people hell-bent on killing him, that there were substantial rewards out for him, dead or deader. His answer? *There are some feelings for which words are utterly useless.* And remember, Salman Rushdie is a damn fine writer who had obviously done his research on the subject of death threats.

As I continued to stare at my blank computer screen, I now fully understood what he'd meant. Of course, it didn't help matters that even if I could write the article, I no longer had *Citizen* magazine waiting to publish it. In case I'd somehow forgotten that, all I had to do was turn on the television.

So much for TV as a diversion.

"...For that story we turn now to Brenda Evans, who's outside the *Citizen* magazine building."

There she was, the "Bull and Bear Babe," my ex-girlfriend reporting for the World Financial

Network on Thomas Ferramore's "stunning announcement" that he was folding *Citizen* magazine.

"Stunning, of course," said Brenda, holding her microphone as if it were one of her News Emmy Awards, "because *Citizen* has been a profitable holding for Mr. Ferramore. Selling it would be one thing, but *folding* it?"

I'd known Brenda long enough to know what was coming next. The gleam in her eye. The tilt of her head. It was gossip time.

"Speculation is rampant," she continued into the camera, "that the move is merely one of spite in the wake of Ferramore's broken engagement to *Citizen*'s editor in chief and driving force, Courtney Sheppard. There's been no official statement from either side, but my sources tell me that it all ended very, very badly."

Click!

I'd seen enough, heard enough. Not just of Brenda but of any more television. If the news wasn't about Ferramore and *Citizen* magazine, it was about the "Murder in Riverdale" of a state prosecutor. It hurt too much. I couldn't bear to look at one more picture of Derrick Phalen.

Clearly neither could Courtney. As usual she'd decided not to take my advice about staying away. We'd spoken on the phone just before I'd turned on the television.

About twenty minutes later, she showed up at my door. She was two hours early. I had had to ask the doorman in the lobby, "Are you sure?" when he'd buzzed me that Courtney had arrived. All she and I had discussed on the phone was that she wanted to bring me dinner, the subtext being that we had a lot to talk about, too much to get into over the phone.

But as I opened the door, Courtney didn't say a word. She looked, I don't know—the word *humbled* came to mind. She stepped into the apartment, closed the door behind her, and stared deep into my eyes while biting her lower lip. Then she kissed me like I have never been kissed before in my life.

Finally she said, "Hey, Nick, what's new?"

I shrugged. "Same old, same old."

The small talk out of the way, we moved into the bedroom. We stripped away each other's clothes. Then we couldn't hold each other tightly enough. I didn't have to tell her how much I wanted and needed her, and she didn't have to tell me. *Thankfully, Mr. Rushdie, the door swings both ways.* Extreme fear, yes, but also intense passion.

There are some feelings, and actions, for which words are utterly useless.

But words do have their place, especially when Courtney said, "You were right, Nick."

I grinned as I said, "First time for everything."

Chapter 76

SO MUCH FOR joy and happiness and all that.

I closed my eyes and drew a deep breath down close to the bottom of my lungs. I was hoping that when I opened my eyes I'd no longer be standing at Derrick Phalen's grave site under a sea of gray clouds at Trinity Church Cemetery. I was hoping that this was all just a dream.

But no, it was as real as real gets, and it was also heart-wrenchingly sad. Dwayne Robinson may have had a host of Yankees at his funeral, but Derrick's service overlooking the Hudson River was no less shy of New York's heavy hitters. In attendance were the mayor, the Bronx borough president, the Bronx DA, and two congressmen, both of whom had campaigned heavily on fighting organized crime. Derrick's victories in the courtroom had helped bring them victories at the polls, and they knew it.

Of course, David Sorren—the mayor in waiting—was on hand, as was Ian LaGrange. I avoided any eye contact with LaGrange while noticing that Sorren seemed to be keeping close tabs on him. Was he worried that LaGrange would take another swing at me?

If so, he should've also been checking out the other prosecutors from the OCTF. I was getting some serious dirty looks from more than a few of them.

Ironically, it was Derrick's family—his parents and sister—who proved to be the most forgiving. Or maybe they were just too numb to be angry. I couldn't tell when Courtney and I approached them to offer our condolences.

Given the incessant media coverage, along with the usual gossip mill churning out whatever tidbits the press didn't, my connection to Derrick Phalen was pretty well established. What wasn't known was exactly *why* I was connected to him.

That's the question I thought I was about to

be asked when Derrick's sister, Monica, caught up to Courtney and me a few minutes later. She wanted to know if she could speak to me alone for a moment.

Never was I so relieved to be wrong. It was an *answer,* not a question, that Monica had for me.

Scratch that. It wasn't just an answer. Hopefully it was *the* answer.

Chapter 77

"I'LL BE OVER here when you're done," said Courtney, who had never been more understanding, and kind of selfless, in all the time we'd known each other. I had never felt closer to her either, or more in love. Bad timing, I know, but there it was.

I watched as she walked over to the shade of one of the immense oak trees that were scattered across the cemetery's lawn. She always looked great in black, and today was definitely no exception. How could anybody *ever* cheat on her?

Nearby, David Sorren was chatting with the Bronx DA. He gave me a quick nod of recognition as our eyes met briefly. *Yes, David, I'm still on the right side of the grass.*

I turned back to face Monica. She was tall and slender, with auburn hair cut straight around her shoulders. A few dozen freckles dotted the bridge of her nose.

The only thing I knew about her was what Derrick had mentioned that one time we'd had lunch. We'd been discussing his reputation as a tough prosecutor. *"If you think I'm tough, you should talk to my sister,"* he'd said with a laugh.

Now here I was, doing just that. What I wouldn't give for our meeting to be under different circumstances.

"I wanted to let you know how sorry I am about Derrick," I told her.

"You feel partly responsible, don't you?"

I nodded. "Yes."

"You shouldn't," she said matter-of-factly. "It's not like Derrick was an accountant or a plumber. His job was trying to put mob guys behind bars. Serious, big-time hoods, the worst of the worst. Did you know he had to wear a bulletproof vest?"

Again I nodded. "Yes. I knew that."

"A lot of good that did him in the end, huh?"

Derrick was definitely right about his sister being tough, or maybe, like Courtney, she just compartmentalized very well. But what I was hearing more from her was anger. She was so angry, in fact, that some of it was spilling over onto Derrick.

"Anyway, that's not what I wanted to talk with you about," she continued. "It's about something I found the other day, something belonging to my brother."

She reached into her black purse, removing something. It was so small, though, I couldn't see it in her clenched fist.

"What is it?" I had to ask.

"If you were ever in Derrick's office, then you know he had this crazy thing for Post-it notes. Those little yellow stickies were everywhere around his desk."

I remembered. "Yes, I know. I saw them when I visited Derrick in White Plains."

"Well, they were all over his stupid apartment, too," she said. "Last night I was over there going through some of his files, trying to find Derrick's life insurance policy. That's when I came across this."

She opened her fist to reveal a small USB flash drive, the kind you can pick up at any computer supply store for about twelve bucks. It was barely over an inch long.

"What's on it?" I asked.

"I have no idea. I didn't look at it—but I'm pretty sure Derrick wanted you to have it."

"How do you know that?"

"Because there was a yellow sticky on it. He'd written your name." She extended her hand, placing the flash drive in mine. "Promise me one thing, though, okay? You have to promise. That's the quid pro quo here."

Hell, I'd pretty much promise her anything to see what was on that flash drive. How could I not think that it was what Derrick had wanted to tell me the night he'd died?

"Sure," I said. "What is it?"

"Out of respect for my brother, could you not tell anyone you have this until you've had a chance to look at it?"

"Absolutely."

"Good," she said, but I could tell there was something else she wanted to say. She seemed unsure about it.

"Go ahead," I said. "It's okay. I owe your brother, and I feel like I owe you."

"You don't. It's just that I was..."

She stopped. A tear formed in her eye, and she quickly wiped it away. "Everyone who worked with Derrick said all the right things, that he was really good at his job and was a great guy and all that. What I want to know, though, is that he didn't die in vain. Can you promise me that, too?"

I reached out and took Monica's hand, squeezing it tight. "Yes, I can promise you that, too. I'll make sure of it," I said.

If it's the last thing I do.

Chapter 78

OFFICER KEVIN O'SHEA turned to his partner, Sam Brison, in the lobby of my apartment building as I looked on. "Heads or tails?" asked O'Shea, tossing a shiny quarter in the air.

"Tails," said Brison.

Apparently, this was what my first shift did every morning when they arrived. Instead of taking turns standing guard in the lobby or outside my door, they flipped for it.

O'Shea caught the quarter and sneaked a peek. "Shit," he muttered underneath his square, bushy mustache. *Tails it is.*

"Ha!" said Brison, heading for the comfortable couch in the lobby. Outside my door there was only a metal folding chair with no padding. Enough said.

I rode the elevator up with O'Shea, continuing with what I thought was my stellar acting job since the funeral. I didn't want to seem overly anxious, but I absolutely couldn't wait to get home so I could plug in that flash drive.

"Hey, are you okay?" O'Shea asked me, leaning against the back of the elevator. "You seem a little jumpy today. You jumpy? Something the matter, Nick?"

So much for my acting. Clearly I wasn't the Second Coming of Sir Laurence Olivier.

"Yeah, I'm fine," I said. "Rough morning, that's all. I don't like funerals much."

"Nobody likes funerals," O'Shea agreed, nodding but continuing to eye me as if his bullshit meter was ticking in the red zone. I was sure he was about to press the subject when I was saved by the bell of the elevator. We'd arrived at my floor.

O'Shea stuck his head out, peering left and right. "Okay," he announced.

I fell in line behind him as we walked the beige and white wavy-striped carpeting of the hallway. The rug was kind of trippy. Staring at it was enough to give you some serious vertigo.

"What do you think you're doing?" asked O'Shea as we reached my door. I'd taken out my key and made a move for the lock.

"Oh yeah, I forgot," I said.

He shot me a look like a disapproving parent. "Sometimes that's all it takes—forgetting one time, Nick."

I handed him the key so he could scope out my apartment before I entered.

"Out of curiosity," I said, "while you're in there checking to make sure the coast is clear, who's watching me here in the hallway?"

He didn't hesitate. "That's why Sam is in the lobby."

"But what if, say, there's someone waiting for me behind the door to the stairwell?"

O'Shea chuckled. He realized I was just busting his chops. "Would you like me to go check for you?" he asked slowly.

"No, that's okay," I said, and laughed lightly. We both did. O'Shea was a pretty good guy actually. I liked him and his partner, too. Hey, they were trying to keep me alive.

"Good. Now stay here," he said with a grin as he unlocked my door. "Try not to get in any trouble."

"Yeah, sure. That'll be a first."

Chapter 79

THE SECONDS OUTSIDE my door went by slowly, and I couldn't help wishing that I could get back my old life, that none of this had happened. Except maybe Courtney breaking up with Ferramore.

"You better not be raiding my fridge!" I called to O'Shea from the hallway.

I'd been eating takeout for three days straight. With all the containers of Chinese, Japanese, Mexican, and Italian, I was just about housing the United Nations of leftovers.

"Hey, did you hear me?" I said.

O'Shea had been checking my apartment for about a minute, roughly a half minute longer than it usually took him or Brison to comb my twelve-hundred-square-foot one-bedroom apartment.

An uneasy feeling suddenly came over me, my mind starting to race.

Instinctively, I took a step forward to peek in around the doorway, only to catch myself. That was the last thing I should be doing, right?

Instead, I looked down at my striped tie, pushing it to the side. Behind it I could feel the outline of the alarm around my neck. Even underneath my dress shirt there was no mistaking the large panic button.

Shit, what do I do? Do I press it?

No. Not yet.

"Kevin?" I called out again, this time louder. No more joking around about my fridge. "Everything all right in there? Hey, Kevin?"

I heard nothing back. I heard nothing, period. My apartment, the hallway—everywhere was quiet.

Then, finally—*thank God!*—I heard him.

"Yeah, everything's fine," came O'Shea's voice.

I couldn't see him yet but I could tell he was walking toward me. He drew a deep sigh before explaining, "For a moment there, I thought I heard—"

Pffft! Pffft!

Before another sound came, I saw the blood, a bright red spray splattering across the hallway in front of the door. Then Officer Kevin O'Shea's body came crashing down at my feet, the back of his head blown wide open.

Oh no! No! No! No!

I took a clumsy step backwards, nearly tripping over my own heel. My knees were beginning to buckle and I couldn't think straight. My thought process felt completely fractured.

Run, Nick! Run now!

I turned, sprinting down the hallway as those crazy beige and white stripes of the carpet blurred before my eyes. I was ten feet from the stairwell. Could I make it?

Barely!

I pushed through the door to the stairs. For a split second I allowed myself to look back. Just one glance.

It was all I needed. Make that *much more* than I needed.

Storming out of my apartment, a gun fitted

with a suppressor snug in his hand, was the man who should've killed me when he'd had the chance in that alley next to the pizza place in the South Bronx.

At least I'm sure that's what Carmine Zambratta, the Zamboni, was thinking as his eyes met mine.

He raised his gun and my heart nearly stopped.

Keep running, Nick!

Chapter 80

I PRACTICALLY FLUNG myself down the stairs, my feet barely keeping up with the rest of me. Could I outrun him? Would he get a clear shot at me? I didn't see why not.

I was about to press the hell out of my panic button to alert Brison in the lobby, when a voice kicked in from the one brain cell remaining that wasn't drowning in adrenaline. *No, wait! Don't come to me, Brison—I'm coming to you!*

And I'm bringing company.

I kept flying down the stairs—the ninth floor...the eighth—my shoes pounding away on the concrete steps, my heart pounding away at my chest.

How far back was he? Was he gaining on me?

That's when I heard it.

Nothing.

There were no footsteps from above, no sound of the Zamboni gaining on me. I was alone in the stairwell and that one working brain cell of mine immediately figured out why.

He was taking the elevator.

Shit!

On the landing of the sixth floor I skidded to a stop, gasping for air, trying to think in straight lines.

Up?

Down?

Stay put?

What do I do?

In a flash, I thought I had the answer. I'd go hide in someone's apartment—just keep banging on doors until somebody let me in. Then I'd call the police.

Oh no! The police.

The image of Brison on that couch in the lobby suddenly came crashing into my head. He was a sitting duck down there. I had to warn him.

You know that company I'm bringing, Brison? He might get there first!

I jammed my thumb against the panic button as I took off again down the stairs.

The fifth floor...

The fourth floor...

My lungs were on fire, my legs aching—but what hurt the most was not knowing what was going to happen.

How would Brison respond to my hitting the panic button? Would he head straight for the elevator and Zambratta?

"Will you walk into my parlor?" said the Spider to the Fly.

The third floor...

The second floor...

I had to get to the lobby first!

Nobody else could die on my watch.

Chapter 81

THE LITTLE THINGS we take for granted.

Like the glass window cut into the door between the stairs and the lobby. Seven years living in the building and I'd never once noticed it. Not one time.

But there it was, no bigger than a loaf of bread—hell, even smaller; make that a *slice* of bread—but still big enough to catch a glimpse of Brison as I raced down the last set of stairs.

He had his gun drawn, his mouth twisted into a scowl so tight I thought his face would crack.

He was aiming the gun dead square at the elevator. Watching. Waiting.

I did neither.

I bolted straight through the door like ... well, like the crazy, panicked guy I was. Only when Brison turned on a dime and nearly blew my head off did I realize that maybe that hadn't been such a good idea.

"Jesus fucking Christ!" he said, his trigger finger still twitching. "I could've killed you!"

"Sorry." What the hell else could I say?

Brison swung his gun back at the closed door of the elevator, and I followed his eyes to the line of floor numbers above it. The five was lit up. Then the four.

"It's Carmine Zambratta," I said quickly, still out of breath.

"I know."

"He shot O'Shea."

I could tell from Brison's face he knew that, too. Or at least was assuming it. "Is he still alive?" he asked.

"I don't know," I said, shaking my head. "I don't think so."

Brison swallowed hard, digesting the news like the bitter pill it was. But that's all he had time for. Otherwise both of us would end up just like O'Shea.

"Get the hell behind the counter!" he yelled at me. "Hurry! Stay down!"

I dashed behind the doorman's desk—which looked more like a counter you'd see at an airline gate—while wondering how Brison had known Zambratta was in the elevator or that it was Zambratta at all.

That's when I saw the closed-circuit monitor with a split screen on the wall right above me. Brison had obviously checked it when I had hit the panic button. He also must have told the doorman to skedaddle out of there. And call for help?

I stared at the monitor, my eyes bouncing back and forth like a game of Pong. On one side was the revolving door of the front entrance. On the other was the inside shot of the elevator.

And there he was in black and white. Grainy and fuzzy, too. Not to mention scary as shit.

The Zamboni.

For sure Brison had recognized him right away. How could he not? The guy was the poster boy for mob enforcers. A celebrity, practically. He killed people and got away with it. Probably have his own show on cable soon.

I could see the gun with the suppressor in his meaty hand, his huge shoulders pressed tight against the side of the elevator wall. Carmine Zambratta was coming for me, and he wanted me dead. Very badly.

Yet he couldn't have looked more relaxed and in control. How freakin' screwed up was that?

"What's he doing? Is he still on the side of the elevator?" asked Brison, his voice clipped. His throat must have been dry as dirt. If he was trying to sound calm, it wasn't working—and I was the last person on earth who could blame him for some nerves and high anxiety.

Crouched low and out of sight, I could still see the monitor perfectly. From where Brison was positioned, he couldn't. Not at all.

I would have to be his eyes.

Don't blink, Nick.

Chapter 82

"YES," I TOLD BRISON, quickly wiping away the sweat dripping from my forehead. Zambratta was still hugging the side of the elevator. He hadn't moved. What was he up to?

And where the hell was the elevator?

The damn thing should've reached the lobby by now, right? And then—

DING!

Right on cue. The elevator landed, the sound of the high-pitched bell cutting through the silence of the lobby. *Here we go...*

I braced myself, my eyes glued to the closed-circuit monitor. No need to look at Brison now.

"He's raising his gun!" I called out.

I listened to the squeak of Brison's shoes

against the white marble floor of the lobby as he shifted his stance. I was waiting for the next sound — the elevator door opening.

It didn't come!

Brison called again, *"What's he doing?"*

I squinted at the monitor. I couldn't tell at first — the image was flickering all over. When it finally steadied I could see Zambratta's hand against the panel of buttons inside the elevator.

"He must be holding the door closed," I said. "He's got his — *oh, shit!*"

"What? What's the matter now?"

It happened so fast.

Zambratta shot the lens of the security camera, the muffled sound of the smashing glass and metal followed by the monitor in front of me — half of it, at least — going black as night.

I poked my head up above the counter to tell Brison I was no longer his eyes.

"STAY DOWN!" he yelled at me as he dashed for the couch on the opposite wall. He ducked low behind the armrest, his gun and eyes never leaving the door of the elevator.

I dropped below the counter, holding my breath. The showdown had turned into a stalemate. Something—or someone—had to give. So what did it come down to? Who was the better shot?

Then I heard it. Off in the distance, the sound of the cavalry. Police sirens. Beautiful sirens. Brison must have called for backup. Or maybe it was the doorman, who'd dialed 911 out on the street. Either way...

What are you going to do now, Zamboni?

Little did I know, he'd already done it.

Chapter 83

WOULD ZAMBRATTA TRY to shoot his way out of here?

Would he take the elevator back up to another floor, maybe even grab a hostage from one of the apartments? That wouldn't be very hard to do.

I wondered if he could hear the approaching sirens. Even if he couldn't, he had to know that staying put in the elevator wasn't an option. It was his move, but he had to do something.

Clearly, Brison was on the same page.

He shouted at the closed door of the elevator, "You can't stay in there, Zambratta! Come out, hands high."

It was wishful thinking, I guess, but I couldn't blame Brison for trying.

"You gave us too much time," Brison contin-ued, his voice growing more confident. "We've got men on every floor now. There's nowhere for you to go."

"Will you walk into my parlor?" said the Spider to the Fly.

I'd been so wrapped up in the moment that I almost didn't see it. Out of the corner of my eye I caught a glimpse of something on the monitor above me. It was the half screen that still had a picture—the revolving door at the entrance to the building.

The door was moving.

At first I thought it was Brison's backup push-ing their way in. The cavalry had arrived!

But, no—I could see only one person and he wasn't in uniform. He was in a business suit.

Oh, shit! It's someone who lives in the building, someone coming home. This is bad!

"Go back outside!" I was about to yell.

Then I changed my mind.

The man spinning through the revolving door didn't live in the building, but I recognized him.

"Brison!" I shouted instead, jumping up from the counter. *"Behind you!"*

It was too late, though.

It was Brison who had given Zambratta too much time. The killer had called in his own cavalry—his own backup.

How could I ever forget this man? It was the cold-blooded killer from Lombardo's Steakhouse.

I watched in horror as he calmly pumped two bullets into Brison. Jesus, he was good with that gun of his.

To my left I could hear the elevator door finally opening. Zambratta strolled out.

"About time," he muttered to his cohort.

The sirens in the background were getting closer, but they weren't close enough as Zambratta walked right up to me.

"Police protection. Highly overrated, if you ask me," he said, raising his gun to my face.

Chapter 84

I SLOWLY OPENED my eyes, kind of glad that I still had eyes to open. My lashes flickered like a silent movie. Everything was blurry. Even the voices around me seemed blurry, if that made any sense.

Where was I? Well, at least I was somewhere.

My head was killing me, and as I slowly reached up and felt along my hairline, I found a lump the size of a tennis ball. I guess I'd been walloped by the butt of Zambratta's gun.

"Look who's up," someone said. "It's Sleepin' Beauty."

All at once everything came into focus. I saw exactly where I was. I saw whom I was with. And I wished that I hadn't seen any of it.

I was riding in the back of a stretch limousine, somewhere outside the city, judging from the speed of the vehicle. To make things a little worse, the car reeked of cigar smoke and gaudy aftershave.

To my right was Zambratta, and across from both of us, legs crossed and arms folded in satisfaction, was his boss. *The* boss.

Joseph D'zorio.

"Do you know who I am, Nick?" asked D'zorio. I was noticing that his ruddy complexion went well with his combed-back silver hair. The guy literally had a glow about him.

I nodded. "Yes, I know who you are."

"Of course you do," he said before cracking a smile. "But I bet you wish you didn't right now. In fact, that's your problem, isn't it? You know me all too well."

My shirt had been ripped open and there was no longer a panic button for me to press. Believe it or not, I was more concerned about something else.

Ever so casually I slid my hand over the pocket of my pants, feeling for the outline of the flash drive Monica Phalen had given me.

"Looking for this?" asked D'zorio.

He opened his clenched fist and I saw the flash drive nestled in the palm of his hand.

"I'm guessing, Nick, that you haven't had the chance to see what's on here."

"No," I said, "I haven't seen it."

"Neither have I. I imagine if we were to watch it together, we'd see things that we both already know."

I didn't say anything.

"Of course, what I *don't* know is who else has seen what's on here," said D'zorio, tapping the flash drive with a knuckle.

I realized that this explained why I was still alive. It's hard to get information out of a dead man.

"The only person who knows what's on that drive was murdered," I said. "On your orders, I'm sure. He was a good man, by the way."

D'zorio rocked his head back and forth as if mulling things over. "You might be right," he said. "Then again, you might be wrong. Maybe Derrick Phalen made more copies. What do you think, Carmine?"

Slouched back in the leather of the seat next

to me, Zambratta shrugged. "It's tough to say. But you can never be too sure with these things, no?"

"Is that why?" I asked D'zorio.

"Is that why *what*?" he asked back.

There was no point in playing dumb anymore. Regardless of what was on that flash drive and who else might have seen it, I knew more than enough on my own. "Is that why you framed Eddie Pinero instead of killing him outright? Less chance of retaliation? Because you can never be too sure?"

"No, that's not it," D'zorio said with a wave of his hand.

"Then what?" I asked.

"You wouldn't believe it if I told you."

"Don't be so sure. Try me."

D'zorio let go with a laugh as the limo suddenly came to a stop, the tires skidding on top of what sounded like gravel. Wherever we had been heading, we were there.

"Sorry, Nick," is all he said.

But it was the way he said it, with a sense of finality. Joseph D'zorio wasn't saying that he wouldn't tell me his secret.

He was saying good-bye.

Chapter 85

THE DOOR NEXT to me swung open with such force that I thought it might have been ripped from its hinges. D'zorio's driver, who looked like he could bench-press New Jersey, said nothing as he waited for me to step out. Behind him I caught a glimpse of an abandoned warehouse, half burned to the ground. It had that look to it, anyway. Desolate and isolated. *The kind of place where no one can hear you scream.*

"Do you need some help getting out?" asked Zambratta. "Maybe a kick in the ass?"

"You don't have to do this," I said.

He pulled out his gun, jamming it hard against my head, just like he had in the alley by the pizza place.

"Actually, I do," he said. "Your time has come."

I swung one foot out of the limo, and then I stopped because of the sound I heard. An unexpected but quite wonderful sound.

Sirens.

D'zorio's driver immediately slammed the door shut, nearly taking my leg off. Before I'd even landed in my seat he was back behind the wheel.

These sirens. They were real.

Real close, too. Not like the ones I had heard from the lobby of my building before Zambratta had knocked me senseless. It was as if this time the cavalry had snuck up from behind, turning the sirens on at the last possible moment. *Surprise!*

"Christ!" yelled Zambratta. "How?"

As in, *how the hell could they have found us here?*

Zambratta raised his fist to bang on the glass divider — "Let's go!" — but D'zorio's driver was already a step ahead. We peeled out so fast I couldn't help but think back to that night on the run in Darfur.

Hold on tight, because this is going to be one hairy ride...

Chapter 86

I HAD GOTTEN that much right, no doubt about it. The limo swerved wildly right and left in a series of turns, the three of us getting tossed around in the back like salads. I still had no idea where we were, and the heavily tinted windows and all the contortions didn't help. What little I could see was a continuous blur.

How fast were we going? Ninety miles an hour? A hundred? On a side road?

Even faster as we hit a straightaway.

The crystal glasses in the bar next to D'zorio were rattling louder and louder, but my ears remained trained on the police sirens. Were they getting closer—or farther away?

There was a chorus of them, and all I could

hope was that no matter how fast we were going, the guys underneath those sirens were going just a little bit faster. *C'mon, boys, let 'er rip! Don't be shy!*

They weren't.

Pop! Pop-pop!

Ping! Ping!

"They're trying to shoot out the tires," said Zambratta. As fast as you could say *double fisted*, the gun from inside his jacket was joined by the one that had been tucked into a shin holster.

"Wait!" said D'zorio. "Don't."

Don't?

Zambratta looked at his boss like he had three heads. "This asshole has seen me kill two guys," he said, waving what looked to be a Glock 9mm in my face. "They've got to know he's in here."

"It doesn't matter," said D'zorio. "If we pull over, no charges will stick. I can protect you, Carmine."

Now it was my turn to look at D'zorio like he had three heads. *No charges will stick? How do you figure that one?* There I was, sitting on the wrong end of two guns and in the wrong car of a police chase, and *that's* what I was wondering about? How D'zorio could protect his favorite henchman? But I couldn't help myself. It seemed like such a bizarre thing for the boss to say. Like everybody but him was stupid.

I looked over at Carmine Zambratta, who was clearly thinking the same thing. Not for long, though. He just wasn't buying it.

Instead, he began opening the sunroof.

"I'm telling you," implored D'zorio. "I can protect you."

"No, you can't," said Zambratta. "But I can protect myself."

He jumped up through the open sunroof, guns blazing. Between the bullets flying and the wind whipping through the limo, I could barely hear myself think.

But I could *see* what D'zorio was about to do.

I just couldn't believe it.

Chapter 87

IT WAS AS IF D'zorio had been counting the shots like Dirty Harry, waiting for the moment when Zambratta would need to reload. That's when he lunged forward and punched the sunroof button, the sliding glass panel trapping Zambratta half in and half out of the speeding car.

"What the fuck!" Zambratta yelled, his legs twisting helplessly beneath him. The Zamboni, D'zorio's prized enforcer, was out of bullets and fully exposed up there. The rest was target practice for the police.

For the next few seconds, Zambratta screamed horribly as several bullets, maybe half a dozen, ripped through his flesh and bones. Then, *thump!*

His lifeless body fell over against the top of the limo as one of his hands, the Glock 9mm still gripped in the palm, plopped down through the narrow space of the sunroof. I watched the blood trickle off his fingertips.

D'zorio shook his head. "The guy never god-damn listened," he said. *Oh, I see. So you killed him?*

The limo suddenly swerved hard to the right, sending me tumbling across the seat. Pushing myself back up, I squinted through the dark tint of the windows. Those were no longer trees we were passing. They were cars.

We were getting on a major highway, picking up even more speed.

I yelled to D'zorio over the sirens. "So we pull over now, right? That's what you said!"

"Not quite yet," he answered.

He reached for a small compartment by his right arm that was no bigger than a box of tissues. If only that's what was in it. *Christ, why does everyone have a gun except me?*

Grabbing the handkerchief tucked into the

breast pocket of his suit, D'zorio draped the cloth over his open palm.

"What are you doing?" I said.

But I knew what he was doing. He was making sure there'd be no gunshot residue on his hand. *When he killed me.*

"It's like I said before, Nick. You wouldn't believe me if I told you."

With that, he aimed the gun at my chest. Meanwhile, the limo was weaving like crazy in and out of lanes, but D'zorio's hand was surprisingly steady. He'd done this before.

"Wait…WAIT!" I yelled. "You heard Zambratta—the police know I'm in here."

"Yes, and when I'm done explaining everything to them, they'll know he's the one who shot you."

Checkmate, Nick. Game over. No way out, not this time.

I closed my eyes, swallowing my last breath.
Pop!

Chapter 88

IT SURE SOUNDED like a gun—only it wasn't. Not this time. Actually, it was one of the limo's tires exploding, maybe from one too many hairpin turns, or maybe from a bullet during the chase.

Of course, I didn't know that right away—I was too busy spinning around like laundry in a dryer as the limo flipped over.

And over and over and over. High bouncer, too. Possibly some cartwheels.

Call it the worst car crash I'd ever been in and—as crazy as it gets—the luckiest break I'd ever been handed, even though it hurt like hell.

My body slammed against the ceiling, the door, the bar. It was happening so fast, my hands were useless to protect me. There was nothing to hold on to, nothing to grab.

Somehow in all that flipping around, amid the crushing of metal and shattering of glass, I managed to stay conscious. And when the limo finally came to a stop—upside down, no less—my vision was going in and out as if I were looking through one of those View-Master toys.

Click! Where am I?

Okay. I was lying facedown on what I guessed was the ceiling of the limo. Slowly, I lifted a hand to my forehead, swabbing it with my palm. I didn't have to see the blood; I could feel it, warm and gooey. It was as if the huge lump I had gotten from the butt of Zambratta's gun had erupted. It hurt like hell.

But the worst pain was lower in my body. The right side of my chest, my ribs. Every breath felt like I was being stabbed with a knife.

I was about to call out for help when I heard a moan a few feet away. It was D'zorio. As bad off as I was, he looked even worse.

There were shards of glass wedged into his forehead and cheek, and I was pretty sure a bone was protruding through his sock right

below his ankle. He was wheezing and cough-
ing up blood.

He looked at me. I looked at him. We both
looked at his gun. It was maybe six inches from
his hand.

Make that four inches.

He was reaching for it, his perfectly mani-
cured nails now covered in blood, but clawing
their way toward the grip of the gun.

Then, out of the blue, I heard a voice. "Go
ahead, Joey, give me a reason!"

Wait! I know that voice...I absolutely do.

I craned my neck to see the man kneeling
beside the limo. The barrel of his Smith and
Wesson .40 caliber automatic was trained on
D'zorio.

*Wait! I know this man. He's the guy from the
diner. And my sister's house.*

I thought he had wanted to kill me, only now
here he was saving my life. He wasn't with the
mob. He was against them. It was as clear as the
three letters emblazoned on his jacket.

FBI.

Chapter 89

I HAD A broken rib for sure, maybe two. There were deep cuts and gashes on my forehead, my ear, and my right arm, all of which would definitely require stitches.

As the EMT finished examining me, Agent Douglas Keller of the FBI folded his arms and gave me a look that reminded me of my father, who'd been a junior high principal. "You need to get to a hospital, Nick," he said. "We'll talk about all this afterward."

"We'll talk now," I said. "Or we won't talk ever again. I'm not kidding—*Doug*."

We were standing in the middle of the south-bound side of the Pelham Parkway in the Bronx. Behind me, for several miles, was a parking lot of cars that weren't going anywhere for a while. To my left, on the northbound side, was a slow parade of rubberneckers, each and every face asking the same question with a wide-open mouth: *What on earth happened over there?* I could see the details they were taking in and trying to figure out: *A flipped limo—with bullet holes? Police everywhere—and FBI, too?*

Not to mention that NYPD photographers were taking pictures, measuring skid marks, and drawing a chalk line around D'zorio's driver, who, despite his size, had somehow been thrown to his death. *Remember, folks, always wear your seat belt.* As for what remained of Zambratta's body trapped in the sunroof, you don't want to know.

"You do realize, Nick, that I'm not required to tell you anything," said Agent Keller.

"That's right. I get that much, Doug. Just like I'm not required to write about the FBI agent who stalked me for two weeks while threatening my life," I shot back. "Is that 'Keller' with two l's?"

He smiled. "Glad you find all this funny," I said.

"For the record, I never actually threatened your life, Nick."

"No, but that's what you wanted me to think. You said I was in a shitload of danger."

"You *were* in a shitload of danger. You still may be."

"Yeah, but not from the FBI. Not from you. So why were you trying so hard to scare me?"

Keller shook his head as if to say, *I can't freakin' believe I'm about to tell you this.*

But he did.

It seems that one Vincent Marcozza, Eddie Pinero's attorney, had been cooperating with the FBI for the past ten months, although not by choice, of course. He had been about to get nailed for income tax evasion, so Marcozza had cut a deal.

"What kind of deal?" I asked.

"Let me put it this way," said Keller. "Marcozza agreed not to bring his 'A' game to the courtroom. He basically let Pinero get convicted."

My jaw dropped and I must have looked like one of the rubberneckers passing us. "Did the Organized Crime Task Force know about this?" I asked next.

"You mean, were their prosecutors in on it?"

"Yeah. That's exactly what I mean."

"No, they had no idea," said Keller. "I mean, maybe privately they were scratching their heads over Marcozza's crummy performance during the trial, but that was it. Nailing Pinero was a huge victory for them. They took it and ran."

And that's where I had come into the story. Literally. I had walked into Lombardo's and right into Eddie Pinero taking his revenge on Marcozza.

Only it *wasn't* Pinero, as we later found out. It had just looked that way because it was supposed to.

"How did you know it was D'zorio—that it was a setup?" I asked Keller now.

"We didn't know. That is, not until you did." He motioned with his hand. "Give me your phone for a second," he said.

I gave him a quizzical look. Then I handed over my iPhone.

Keller unlocked the touch screen and went into the settings. I watched as he scrolled down, then tapped into my "Password Lock" and entered a four-digit code.

"There," he said, giving it back. "Good as new."

Huh? "What was it before?" I asked.

Keller didn't answer me. He didn't need to. That's how he had found me at my sister's house. The FBI had turned my phone into a tracking device. But how? When? Who had done that?

"Yeah, you were pretty wrapped up in your newspaper that morning," he said, playing off my expression. I flashed back to the Sunrise Diner and the first time Keller had approached me. *"Is this your phone?"* he'd asked.

"So, let me guess," I said. "Because you saved my life, in return I never go public...I never write this story?"

"That's the basic plan," he said bluntly. "Especially given one other little thing I ought to mention."

"What's that?"

"The story's not over, Nick."

Part Five

IT AIN'T OVER TILL IT'S OVER

Chapter 90

I FELT LIKE a cat must after using up eight lives. In other words, *no more messing around*. Right smack in the middle of the Pelham Parkway I cut my own deal with Agent Douglas Keller. *Keep me alive and the story I could write dies. If I die, the story lives.* I would see to that—pronto, I promised him.

"Here's where I keep my former editor's number." I pointed to the number two on my phone. "She's on speed dial. She's a better writer, and reporter, than I am. Hard to imagine, I know."

Keller pinched his lips while nodding slowly. Weird, but I could tell there was a part of him that liked my playing hardball. He could relate.

"Okay," he said. "Deal." He handled it from

there. And faster than I would have thought possible.

By the time he met me at the emergency room of the closest hospital—Jacobi Medical Center— he'd already informed the NYPD that the FBI would be taking over my protection. Two cops had already been murdered trying to protect me. Enough said, enough damage done.

"After you get stitched up here, another agent and I will take you back to your apartment. You'll have a few minutes to pack a suitcase," said Keller.

We were in a curtained-off area of the ER, waiting for one of the doctors to show up. Were it not for about a dozen butterfly bandages holding me together, I might have already bled out.

"Once I pack, where do I go?" I asked. "Sorry if I don't entirely trust protective custody schemes."

"We're going to a real safe place outside the city. Trust me on this one, Nick."

"Where's that? The real safe place?"

"Now, if I told you, how safe would it be for the next guy?" said Keller.

"What about David Sorren?" I asked next.

"What about him?"

"Does he know you're taking me to the Batcave? He won't appreciate that. Sorren can play tough, too."

Keller cracked a slight smile. It was good to know he had one. "Sorren will find out soon enough," he said. "If there's anybody who might be even *more* concerned about your health than us, it's the Manhattan DA. Mr. David Sorren needs you alive to prosecute D'zorio."

"If the devil doesn't get him first," came a voice on the other side of the curtain.

Sorren.

He took one look at me as he yanked back the curtain and immediately shook his head. "Man, when this is all over, you're going to have a hell of a story to write."

"I guess so. *If* this is ever over, and if I'm in any condition to write it. Not to mention, if I'm actually allowed to write about any of this."

I shot a quick, uncomfortable glance at Keller.

Sorren promptly introduced himself to Keller. Then he asked how and why the FBI was involved, the unspoken subtext being *How and why is the FBI involved without my knowledge?*

Keller didn't skip a beat. "Bruno Torenzi," he said.

"Who's Torenzi?" asked Sorren. "I don't know that name."

"Your scalpel-wielding psychotic contract killer. He took out Vincent Marcozza, Derrick Phalen, and two cops."

"Make that three cops," I said. "Torenzi showed up at my building to help out Zambratta. He's the one who shot Officer Brison."

"This Torenzi...I'm guessing he isn't from around here," said Sorren.

"Originally from Sicily. But he's worked in the States before. We were wondering where he would surface next. Now we know."

"Do you think he's got one more assignment?" I asked.

Sorren rubbed his chin. He knew what I was asking. *Is Torenzi coming after me?*

"That might depend on what's going on upstairs," he answered. "D'zorio's in surgery. He has massive internal bleeding. It's a coin flip whether he makes it."

"Which is why we don't want to take any chances here with Nick," said Keller, peering around the curtain at the rest of the ER. He sighed impatiently. "Where the hell is that doctor?"

I was getting impatient myself.

Then suddenly my phone rang.

Chapter 91

I GLANCED AT the caller ID expecting it to be Courtney. Or maybe my sister. Or anyone else, for that matter. I didn't expect it to be my niece, Elizabeth.

Especially because she was calling from her Braille cell phone, which she rarely used. "Mom said I'm only supposed to use it in case of an emergency," she had once told me.

I could hear her saying those exact words as I answered.

"Elizabeth? Is everything all right?"

"Yes," she said.

That's all it took. One word from my niece, the fourteen-year-old girl with the freckles who

I'd first held in my arms when she was a mere two days old.

One word.

Something was wrong. Elizabeth has never been at a loss for words. The girl was a total motormouth.

"Are you okay?" I asked.

"No."

"What's wrong, honey? Is it your mom? What happened?"

"Can I come into the city to see you?"

I could tell, or at least sense, that she was fighting back tears. Her voice was cracking. Quivering, actually.

"Elizabeth, what happened?" I repeated.

I pressed the phone hard against my ear as I exchanged looks with Sorren and Keller. They'd been talking, not paying any attention to what I was saying. Until now. Now both of them were staring at me. *Who?* Sorren mimed.

"I got into a bad fight with Mom and I'm really upset," said Elizabeth. "I need to talk to you. You're the only one I can talk to."

A fight with her mother? It was certainly within the realm of possibility, I guessed.

Elizabeth was a teenager and her mother was... well, her mother. Normally they were the best of friends, but even best friends fight.

So why wasn't I buying any of this? Probably because Elizabeth wasn't sounding like... Elizabeth.

"Where are you now?" I asked.

"I had to get out of the house, I was so mad," she answered. "So can I please come into the city to see you? Please, Uncle Nick."

"Here's the deal, honey," I said. "Any other time I'd probably say yes, but right now is really bad for me. I can't get into the details, but you may hear about it on the news later." I paused to put a little extra emphasis on my next sentence. "In fact, maybe you've already heard about what happened to me today. Is that true?"

Elizabeth was silent for a few seconds. "No, I haven't heard anything," she said.

But it was what she didn't say—she didn't ask me what had happened.

"This is what I think you should do," I said. "You need to go home and try to patch things up with your mom. Whatever it was you were fighting about, I'm sure you both can work it out. It's going to be okay."

"No, it won't be," she said, adamant. "She's going to tell my father and I'm afraid of what's going to happen when he gets home."

She was flat-out crying now, and I wasn't sure what to say next because I was about to throw up. Elizabeth wasn't alone. I was sure of it—as sure as the sound that came next. Someone was grabbing the phone away from her.

"That's a smart little niece you have there, Nick. But we all know her daddy's dead," he said. "And unless you come alone to Grand Central Station in one hour, this little girl will be dead, too. And remember this, Nick. I have no reason to hurt her. *She hasn't seen a thing.*"

Chapter 92

I COULD FEEL the blood forcing its way through the butterfly bandages on my head and arm as I walked into Grand Central Station a little less than an hour later. But I could give a damn about needing more stitches. What I really needed was Elizabeth back safe and sound. Nothing mattered more. How could it?

Above me in the Main Concourse of the station was the giant display board listing the arrival time and track information for every train. Scores of people were stopping to look up at it.

Not me. I never even gave it a glance as I kept walking, fast. That board couldn't tell me anything that I didn't already know.

An unidentified man with an unidentified teenage girl in tow hijacked the 5:04 southbound Metro-North train from Westport, Connecticut. Instead of taking hostages, he let everyone else go. Except for the girl and the train's engineer...My mind had raced. Jesus, what kind of plan is that? What does it tell me about Bruno Torenzi?

That had been the gist of the first report from the local police in Westport, the sister town to Weston, where Kate and Elizabeth lived. The only other thing they could tell Agent Keller on the phone was that the train was heading into New York City.

Yeah, we know. The unidentified man told us. He also said that the train was making no other stops.

It was hurry up and wait as I stood on the empty platform of track 19. The image of Bruno Torenzi had been seared into my brain so deeply that I could hardly focus on anything else. I could see him at Lombardo's, and I could see him in the lobby of my apartment building. Now I was about to meet up with him again. One way or the other I figured this would be the last time. But what the hell was his plan? I just couldn't figure that out.

I definitely wanted to kill the bastard, though. Never in my life had I felt such hatred, such loathing, toward anyone.

Easy, Nick. Keep it in check.

But it was near impossible. Not when I thought about Elizabeth and how scared she must be, or, for that matter, how absolutely terrified her mother was. Only minutes after bolting from the hospital I had reached Kate on her cell phone. She'd been food shopping, a simple half-hour errand, and then back home in a jiff to Elizabeth. Solemnly, I broke the news that Elizabeth wouldn't be there when she arrived.

"My baby!" she said over and over. It was just crushing.

That's when I called Courtney to ask a favor that wasn't really a favor at all, not as she saw it. As soon as I had told her what had happened, and she knew there was nothing she could do for me here in the city, Courtney had immediately read my mind. My sister was in the good hands of the local police while she waited for this all to play out.

"But she needs to be with someone she knows, a familiar and friendly face," said Courtney. "I'm on my way, okay?"

Yes, thank you! And when this is all over, I need to be with you, Courtney. Okay? Nothing and no one is going to stop me.

Right on cue, I heard the rumbling in the distance. Then I saw it.

The 5:04 train from Westport was pulling into the station like a slow-moving snake made of metal and steel. As the air brakes grabbed the rails, a piercing hiss echoed between my ears.

This is it. The end of the road, tracks, whatever.

Immediately, the sliding doors opened in unison. But the familiar sight of lots of people bustling out didn't follow. There was only silence, creepy as hell. I held my breath. I could barely stand it. And then—

Tap. Tap-tap-tap...

I finally saw her all the way down the platform. Elizabeth was stepping off the first car of the train, her cane leading the way. My niece was dressed in faded jeans and a lime green zip-up sweater, her hair pulled back in a ponytail. Everything about her looked so young and innocent—except her face, her expression. Her mouth was closed tight, her freckled nose scrunched in fear—she looked petrified.

Still, I was so relieved to see her—to see her alive—that the incongruity didn't dawn on me at first.

She was alone. No Bruno Torenzi.

"Elizabeth!" I called out.

I started running toward her, flying down the platform. It was a knee-jerk reaction. There was no thought, only instinct. How could I not go to her?

She was about to tell me why. My niece stopped, raising her palm. "Wait, Uncle Nick!" she yelled at the top of her voice. "Stop right there! I'm serious!"

Chapter 93

OH GOD NO. This can't be happening. Only it definitely was happening. I was watching it happen from maybe fifty feet away.

All I needed to see were the red wires peeking out of her sweater. My mind connected the dots from there. *Just like the red wires are connecting the blocks of C-4 explosives strapped to Elizabeth's chest.*

"YOU SON OF A BITCH!" I yelled, or more accurately screamed. I couldn't see him but I knew Torenzi was there. Somewhere. Then, suddenly, he was *everywhere.*

The air crackled with the sound of the train's public-address system, a thick static followed by a thick Italian accent. "What did I say about you coming alone?" he asked, sounding like the voice of God.

"I did come alone!" I shouted.

"Lie to me one more time and you watch your niece die. In a horrible way."

I stared at Elizabeth. Her eyes were staring right back but I knew of course she couldn't see me. That only made things worse, made my guilt worse.

"It's going to be okay," I said. "You're not going to die."

Then I turned around, looking at nothing but the empty platform behind me. But it wasn't empty. I knew it, and Torenzi sure as hell knew it.

Slowly, the six-man SWAT team that Keller had employed stepped out from the shadows and the rafters, one by one. They were armed with assault rifles equipped with high-power scopes. The original plan had been to take out Torenzi the second he stepped away from Elizabeth.

But now Torenzi was calling all the shots. "Get on the train with the girl," he ordered. "First car."

It was so damn unnerving not being able to

'see him. I could still see just Elizabeth, standing up ahead with her walking stick. What an unbelievable coward this bastard was and had been, right from the start. And not just Torenzi, because D'zorio had to be involved in this. His people, anyway. Torenzi couldn't be working alone here. Could he?

I walked down the platform, reaching for Elizabeth's hand. "I've got you," I said.

"Don't let go," she whispered.

"I won't," I said.

Together, we stepped back onto the train, the doors immediately closing behind us. The idling diesel engine kicked in, shaking the wheels into motion. And then we were off.

To where, though?

Not to mention, where the hell was Torenzi?

"Welcome aboard," came his voice suddenly. Only it wasn't over the PA. It was from the front of the train.

I turned in the vestibule to see him standing about a dozen feet away, next to the conductor's cabin. He was wearing the same suit, same sunglasses, same "don't screw with me" attitude. In one hand he was holding a small device that looked like a flip-top cell phone without the flip top. It was the detonator.

In the other hand was a gun. It was aimed at the conductor's head.

"What now?" I asked Torenzi.

He nodded slowly. "You'll see. Let's not get ahead of ourselves."

Chapter 94

TORENZI WAS CERTAINLY on top of everything, and that was really scary. He'd kept a
watchful eye on the security monitors inside
the conductor's cabin, checking every camera
focused on every door of the train. There would
be no uninvited guests stepping on board with
him, no front-page heroes. It would be just the
conductor, Nick Daniels, and Daniels's niece. A
nice little trio, neat and manageable. That is,
until he no longer needed them.

Yeah, Torenzi was on top of everything.
Except the train itself.

That's where Agent Keller was.

There were no cameras pointed up there.
Better yet, there was a ceiling panel on top of the

engine car that could be opened from the outside. At least that's what the Metropolitan Transportation Authority official had assured him while presenting a crash course outside Grand Central Station on the M7 electric multiple-unit railroad car, otherwise known as the 5:04 from Westport.

"Trust me, you'll see the panel once you're up there," said the MTA official.

The guy was right.

As soon as Plan A had fizzled, Keller had rappelled down from the rafters above the train on track 19. The last time he had done anything like it was twelve years ago during his training at Quantico. "You never know," his instructor had said.

That guy had been right, too.

Keller had landed on the roof less than a minute before the train had sputtered forward, pulling out of the station. Unclipping his rope, he crouched down low, something like a surfer riding a monster wave. There was no turning back now.

Next, Keller spotted the roof panel. It was no more than ten feet away. Edging toward it, he reached for the two tools given to him by the MTA. The first was a 3200-rpm power screw-driver equipped with a half-inch flat-head bit to maximize the torque. The second was a tad more primitive: a crowbar.

"Once you remove the four screws you're going to need some elbow grease prying open that panel," an MTA engineer had warned. "It's a heavy mother."

It was also the only way to get inside that train undetected. "Anything else I need to know?" Keller had asked the engineer.

"No, I think that's it."

Think again.

Channeling his inner carpenter, Keller quickly dispatched with the four screws holding down the panel. No problem there. The real trick was keeping his balance on top of the train. It was zipping along at full throttle, relentlessly rocking back and forth on the tracks. Still, he was managing. So far, so good.

"Crowbar time," Keller mumbled, hoping he had a good supply of elbow grease.

Immediately, he knew that the MTA mechanic hadn't been kidding around. The panel was a heavy mother, all right. It wouldn't budge. Not an inch. Was it stuck?

Maybe.

Keller tried again. He could almost hear the clock in his head ticking away as he pressed down hard on the crowbar.

"Shit!"

The panel still wouldn't budge. This was definitely a problem, a big one.

Then, turning his head, Keller had an even bigger problem—if that was possible.

A ray of light had caught the corner of his eye. It was literally the light at the end of the tunnel, which also marked the end of the underground tracks. So much for that old cliché meaning good things were coming his way. That MTA official had forgotten to mention a little thing called clearance.

There wasn't any.

The loading gauge of the tunnel looked to be only a few inches higher than the train itself. Even if he lay flat, he still wouldn't clear it. It was either jump or *splat!*

Or get inside that damn train in a hurry.

Keller shifted his body alongside the panel,

desperately throwing his weight into the crowbar as the tunnel kept getting closer and closer to its end. The vibration of the train felt like an electric shock through his body as the air whipped over him, blasting his face, pushing the beads of sweat off his brow like rain on a windshield.

"C'mon, you son of a bitch!" he yelled at the panel. "Move!"

Chapter 95

TIME WAS MEANINGLESS—and I had no idea how many minutes, how many seconds, had actually passed so far. A burst of late afternoon sun hit my eyes as we shot out of the underground tunnel leaving Grand Central Station. It felt like we were practically flying off the tracks.

Torenzi had barked at the engineer to "gun it" and that's obviously what he was doing. Given that the poor guy had a gun aimed at his head, I could hardly blame his accommodating nature. *Funny how that works.*

I squeezed Elizabeth's hand. "Stay behind me," I whispered, stepping between her and Torenzi.

I wasn't expecting any small talk or chitchat

from the bastard. Whatever his plan was, it didn't include telling me all about it. He'd come to kill me, and the only reason he hadn't done it yet was to make sure he wouldn't get caught. But I had to die—I knew too much.

I figured we weren't about to pull into some town in Westchester and step off the train, la-di-da. Agent Keller had seemed sure of it, too. Still, he had plotted every scenario the moment Torenzi had hung up on me at the hospital and had arranged for local police to be camped out at every station all the way up to New Haven, the end of the line.

"Just in case Torenzi's stupid," Keller had said.

But we both knew he wasn't. He was daring as hell, and he was smarter than I would have thought. Actually, I've noticed that before about professionals in Europe. They work hard; they learn their craft—even the hit men, apparently.

Torenzi turned to the engineer less than a minute later. "Stop the train," he ordered. "Right here! Now."

The engineer slammed the brakes like . . . well, like a guy who still had a gun aimed at his head.

We skidded along the rails, the train wheels scraping like countless fingernails on a blackboard. I spun around to catch Elizabeth, who was hurtling toward the ground. *Not a good thing when you're wearing a bomb*, I was thinking. All I'd been focused on while on that train was how to make sure Elizabeth survived this. I was the reason Elizabeth was here, and so far there was nothing I could do to help her.

Torenzi held every advantage, literally. The gun. The detonator. A plan to kill me. I held nothing. Except a very scared little girl's hand.

Out the window I could see dense trees on both sides of the track. We were shielded from view and it wasn't by accident.

"Please, leave the girl alone!" I shouted. "You've got me. I'm the one you want."

"You're right," said Torenzi calmly, reaching into the engineer's cabin.

He hit the button for the doors to open. Then he raised his gun and aimed it dead center at my chest. For the first time, I let go of Elizabeth's hand.

"GET DOWN! GET DOWN, DANIELS!"

Out of nowhere came a voice from the back of the train car. I didn't know who it was at first, and I didn't care. It was someone!

And suddenly that someone was shooting at Torenzi! I grabbed Elizabeth and yanked her down to the floor with me as Torenzi fired back. Bullets whizzed over our heads as I connected the voice to Agent Keller. But how did he get on the train? And did I really care how?

Looking up from the floor I saw Torenzi grab the engineer in a choke hold. Next, he jammed his gun right into the man's ear.

Keller stopped firing.

"Stay where you are, asshole!" Torenzi warned as he forced the engineer up the aisle in front of him. The closer he got, the more I tried to cover up Elizabeth with my body.

The train fell nearly silent, the only sound the low hum of the idling engine. I didn't dare look at Torenzi as he came toward us, not even a glance. All I wanted was for him to get off the train, even if it meant he'd never be caught.

But as he reached the open door right by us in the vestibule, he kicked me in the ribs. "Get up!" he said.

He kicked me again even harder, to make sure I had heard him and was getting up.

Slowly I began to stand, and before my knees could even straighten, Torenzi pushed the engineer down and grabbed me in his place. I was his new hostage, his ticket off the train, and of course I was his target as well.

But Keller had other ideas. What was he doing now?

His gun gripped tight in his outstretched hand, he began walking toward us down the aisle.

Torenzi barked. "STAY WHERE YOU ARE!"

Keller didn't. He kept walking, his mouth clenched so tight I could see his jawbone rippling along his cheeks. He seemed like a man possessed. What was he doing? Didn't he see the gun to my head?

In fact, that's all he saw.

Right before Keller shot me in the chest.

Chapter 96

THE FORCE OF the bullet's impact knocked me out of Torenzi's grasp. It happened so fast that even if he'd pulled the trigger and tried to blow my brains out, he probably would've missed. Besides, what was the point? Why bother killing me when the FBI was doing it for him?

As I fell to the ground, Torenzi thrust his gun forward and opened fire on Keller. I couldn't see much, though. *Shit! Did he get Keller? Did Keller get him?*

No! And—*no!*

I saw Bruno Torenzi dive behind the row of seats across from where I lay wounded. I looked over at Elizabeth. "Don't move!" I said to her.

She nodded, tears streaming down her cheeks. "I won't, Uncle Nick. Are you okay?"

Next to her was the engineer, clinging to the floor. Our eyes met for an instant and it was as if I could read his mind. *I should've called in sick today!*

I hear you, buddy. Me too.

I could see enough of Torenzi to tell he was reloading. One hand was holding his gun, the other removing the magazine.

Wait! Where is the detonator?

My eyes searched the seat next to him. There it was.

I didn't stop to think. I didn't stop at all. I pushed off the floor with both hands. Then I lunged for the detonator, scooping it up in my hands.

I had it! But now what could I do?

Torenzi turned to me and I was maybe four feet away from him—point-blank range.

That's when Keller shot him for the first time.

Blood sprayed as Torenzi took a bullet above his elbow. He let out a horrific grunt and spun around to shoot back at Keller, only to take another bullet higher on the arm, somewhere just below his shoulder.

But the killer didn't go down. Instead, he fired back at Keller.

Then Torenzi bolted off the train. The last sound I heard was his footsteps on the gravel around the tracks as he raced into the woods.

Chapter 97

KELLER LOOKED LIKE a blur in a comic-book-inspired movie as he came sprinting down the aisle.

"I've got the detonator!" I yelled, holding it up. With the other hand I was pointing out the door of the train. "Don't let him get away!"

But Keller went nowhere except down on one knee, right by my side. "Suspect armed and on foot," he announced into his radio. "You okay?" he asked me.

My chest felt as if I'd just danced with a wrecking ball, but all things considered? "Yeah, I'm okay," I said. I handed him the detonator.

Then I lifted up my shirt and we both stared

at the bullet lodged in the Kevlar vest that he had insisted I wear.

"Bull's-eye," he said with a smile.

"Oh, that's funny," I said. "You could've killed me!"

"You're right, I could've," said Keller. "But Torenzi? He would've for sure."

"Uncle Nick?"

We both turned to Elizabeth, who was still on the floor about six feet away. *She was still wearing a bomb.*

Keller went over to her and helped her to her feet. "Honey, that's Agent Keller, with the FBI," I said. "He's going to get that bomb off you."

My eyes went to Keller. He gave me a nod somewhere between hope and confidence: *I'll do my best*.

Then he held the detonator up like a Fabergé egg, quickly studying it front and back. It actually *was* a flip-top cell phone without the flip top.

"So he dials some numbers and we all go boom—is that how it works?" I asked.

"Only one number…speed dial," said Keller. He motioned to Elizabeth. "Somewhere on her is the ringer of another phone that's wired to a detonating cap. Simple. ETA pioneered it before it was adopted by jihadists, and now apparently Italian hit men."

Keller assumed I knew what ETA was, given my profession. He was right, and it didn't stand for "estimated time of arrival." ETA was Spain's homegrown terrorist network.

"Uh, excuse me, but shouldn't we be calling the bomb squad or something?" asked the engineer. He was still sitting on the floor of the train, a little dazed but clearly comprehending the situation.

"Trust me, they're already on their way," answered Keller. "The problem is, we can't wait for them."

It wasn't exactly the answer the engineer was looking for. "Why not?" he asked, half a beat before I did.

"Because right now any phone can detonate this bomb," said Keller. "All Torenzi has to do is get to one."

"So what do we do?" I asked.

"*We* don't do anything," said Keller. "I need both of you guys to clear out of here right now. A hundred yards, no less than that. Move it. Go."

"I'm not going anywhere," I said flatly. "I'm staying right here. Period."

It was the easiest decision I'd ever made, and it didn't seem to surprise Keller that much. He didn't bother fighting me on it. Instead, he turned to the engineer and cut straight to the chase.

"You married?" asked Keller.

The guy wasn't quite ready for a pop quiz, easy as it was. He was still rocking and reeling from all the action he'd had in the past hour.

"I said, are you married?" repeated Keller.

"Yes," said the engineer.

"Any kids?"

Keller didn't say another word.

He didn't have to.

"I'm out of here. Good luck," said the engineer. "I'm praying for you."

Chapter 98

I WATCHED THROUGH the window for a few seconds as the engineer did the right thing and got the hell away from the train. Then Keller got down to business. Very tricky, very risky business.

"Okay, Elizabeth, all you need to do is relax," he said in a soft voice. "The first thing we're going to do is take off the sweater you're wearing. Okay with you?"

She clenched her fists and nodded. "Okay." What a trouper. Like I said, the bravest kid I know.

Ever so slowly, Keller unzipped the rest of Elizabeth's green sweater, past the little embroidered flower and all the way to the bottom. The farther down he went, the more I had to stifle my urge to gasp at all the wires—and the bomb attached to them.

"You're doing great, Elizabeth, really great. This should be no problem at all," said Keller. He wasn't about to scare her any more than she already was, but I could tell from his face that the "no problem" talk was just that. Talk. Probably to keep Elizabeth's *and* his mind off what was actually happening.

Of course, the one thing he hadn't factored in was Elizabeth's amazing sense of smell. As in, she could smell bullshit from a mile away. Even more so when the person was right in front of her.

"It's worse than you thought, isn't it?" she finally asked.

"Not necessarily," said Keller, peeling the sweater off her shoulders. Then he pushed around a few of the wires for a better look at the explosives. They literally crisscrossed the front of Elizabeth's undershirt like an *X*.

"Are you sure you should be doing this?" I asked.

Keller kept poking and prodding while answering me, as if to make his point. "This C-4 stuff is as stable as it comes. You could shoot it with a gun and it wouldn't explode."

You learn something new every day. Even when it could be your last.

"So, what *does* make it explode?" I asked.

"A shock wave combined with extreme heat," said Keller, "created by triggering these wires connected to the detonators imbedded in C-4."

"Couldn't we just slip everything off her? Right up over her head?"

"That's what I'm checking to see," he said as he continued to poke and prod. "The way whoever built this has it configured, though, I'm not sure—"

Keller suddenly stopped cold, and he looked as if he'd seen a ghost.

"What is it?" I asked. *"Tell me."*

Instead, he showed me. He pulled me closer and pointed at it, clear as could be.

It was worse than a ghost, actually.

It was a timer—ticking backwards.

Chapter 99

"UNCLE NICK? WHAT'S happening? What's going on? Why aren't either of you talking?"

Elizabeth reached out for me, her pale, slender hands waving helplessly in the air. She started to move toward me but Keller held her back.

"Nick, come hold Elizabeth," he said. "Can you do that? Keep her hands up."

I swung around behind Elizabeth, doing exactly as Keller said. "Don't move," I whispered in her ear. "I'm right here with you."

Over her shoulder I could still see the timer, a cheap plastic stopwatch that was taped to the cell phone behind one of the blocks of C-4.

Fifty-four seconds!

And heading in the wrong direction...

Keller had no time to think. He was winging it, fast and furious. Then, like a switchboard operator on speed, he began pulling out the detonator wires one by one.

"How much time?" he asked.

"Forty seconds!" I said.

He pulled out another wire. There were three to go. Then two. My eyes were pinballing back and forth between the timer and his hands.

"Talk to me," he said.

"Thirty seconds!"

Keller was down to the last wire. "Just one more," he said under his breath. "C'mon, now…"

He gripped the C-4 to hold it steady. All he had to do now was pull on the wire and ease it out like he'd done with all the others.

"Shit!" said Keller.

The wire wasn't moving.

"Pull harder!" I yelled.

"I am!" he yelled back. "He must have glued it."

Twenty-five seconds!

Keller looked at me and then out the door of the train. I saw the spark of an idea light his face. A last-gasp idea? Probably.

"Wait! Where are you going?" I said.

He was already sprinting toward the front of the car, heading for the engineer's cabin. Seconds later, the train jerked and sputtered. It was moving along the track again.

"Pick her up!" he barked, running back toward us.

"What?"

"Lift her off the ground! Do it! Right now!"

"Please do it!" Elizabeth joined in.

I grabbed Elizabeth by the elbows and hoisted her up. Suddenly Keller pulled the bomb over her waist and down her legs, sliding it off her feet.

Damn it! I couldn't see the timer anymore. All I could see was Keller pointing out the door of the train at the green of trees. The train was gaining speed.

"Jump!" he yelled. "Jump now!"

I scooped up Elizabeth, cradling her in my arms as I turned toward the door—and then leaped through the air after him.

There was no tuck and roll, only a thud—my feet barely hitting the ground before I fell onto my back to shield Elizabeth. The *snap!* I heard was another one of my ribs, the pain shooting through my body like an angry rocket.

Still cradling Elizabeth in my arms, I turned to watch the train zoom by us, the head car that was carrying the bomb getting smaller and smaller. But not small enough.

"Get up!" barked Keller. "Run!"

I scrambled to my feet with Elizabeth as Keller grabbed my arm to lead the way. We raced along the tracks, putting as much distance as we could between us and the—

BOOM!

Chapter 100

"*DARK SIDE OF the Moon* or *Wish You Were Here*?" asked Anne Gram, one of the two surgical technologists prepping the OR at Jacobi Medical Center. She was cueing up the iPod of Dr. Al Sassoon, the attending surgeon—and massive Pink Floyd fan—who was still scrubbing.

Ruth Kreindler, the frick to Anne's frack, looked up from the sterile surgical drape she was laying over Joseph D'zorio's groin area. It was the only part of the guy that wasn't broken, punctured, lacerated, or ruptured.

"The way this is shaping up," said Ruth, shaking her head, "we'll hear both albums and some of *The Wall* as well. Al and his Pink Floyd."

"Hey—he's good, and he's fun to work with."

The two women, both in their early forties, were done with their pre-op checklist, even twice testing the suction machines as they'd been clogging as of late. All in all, it was business as usual, although they both knew that the man on the table, unconscious and breathing oxygen, was no ordinary patient.

"Do you believe all people deserve to be saved?" Anne finally asked.

Ruth looked over her shoulder to make sure the two of them were still alone with the infamous mob boss. They were. "Are you speaking medically or spiritually?" she asked. "It might make a difference in my answer."

Anne shrugged. "Medically, I suppose."

"I know what you're saying, but a hospital isn't a courtroom. Know what I mean?"

"I do. *Still.*"

Ruth glanced down at D'zorio. "I'll put it to you this way," she said. "A guy like this puts my faith to the test. It's righteous anger versus forgiveness."

"Who wins?" asked Anne.

"Forgiveness, I suppose. Spiritually, all people can be saved."

Anne nodded but there was little belief in her eyes. She could never say it out loud, but she was secretly hoping that Dr. Sassoon would have an off day, or at least not bring his "A" game to the table.

"What did you say?" asked Ruth.

Anne hadn't said anything. She was too busy envisioning Dr. Sassoon "accidentally" leaving a sponge in D'zorio's chest.

But she'd heard it, too. Someone had said something in the operating room.

Simultaneously, they both looked down at D'zorio on the table. His thin, bluish lips were moving. He was mumbling.

"What did he say?" asked Anne.

"I'm not sure," said Ruth, leaning down toward his mouth. Anne joined her.

"Sorr—" said D'zorio, his voice barely above a whisper. "*Sorry.*"

At least, that's what the two heard.

"He's confessing his sins," said Anne.

"Or trying to," said Ruth, walking over to the phone on the wall.

She called down to the staff chaplain's office to see if D'zorio's priest had arrived yet. They had been told he was on his way to administer the anointing of the sick, otherwise known as the mob boss's last rites.

Apparently, D'zorio was starting without him.

Ruth was still waiting for someone in the chaplain's office to pick up when the heart monitor alarm sounded.

"Oh, Christ!" said Anne, back at the table with D'zorio. "He's flatlining!"

Ruth hung up the phone and ran out to where Dr. Sassoon had just finished scrubbing.

But it was too late. There would be no Pink Floyd played in the OR that afternoon. Joseph D'zorio had receded into death.

Like a distant ship's smoke on the horizon.

Chapter 101

BRUNO TORENZI WAS steamrolling his way through the brush and branches, his hands clearing the way forward while his ears listened for anyone coming up behind him.

He was waiting for the explosion back on the train tracks, and with a quick glance at his watch he knew it wouldn't be much longer. Any second now, really. It was so close to happening, he could practically hear the entire sequence in his head—a symphony of sounds, from the initial thunderous clap to the seemingly endless echo to the relentless squawking of every bird knocked off its perch within a square mile.

Finally, it came. The bomb, the echo, the

birds...everything. Almost exactly as he'd imagined it would be.

But Torenzi didn't stop and look back, not for a second. He had no interest in taking it all in. He didn't feel the need.

He didn't *feel* anything.

There was no glee, no satisfaction, and certainly no remorse—not even the slightest twinge of guilt over the innocent little girl. She had flushed out her uncle as he'd planned. She'd served her purpose from his viewpoint. That was all there was to it.

As for the Rambo who'd crashed the party on the train, Torenzi still had no idea who he was. In hindsight, though, the guy must have known Daniels was wearing a bulletproof vest. There was no way his aim was that bad, the two shots he tagged Torenzi with being evidence of some skill on his part.

Speaking of not feeling anything...

Torenzi had yanked the black leather belt from his pants, making a tourniquet and cutting off the circulation directly below his shoulder. For now, his arm was as numb as rubber in December. Later, he'd tend to it. He'd dig out the bullets with the stiletto blade he kept strapped to his shin and then stitch himself up with a dime-store needle and thread, leaving two more scars on a body littered with them. No big deal. Just another day at the office.

As Hyman Roth said to Michael Corleone in *The Godfather: Part II,* "This is the business we've chosen."

Now Torenzi's business was done. Once again, he had won the game.

Finally, he emerged from the trees and saw the car waiting for him. Perfect timing. Things were going his way again—as they always did.

"Is he dead?" he heard as he approached the white Volvo S40.

Torenzi leaned down into the open window of the front passenger side. He smirked. "What do you think? You heard the explosion, didn't you?"

Ian LaGrange smiled wide, his overly large mouth almost cartoonish. "Indeed I did," he said. "Get in."

The Volvo was parked on a deserted dead-end road, the only sign of life being two half-finished spec homes that were destined to stay that way because the builder had gone belly-up when the housing market had collapsed.

Torenzi yanked open the car door and stepped in. "Let's go," he said.

LaGrange motioned to Torenzi's arm, the belt, and his bloodstained shirt beneath his jacket. "What the hell happened to you?" he asked.

"It's nothing. There was someone else on the train."

"Who?"

"Does it matter?"

"I'm the head of the Organized Crime Task Force," said LaGrange. "What do *you* think?"

"He was most likely FBI."

"Did you kill him?"

"No, but the bomb surely did," said Torenzi. "What about D'zorio?"

"He didn't make it."

"Lucky break for you."

LaGrange chuckled. "Better to be lucky than good."

"Even better to be both," said Torenzi, meaning every word of it. "You got the rest of my money?"

"Of course I do. In the trunk," he answered

with a throw of his head. "Gave you a little extra for all your troubles. You did a fine job."

Torenzi didn't say thank you. Instead, he was wondering why LaGrange still had the car in park.

"What are we waiting for?" he asked.

"There's one other piece of business we need to take care of."

"What's that?"

"Me," said the man outside the open car window.

How do you say revenge *in Russian?*

Chapter 102

BRUNO TORENZI DIDN'T recognize the voice, but there was little doubt about the barrel of a gun jammed against the side of his head.

"Put your hands on the dashboard," ordered Ivan Belova. "Slowly. Very, very slowly."

Torenzi complied with disgust as LaGrange removed the keys from the ignition and opened the driver's side door. "I'm sorry, Bruno," he said before stepping out. "Remember the San Sebastian Hotel? You fucked up, you horny bastard."

Belova, a better-dressed and slimmed-down version of Boris Yeltsin, kept his eyes squarely focused on Torenzi. He had no intention of giving the professional killer any opening. It was a lesson his two sons had learned the hard way at that hotel in Manhattan where they'd tried to run their scam on the Italian.

"Do you know who I am?" he asked in his heavy Russian accent. He was the head of the Belova crime family, that's who. They were the U.S. arm of Solntsevskaya Bratva, one of the most powerful crime families in Moscow.

"No," answered Torenzi, who knew enough to keep looking straight ahead out the windshield.

"Those were my boys you killed in that hotel room, my flesh and blood," he said with equal parts anger and despair. He was his own Molotov cocktail ready to explode.

Belova waited for some type of reaction from Torenzi. A look of surprise, maybe even regret. "Sorry" was a long shot, as was anything else approaching an apology—Belova had no delusions about that. Not that it would've made a difference. There was no changing his plans. No chance of mercy for the Italian killer.

Still, Belova never would've imagined the response he did get from the man.

"They were punks," said Torenzi. "They had it coming."

"Motherfucker!" yelled Belova, pulling back the hammer on his Makarov PM.

"Wait!" yelled LaGrange even louder. He was standing behind Belova.

"What?" asked Belova impatiently over his shoulder. He still wasn't about to take his eyes off Torenzi. He knew how lethal this man could be.

"For Christ's sake, not in the car," said LaGrange. "Not unless you want to clean up afterward."

Belova reluctantly nodded, reaching out with his free hand. He opened Torenzi's door and backed up a few steps, just to be safe.

"Get out," he said.

For the first time, Torenzi turned to Belova. But all he gave him was a quick glance as he stepped out of the car. LaGrange, on the other hand, received a glare that would have made even the devil stutter.

"How much?" asked Torenzi. *For how much did you sell me out?*

LaGrange didn't answer. He could only look down at the dirt beneath his feet.

Torenzi stared back at Belova now, unblinking. There was no plea for mercy, no begging for forgiveness.

"Turn around," ordered Belova. "Let me see the horse's ass."

Torenzi shook his head adamantly. "No. You look at me when you do it," he said.

With that, he linked his hands behind his back and dropped to his knees. As if that weren't enough, he opened his mouth wide.

Sick and twisted to the bitter end.

Belova stepped forward, shoving the barrel of his Makarov PM straight back to Torenzi's molars. He was the boss of his family; it had been more than a decade since he'd killed anyone himself. He was far more accustomed to giving the order, not seeing it through.

The result was a split second's pause. A blink of the eye. The chance Torenzi was banking on, or at least hoping for.

Now!

Torenzi whipped his head to the side, forcing the gun against the inside of his cheek as a startled Belova pulled the trigger. The bullet blew a quarter-size hole in the hit man's face, but only his flesh went flying, not his brains.

Falling backwards, Torenzi reached under his pant leg for the stiletto strapped to his shin.

With the grip clenched in his fingers he lunged for the Russian asshole, stabbing him so deep in his thigh that the tip of the blade struck bone.

Belova screamed in agony as he collapsed to the ground. The gun dropped from his hand. Torenzi scooped it up and fired straight into Belova's throat before whipping his arm around at LaGrange for his second shot.

But LaGrange had other ideas.

He had already fired his Ruger SR9, the oversize trigger an easy squeeze in his large hands. The round caught Torenzi in the stomach, sending blood spurting out of his mouth as he keeled over on one side.

Stepping forward, LaGrange quickly pumped two more shots into Torenzi's chest before waiting to see if yet another would be required.

It wasn't.

Torenzi had slid onto his back, arms spread, the gun resting in the palm of his hand, never to be fired again. His eyes flickered as he drew a last breath, his chest heaving upward before slowly deflating.

Then he was gone, straight to hell. *Do not pass Go.*

Chapter 103

"HELLO, MR. DANIELS, I'm Marie McCormick," said my new nurse for the night. She came into my room at Lenox Hill Hospital with a welcome smile and an even more welcome cup filled with two Vicodin. This was my second hospital of the day. After finally being stitched up, I was being "kept for observation," which I didn't mind so much since my apartment was still a police crime scene.

"Boy, am I glad to see you, Marie," I said.

Not just because of the good meds, either. The day nurse assigned to my room had all the charm and charisma of the leaders of the Spanish Inquisition. She was also a stickler for the rules. Visiting hours ended at 8:30 and at 8:31 she had shooed Courtney out as if she were a fox in a henhouse. How could anybody with a heart do that? Couldn't she see how good Courtney and I were together? Heck, we were holding hands, and had been for half an hour.

Before I could tell Nurse Ratched where to shove her rules, Courtney announced she had to be somewhere anyway. "I've got to go put the finishing touches on something," she said. "Sorry, Nick. I'll be back in the morning."

"What is it?" I asked.

"Something kind of interesting. But I can't tell you yet. I don't want to jinx it."

"So I'm a jinx, huh?"

It's hardly what she meant, but it's not like I could blame her or anyone else for thinking that, especially anyone who happened to tune in to the news.

Clearly, Nurse Marie had watched a little of the coverage before coming on duty.

"You're what my aunt Peggy up in Boston calls a trouble magnet," she joked, wrapping a blood pressure sleeve around my arm. "Of course, she should talk, the big dope. She's been married and divorced three times to the biggest losers on the planet."

My cracked ribs made it hurt to laugh but I couldn't help it. Marie was my kind of woman. Down-to-earth and funny.

"Say, where's that brave little niece of yours?" she asked. "I saw her being interviewed."

"She's back home safe with her mother," I said. "Right where she should be."

Agent Keller had personally driven her back to Weston. He certainly knew the way. For good measure he was spending the night—even though the Bureau had already assigned four agents to guard the house. "Just in case," he said. "I owe Elizabeth."

But if you ask me, I saw the way he'd looked at Kate when she'd arrived at the train tracks with Courtney courtesy of a Connecticut state trooper. Turns out Keller's a single guy. *Hey, you never know.*

Of course, I'm a single guy, too, but that was hard to tell, given the way Courtney and I practically ran into each other's arms and kissed like crazy by those same train tracks. It was movie-of-the-week mushy but I loved every second of it. As for Elizabeth, time will tell how she deals with everything that happened. She didn't have a scratch on her, but the mental scars could be another story. Then again, if there's anyone who can handle it, she's the one. The fact that she wanted to give interviews afterward was a pretty encouraging sign.

I was shooting the breeze with Marie a little more when I heard another voice at the door. "Knock, knock," said David Sorren.

Marie turned to him as he strolled in. "You must be somebody important because that cop posted outside the door isn't supposed to let anyone by him."

"Yeah, he's somebody important," I assured Marie. "In fact, you might be looking at the next mayor of this city."

David introduced himself and was as pleasant as a good politician could be with her. Still, I could tell he wanted to speak to me privately. Marie picked up on it, too. She left us alone.

David removed his jacket, placing it on the chair in the corner. Then he turned to me with what he knew was some very good news.

"Bruno Torenzi is dead," he announced. "I wanted to tell you myself, Nick. Hope that gets your vote come the next election."

I shook my head, but I was grinning. "Sorry. I'm a Democrat, David."

Sorren explained how Torenzi had been found during a sweep of the surrounding area near the blown-up train. He said there had been another dead body with him, a Russian crime boss. Go figure.

"So, wait…who did Torenzi work for? Was it D'zorio—or this guy Belova?" I asked.

"Good question. It was probably D'zorio, but for all I know right now they could've been working together. Setting up Eddie Pinero was in both their interests. Anyway, we'll sort it all out soon enough, especially when we bring in that manager from Lombardo's who mixed it up with you. He was on *somebody's* payroll."

Sorren glanced back at my door. "In the meantime, with Torenzi, D'zorio, and Belova out of the picture, the need for that cop outside your door just went down dramatically. Same goes for at your apartment, Nick."

"Hallelujah," I said. "Oh, and don't forget to put Carmine Zambratta on that list. He's gone, too."

"You're right," said Sorren. "In fact, that reminds me—there's one other thing."

"What's that?"

"It's about Dwayne Robinson. As you probably suspected, he didn't commit suicide. As soon as the news about D'zorio's death hit the airwaves, a guy who lived in the building across the street from Robinson came forward to say he saw Zambratta throw him over the railing."

"Why didn't the neighbor say anything before? Not very neighborly."

"He was too scared. He knew who Zambratta was and what he was capable of. Hell, he witnessed it, didn't he?"

"I guess you're right," I said.

Sorren folded his arms, hesitating for a moment. "Listen, Nick, I owe you an apology. I really do. You were way out in front on this whole thing and I should've seen that better. Instead of helping you at first I gave you a hard time, didn't I?"

I smiled. "Yeah, you did," I said. "What's important now, though, is that it's over."

We shook hands. Then we both shook our heads, chuckling in disbelief. It was an amazing end to an amazing day, and to an amazing story.

But I should've known better, I guess. The day wasn't actually over. It was still a little before midnight. Plenty of time for more fun and games.

Chapter 104

THE VICODIN WERE doing their thing, easing the pain while making me drowsy. Minutes after David Sorren left, I started to doze off. I barely heard the creak of the door opening again.

It was Marie, I assumed. I didn't bother to look over right away—or even open my eyes. But as she walked toward me my ears perked up. This wasn't the sound of soft rubber soles. I was hearing heels—heavy ones. These shoes belonged to a man. What man was that?

My eyes shot open.

"Hello, Nick," said Ian LaGrange. Quick as could be, he grabbed the cord of my call button and sliced through it with a knife.

Then he jammed the tip of the knife

underneath my chin. I could feel the blade pierce my flesh enough to send blood trickling down over my Adam's apple.

"What do you want?"

"You know what I want, Nick. Because you have it. *Where's the flash drive?*"

Jesus Christ. In the chaos, the confusion, and the Vicodin, I'd forgotten about that. Clearly, LaGrange hadn't. But how did he even know it existed? And what was with the knife at my throat?

"What are you talking about?" I asked him. "What flash drive?"

"You stupid bastard, don't even try," he snapped. "I know you had it."

LaGrange twisted the tip of the blade slightly. More blood started running down my neck. Vicodin or no Vicodin, it hurt to get stuck in the throat.

"You're right, I did have the flash drive," I said. "D'zorio took it away from me before I got a chance to see what was on it. I don't have it anymore."

LaGrange squinted, sizing me up. He was trying to decide if I was telling the truth. And I guess he decided that I was.

"In that case, what good are you?" he asked,

snatching the pillow from behind my head. *The pillow? You're kidding me* ...

He wasn't—not one bit. He slammed it over my face, forcing the enormous weight of his upper body against my nose and mouth. I couldn't breathe. That was the idea, of course.

The more I struggled, the harder LaGrange pressed, all three hundred pounds of the bastard. No air was coming in. Whatever was left in my lungs was spilling out of me like life itself. I was losing consciousness in a hurry.

There was nothing I could do this time; I was definitely suffocating to death.

I didn't see what happened next, but I sure heard it. Someone came bursting through the door of my room. Not a word was spoken, but a gunshot was fired.

Ian LaGrange fell to the ground with a horrendous thud. He even took the pillow with him, and as I blinked my eyes into focus and breathed the sweetest batch of air I'd ever known, I got to see who had pulled the trigger.

Not the cop who had been stationed outside the door.

Not Doug Keller of the FBI, either.

Chapter 105

"THIS GUY SHOULD be fitted for a cape!" raved the *New York Post*. David Sorren's timing remained just about perfect two days later as he walked up to a podium on the top step of the Manhattan Criminal Courthouse and, with the sunlight of a beautiful day beaming down on him, looked out at a huge, enthusiastic crowd and announced his candidacy for mayor of New York.

By then, anyone with a pulse had either read or heard the story of how he had come back to my hospital room because he'd forgotten his jacket. That's when he'd seen the cop on duty slumped in the hallway. Sorren had grabbed the gun from the cop's holster, bursting into my room.

Needless to say, he had my vote come November, Republican or not.

Courtney's, too, although she remained a tad suspect of Sorren's judgment given his involvement with Brenda Evans.

"I mean, she can't be *that* good in bed," she quipped, standing next to me as we watched Sorren wrap up his announcement to a chorus of cheers. Courtney glanced to see if I'd take the bait and comment on my firsthand knowledge of the subject.

Instead, I just laughed. Hey, I was feeling pretty terrific. Why not—Courtney and I were holding hands again. Corny? Maybe. But who cares when you're in love?

"So what's the big news you weren't ready to tell me?" I asked, changing the subject.

"I knew you'd ask, Nick," she said, reaching into her handbag. She handed me a press release. "Courtney Sheppard named editor in chief of *New York* magazine," read the headline.

"Wow," I said. "Congratulations. That is great."

"Right back atcha," she said. "Have you met my new executive editor? Cute guy, very talented. Great kisser."

"Really? Do I know him?"

She playfully punched my arm and I grabbed hers in return, pulling her close. "Great kisser, huh?" I said before planting one on her. And right there in the middle of the roaring crowd we made out like a couple of teenagers.

"Does that mean you'll take the job?" she asked as we came up for air.

"Absolutely not," I said.

Courtney rolled those beautiful blue eyes of hers. "Why not, Nick? Because you don't think we can work *and* sleep together?"

"No, that's not it at all. I'm just not the executive editor type. I write stories, that's what I do — and the kind I write you can't find sitting in a corner office."

Courtney smiled and I knew she understood, which warmed the cockles of my heart. "All right. I guess I'll just have to lower my standards and sleep with a regular staff writer instead."

"Correction, missy. Your highest-paid staff writer."

"We'll see about that, Nick. Just remember, I didn't get to be editor in chief for nothing."

We were about to kiss again when we both

realized that someone was suddenly standing next to us. Speak of the devil—it was none other than Brenda.

"Sorry to interrupt," she said, coming very close to blushing. I didn't know she had it in her. "I saw you both here. I wanted to give Nick something."

She handed me a slender rectangular box—gift wrapped, with a red bow on top.

"What's this?" I asked, genuinely surprised.

"A make-good," she said. "Something I've owed you."

I was about to open it when she stopped me. "No, not here," she said. "Open it later, Nick. And Courtney—good luck with this one. He's actually a pretty decent guy."

With that, she turned and walked away. No good-bye or anything. I didn't even have a chance to say thank you.

"Decent guy"? All right, I could live with that. I think she even meant it.

Chapter 106

A LITTLE MORE than a week passed. I was on my first assignment for *New York* magazine, and it was definitely cover material.

"Thanks for doing this, David," I said. "This will be a great story—I promise you."

Sorren leaned back in the chair behind his desk. We were in his office downtown at One Hogan Place and David was a man clearly at peace with himself.

"Are you kidding? Thank *you*," he said. "I know being pushy is the first rule of politics, but given everything you've been through, the last thing you needed was my hitting you up for an article so fast. I didn't want to exploit our friendship that way."

"No problem at all. It's the least I could do. After all, you did save my life."

"Just dumb luck," he said with an aw-shucks wave. "Of course, that's the second rule of politics, isn't it? Dumb luck."

"It's pretty high up there for journalism, too."

"That's you and me, a couple of lucky guys. If we're not careful, we may wind up getting everything we want in life," he said with a wink.

I reached for my beat-up leather bag on the floor, pulling it up to my lap. "Let's get started, then, okay?"

"Sure thing," Sorren said. "By the way, what did Courtney say when you proposed this article? I mean, it's her first issue at *New York*. She have any doubts?"

"Doubts? Are you kidding me? I haven't written a word yet and she's already guaranteed us the cover."

Sorren smiled widely as I pulled out a notepad. It was followed by my tape recorder. Immediately, his smile soured.

"Shit, Nick, I'm sorry. I should've said something on the phone when you called. I've got no problem with your taking notes but I can't let you record me. It's policy here in the DA's office," he explained. "Of course, the mayor's office has no such policy."

"That's okay," I said, placing the recorder on his desk. "Actually, this isn't to record you. I wanted to *play* you something. If I may? That okay?"

"Sure," said Sorren. "What is it?"

I hit the play button and turned up the volume. I didn't want Sorren to miss a single word of Ian LaGrange's voice.

Or his own.

Chapter 107

WHAT WOULD YOU do if you found a flash drive, with blood on it, in your boyfriend's favorite hiding spot in his apartment? In his secret, secret place?

I now knew what Brenda Evans would do. She was a reporter, after all, with a sensitive—some would say suspicious—nose for stories. She couldn't help it—the blood had bothered her.

Not nearly as much, though, as what she had discovered on that flash drive.

Derrick Phalen had uncovered it all, and he'd put it on the drive for me to see. Or, rather, for me to *hear*. There were no pictures, no pilfered secret documents—only an MP3 voice file. And while I may be a purist with my vinyl LP collection, this little digital recording trumped everything I'd ever listened to.

Why had Derrick decided to bug his boss's office? Sadly, I'll never have the chance to ask him. But I'll never forget how he had looked that day he saw Ian LaGrange come walking toward us by the elevator at the OCTF.

"Holy shit," I thought I had heard Derrick say. Like he couldn't believe something.

Soon after that, he had his smoking gun—a conversation between LaGrange and none other than David Sorren.

Blinded by his own political ambition, Sorren was willing to forsake the law he had sworn to uphold. He'd built his reputation battling organized crime, but in a world of hotshot defense attorneys and legal loopholes, guilty verdicts against the mob were tough to come by. There had to be a better way, right?

At least that's what Sorren's twisted mind had been thinking. What he needed were *results*. He didn't care how he got them, or for that matter who paid the price. Because results equaled votes. Today, city hall. Tomorrow, the governor's office. Then one day, maybe, the White House.

A modern-day Machiavelli of the worst order.

So Sorren had recruited LaGrange and made the ultimate backroom deal. They chose sides in the organized crime underworld. They backed Joseph D'zorio and set up Eddie Pinero after his criminal usury conviction.

There was just one problem. *Me.*

I stared at Sorren across his desk as he listened to the recording, the flash drive people had died for. Suddenly, his face was as pale as the ceiling tiles of his office.

"I don't like it," said a nervous-sounding LaGrange. "If Daniels is actually talking to one of my prosecutors, then he knows something."

"You worry too much, Ian," said Sorren.

"No, I worry just enough. You should, too. He's already thinking that his being at Lombardo's was more than a coincidence."

"We can take care of it."

"How?" asked LaGrange.

"Leave it to me, Ian. I'll talk to the manager at Lombardo's, erase Marcozza's name from the reservations on that Thursday, figure out everything. Just consider it done."

There was more on the tape, but Sorren had

heard enough. He grabbed the recorder and stopped the playback. Then, of all crazy things, he started to laugh out loud.

"You haven't heard the rest of it," I said.

"I don't need to. I was there. I know what I said. But no one else will. Do you know why?"

I shrugged. "Tell me."

"You should've gone to law school," he said, shaking his head. "This was illegally obtained. It's inadmissible."

Jesus, he was pirouetting through his own legal loophole. I guess it figured.

But it was my turn to shake my head. "How could you do it, David?"

"Do what?" he said.

"At least explain one thing to me," I said. "Why did you kill LaGrange?"

"Because he was trying to kill *you*. I saved your life," he said. "How soon we forget."

"Do you think I'm that stupid?" I asked him.

"Do you think I am?"

"No, what I think is that somewhere along the way you completely forgot the difference between right and wrong, Sorren. You got as cynical as they come, and I've seen cynical, believe me.

Maybe you actually wanted great things for the city. But for sure you wanted even better things for yourself."

"So now you're a shrink?"

"No, I'm still a journalist. A pretty decent one, I think," I said. "But you? You're a criminal."

Sorren clenched his jaw as he leaned forward in his chair. I could see the veins popping in his neck, just like they had the very first time I'd met him. The anger was building, and he was trying to contain himself.

But he couldn't.

"Fuck you!" he said. "How could I do it? *Do what?* Induce one lousy, stinking mob boss to take out another? I was doing everybody in this city a huge favor. One less scumbag mob lawyer, one less crime family, a lot less crime on the streets…Everybody wins—and with D'zorio dead, we win even more."

He jabbed his finger at me. "So don't give me your sanctimonious bullshit. You couldn't leave well enough alone! You got Dwayne Robinson and Derrick Phalen killed. IT WAS YOU! YOU DID IT! THIS IS ALL ON YOU!"

"That's where you're wrong," I said softly

before pointing at my recorder. It was still in his hand. "You always had a choice. You just got caught making the wrong one."

Sorren shot me a pathetic look. "Didn't I already tell you? What's on this recorder is inadmissible. Illegally obtained. It never happened… *just like this conversation*."

I smiled. "Oh, this is happening, all right. I'm here, you're here, David. This is definitely happening."

With that, I undid the top two buttons of my shirt to expose the wire I was wearing.

"Damn chest hairs. I hope it doesn't hurt too much when they pull off the tape," I said. "Legally obtained, by the way."

In the blink of an eye, the door to Sorren's office burst open as a team of FBI agents came in with guns drawn. Leading the charge? Agent Doug Keller.

"Congratulations, asshole," he said to Sorren. "You just broke the record for the shortest campaign for mayor in history."

Epilogue

NOT BIG ON HAPPY ENDINGS

NOT BIG ON HAPPY ENDINGS

Chapter 108

I'VE NEVER BEEN real big on happy endings. It's not that I'm a total pessimist. I've just found that anything worth cherishing usually comes at a price. In this case, a very steep one. Four good cops lost their lives, as did a brave prosecutor. *I can't thank you enough, Derrick Phalen. You made the ultimate sacrifice. I promised your sister you wouldn't die in vain, and for sure you didn't.*

Now I'll have to compartmentalize like Courtney and figure out a way to move on.

Like with this dinner at my sister's house in the woods of Connecticut.

"How does everyone like their steak?" asked Kate.

"On a plate, and preferably soon," I joked. "I'm starving, sis."

"You were born starving."

"Don't start that 'Mom always liked me best' stuff."

"Enough, you two," said Elizabeth. "Grow up."

Five of us were gathered on the back patio of Kate's house in Connecticut. Courtney and Doug Keller had come out from the city with me to join my sister and Elizabeth for a Sunday barbecue. The sun was shining and spirits were high.

Kate, who insisted on doing the grilling, waved her spatula at me. "You're such a wise-guy," she warned with a smile.

"Now, there's a word I wouldn't mind not hearing for a while," I said. "Wiseguy."

"I'll drink to that," said Keller, clinking my bottle of Rolling Rock with his. It was good to see him out of a suit—and holster—and into a wicker lounge chair and some jeans.

Within a day of Sorren's arrest, Keller had been able to answer the remaining question I had. *Why did Sorren kill LaGrange?* Hadn't they both wanted me dead? Yes, they had. But Sorren had suddenly needed to protect himself.

That's what Keller figured out.

LaGrange had become a liability the minute he'd veered from Sorren's game plan and sold out Bruno Torenzi to line his pockets. But LaGrange's greed got Belova killed and in turn guaranteed some intense heat from the Solntsevskaya Bratva back in Moscow. They would have eventually traced the debacle back to LaGrange and quite possibly Sorren.

So Sorren, clever as always, plotted with LaGrange to kill me once and for all. Under the guise of a visit, Sorren did the reconnaissance on my hospital room and the cop guarding it. He was supposed to be making sure the coast was clear for LaGrange. But all he was really doing was setting him up.

Elizabeth leaned back in her chair on the patio and took a sip of lemonade. She threw me a big, happy smile. "So, when's our next Yankee game, Uncle Nick?"

"Right when I get back," I said.

"Back from where?"

"Oh, he didn't tell you, huh?" said Courtney. "Your uncle's going Hollywood on us. He just sold the film rights to his story."

"Can I be in the movie?" asked Elizabeth excitedly.

"I'll be sure to ask," I said. Right after I insist that Tiffany, the ex-hostess from Lombardo's, gets a part. It was the least I could do for her.

"How long will you be out there?" asked Keller.

"After I meet with the studio, I'm actually taking a drive."

This part I hadn't told anyone, not even Courtney. "A drive? Where?" she asked.

"Up the Pacific Coast Highway, in a rented Ferrari f50. You believe it? Always been a dream of mine. So I'm going to do it."

Kate started to crack up. "Wow. You really are going Hollywood on us."

"Can I come and ride shotgun?" asked Keller.

Kate stepped over from the grill and playfully nudged him. "*You can't*. You're taking me out on a big date next weekend. You forget already?"

"That drive up the coast—in *that* car—is something I've always wanted to do," I explained. "By the way, Courtney, you're invited. You know what else? When I get back from California, I'm taking my first saxophone lesson."

"Gee, just when you think you know some-body," joked Courtney. "By the way, after *our* road trip in the Ferrari, any chance you'll ever find time again to, you know, do what you do for a living? Write?"

"I'll always find time for that," I assured her. "In fact, I've already got my next big story lined up."

"You do? What is it?"

"I can't tell you yet," I said with a smile. "But it's coming. I can feel it coming. Everybody— *duck!*"

They did, too. Everybody there ducked.

"That's so not funny, Uncle Nick," said Elizabeth.

Then she laughed.

We all did.

Kill Me If You Can

James Patterson
& Marshall Karp

**An innocent art student finds $13 million in
diamonds. Let the manhunt begin . . .**

Matthew Bannon, a poor art student living in New York City, finds a
leather bag filled with diamonds during a chaotic attack at Grand
Central Station. Plans for a worry-free life with his gorgeous
girlfriend Katherine fill his thoughts – until he realises that he is
being hunted, and that whoever is after him won't stop until they
have reclaimed the diamonds and exacted maximum revenge.

Trailing him is the Ghost, the world's greatest assassin, who has
just pulled off his most high-profile hit: killing Walter Zelvas, a top
member of the international Diamond Syndicate. There's only one
small problem: the diamonds he was supposed to retrieve from
Zelvas are missing.

Now, the Ghost is on Bannon's trail – but so is a rival assassin who
would like nothing more than to make the Ghost disappear forever.

Kill Me If You Can is a high-speed, high-stakes, winner-takes-all thrill
ride of love, greed, and suspense.

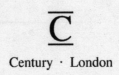

Century · London

Turn the page for a
sneak preview of

KILL ME IF YOU CAN

One

SOME PEOPLE ARE harder to kill than others.
The Ghost was thinking about this as he huddled
in the deep, dark shadows of Grand Central
Terminal. A man named Walter Zelvas would
have to die tonight. But it wouldn't be easy.
Nobody hired the Ghost for the easy jobs.

It was almost 11 p.m, and even though the
evening rush was long over, there was still a
steady stream of weary travelers.

The Ghost was wearing an efficient killing
disguise. His face was lost under a tangle of
matted silver-and-white hair and shaggy beard,
and his arsenal was hidden under a wine-stained
gray poncho. To anyone who even bothered to
take notice, he was just another heap of homeless

humanity seeking refuge on a quiet bench near Track 109.

He eyed his target. Walter Zelvas. A great hulk of a man with the nerves and reflexes of a snake and a soul to match. Zelvas was a contract killer himself, but unlike the Ghost, Zelvas took pleasure in watching his victims suffer before they died. For years, the ruthless Russian had been an enforcer for the Diamond Syndicate, but apparently he had outlived his usefulness to his employer, and the Ghost had been hired to terminate him.

If he doesn't kill me first, the Ghost thought. With Zelvas it was definitely a matter of kill or be killed. And this would surely be a duel to the death between them.

So the Ghost watched his opponent closely. The screen on the departures monitor refreshed and Zelvas cursed under his breath. His train was delayed another thirty minutes.

He drained his second cup of Starbucks cappuccino, stood up, and crumpling his empty cup, deposited it in the trash.

No littering, the Ghost thought. That might attract attention, and the last thing Zelvas wanted was attention.

That's why he was leaving town by train. Train stations aren't like airports. There's no baggage check, no metal detector, no security.

Zelvas looked toward the men's room.

All that coffee will be the death of you, the Ghost thought as Zelvas walked across the marble floor to the bathroom.

A half-comatose porter, mop in hand, was sloshing water on the terminal floor like a zombie tarring a roof. He didn't see Zelvas coming.

A puddle of brown water came within inches of the big man's right foot. Zelvas stopped. "You slop any of that scum on my shoes and you'll be shitting teeth," he said.

The porter froze. "Sorry. Sorry, sir. Sorry."

The Ghost watched it all. Another time, another place, and Zelvas might have drowned the man in his own mop water. But tonight he was on his best behavior.

Zelvas continued toward the bathroom.

The Ghost had watched the traffic in and out of the men's room for the past half hour. It was currently empty. *Moment of truth*, the Ghost told himself.

Zelvas got to the doorway, stopped, and turned around sharply.

He made me, the Ghost thought at first.

Zelvas looked straight at him. Then left, then right.

He's a pro. He's just watching his back.

Satisfied he wasn't being followed, Zelvas entered the men's room.

The Ghost stood up and surveyed the terminal. The only uniformed cop in the area was busy giving directions to a young couple fifty feet away.

The men's room had no door—just an L-shaped opening that allowed the Ghost to enter and still remain out of sight.

From his vantage point he could see the mirrored wall over the sinks. And there was Zelvas, standing in front of a urinal, his back to the mirror.

The Ghost silently reached under his poncho and removed his equally silent Glock from its holster.

The Ghost had a mantra. Three words he said to himself just before every kill. He waited until he heard Zelvas breathe that first sigh of relief as he began to empty his bladder.

I am invincible, the Ghost said in silence.

Then, in a single fluid motion, he entered the bathroom, silently slid up behind Zelvas, aimed the Glock at the base of his skull, and squeezed the trigger.

And missed.

Some people are harder to kill than others.

Two

WALTER ZELVAS NEVER stepped up to a urinal unless the top flush pipe was made of polished chrome.

It's not a perfect mirror, but it's enough. Even distorted, everything he needed to see was visible.

Man. Hand. Gun.

Zelvas whirled on the ball of his right foot and dealt a swift knife-hand strike to the Ghost's wrist just as he pulled the trigger.

The bullet went wide, shattering the mirror behind him.

Zelvas followed up by driving a cinder-block fist into the Ghost's midsection, sending him crashing through a stall door.

The Glock went skittering across the tile floor.

The Ghost looked up at the enraged colossus who was now reaching for his own gun.

Damn, the Ghost thought. *The bastard is still pissing. Glad I wore the poncho.*

He rolled under the next stall as Zelvas's first bullet drilled a hole through the stained tile where his head had just been.

Zelvas darted to the second stall to get off another shot. Still on his back, the Ghost kicked the stall door with both feet.

It flew off its hinges and hit Zelvas square on, sending him crashing into the sinks.

But he held on to his gun.

The Ghost lunged and slammed Zelvas's gun hand down onto the hard porcelain sink. He was hoping to hear the sound of bone snapping, but all he heard was glass breaking as the mirror behind Zelvas fell to the floor in huge fractured pieces.

Instinctively, the Ghost snatched an eight-inch shard of broken mirror as it fell. Zelvas head-butted him full force, and as their skulls collided, the Ghost jammed the razor-sharp glass into Zelvas's bovine neck.

Zelvas let out a violent scream, pushed the Ghost off him, and then made one fatal mistake. He yanked the jagged mirror from his neck.

Blood sprayed like a renegade fire hose. *Now I'm really glad I wore the poncho,* the Ghost thought.

Zelvas ran screaming from the bloody bathroom, one hand pressed to his spurting neck and the other firing wildly behind him. The Ghost dived to the floor under a hail of ricocheting bullets and raining plaster dust. A few deft rolls and he managed to retrieve his Glock.

Jumping to his feet, the Ghost sprinted to the doorway and saw Zelvas running across the terminal, a steady stream of arterial blood pumping out of him. He would bleed out in a minute, but the Ghost didn't have time to stick around and confirm the kill. He raised the Glock, aimed, and then . . .

"Police. Drop it."

The Ghost turned. A uniformed cop, overweight, out of shape, and fumbling to get his own gun, was running toward him. One squeeze of the trigger and the cop would be dead.

There's a cleaner way to handle this, the Ghost

thought. The guy with the mop and every passenger within hearing distance of the gunshots had taken off. The bucket of soapy mop water was still there.

The Ghost put his foot on the bucket and, pushing it, sent it rolling across the terminal floor right at the oncoming cop.

Direct hit.

The fat cop went flying ass over tin badge and slid across the slimy wet marble floor.

But this is New York—one cop meant dozens, and by now a platoon of cops was heading his way.

I don't kill cops, the Ghost thought, *and I'm out of buckets.* He reached under his poncho and pulled out two smoke grenades. He yanked the pins and screamed, *"Bomb!"*

The grenade fuses burst with a terrifying bang, and the sound waves bounced off the terminal's marble surfaces like so many acoustic billiard balls. Within seconds, the entire area for a hundred feet was covered with a thick red cloud that had billowed up from the grenade casings.

The chaos that had erupted with the first

gunshot kicked into high gear as people who had dived for cover from the bullets now lurched blindly through the bloodred smoke in search of a way out.

Half a dozen cops stumbled through the haze to where they had last seen the bomb thrower.

But the Ghost was gone.

Disappeared into thin air.

JAMES PATTERSON

**To find out more about James Patterson
and his bestselling books, go to
www.jamespatterson.co.uk**

Tick Tock

James Patterson
& Michael Ledwidge

Tick – a killer's countdown begins . . .

A rash of horrifying crimes tears through New York City, throwing it
into complete chaos.

Tick – can Michael Bennett catch him before . . .

The city calls on Detective Michael Bennett, pulling him away from
a seaside retreat with his ten adopted children, his grandfather,
and their beloved nanny, Mary Catherine. Bennett enlists the help
of a former colleague, FBI Agent Emily Parker. But as his affection
for Emily grows into something stronger, his relationship with Mary
Catherine takes an unexpected turn.

Tock – your time is up?

All too soon, another appalling crime leads Bennett to a shocking
discovery that exposes the killer's pattern and the earth-shattering
enormity of his plan.

arrow books

THE *SUNDAY TIMES* NO. 1 BESTSELLER,
AVAILABLE IN PAPERBACK FROM JANUARY 2012

Private London

James Patterson
& Mark Pearson

**SOMETIMES WHEN THE NIGHTMARE ENDS – THE TERROR
IS ONLY JUST BEGINNING . . .**

For Hannah Shapiro, a beautiful American student, this particular
nightmare began eight years ago in Los Angeles, when Jack
Morgan, owner of Private – the world's most exclusive detective
agency – saved her from a horrific death. She has fled her country,
but can't flee her past. The terror has followed her to London, and
now it is down to former Royal Military Police Sergeant Dan Carter,
head of Private London, to save her all over again.

In central London, young women are being abducted off the street.
When the bodies are found, some days later, they have been
mutilated in a particularly mysterious way. Dan Carter's ex-wife,
DI Kirsty Webb, is involved in the investigation and it looks likely
that the two cases are gruesomely linked.

Carter draws on the whole resources of Private International in
a desperate race against the odds. But the clock is ticking . . .
Private may be the largest and most advanced detection agency
in the world, but the only thing they don't have is the one thing
they need – time.

arrow books

AN ILLUSTRATED NOVEL

Middle School
The Worst Years of My Life

James Patterson
& Chris Tebbetts

Illustrated by Laura Park

Rafe Kane has enough problems at home without throwing his first year of middle school into the mix. Luckily, he's got an ace plan for the best year ever, if only he can pull it off. With his best friend Leonardo the Silent awarding him points, Rafe tries to break every rule in his school's Code of Conduct. Chewing gum in class – 5,000 points! Running in the hallway – 10,000 points! Pulling the fire alarm – 50,000 points! But when Rafe's game starts to catch up with him, he'll have to decide if winning is all that matters, or if he's finally ready to face the rules, bullies, and truths he's been avoiding.

Containing over 100 brilliant illustrations, *Middle School* is the hilarious story of Rafe's attempt to somehow survive the very worst year of his life!

Are you a parent?

Why not share your favourite author with your kids?

James Patterson is passionate about getting kids reading. Inspired by his own son, who was a reluctant reader, James has written books specifically for younger readers all packed with his trademark page-turning punch.

Check out the **MAXIMUMRIDE** series for some fast and furious bird kid adventures. Max and the flock are kids with wings, who must save the planet as well as themselves before it's too late.

Does your child have a passion for mystery, adventure and magic? Then the brand new series **Witch & Wizard** is perfect.

Aliens are living on planet Earth and

is a boy with a mission – to hunt them down before they destroy life as we know it. Extraterrestrial adventures about one boy in a whole world of intergalactic trouble.

We support

National
Literacy
Trust

I'm proud to support the National Literacy Trust, an independent charity that changes lives through literacy.

Did you know that millions of people in the UK struggle to read and write? This means children are less likely to succeed at school and less likely to develop into confident and happy teenagers. Literacy difficulties will limit their opportunities throughout adult life.

The National Literacy Trust passionately believes that everyone has a right to the reading, writing, speaking and listening skills they need to fulfil their own and, ultimately, the nation's potential.

My own son didn't use to enjoy reading, which was why I started writing children's books – reading for pleasure is an essential way to encourage children to pick up a book. The National Literacy Trust is dedicated to delivering exciting initiatives to encourage people to read and to help raise literacy levels. To find out more about the great work that they do, visit their website at www.literacytrust.org.uk.

James Patterson